The Voice of Angels

A Novel

By Nydia Hadi

Full Quiver Publishing,
Pakenham ON Canada

To God, my dad, my mom, my sister, and my boyfriend, who have been supporting me tremendously and loving me unconditionally.

Chapter 1
Olivier Lefebvre
Plateau Mont-Royal
First Week of March

Two bright lights appear where they shouldn't—on the dark road in front of me. My stomach lurches. Time slows. I slam the steering wheel to the right, but it's too late. The lights blind me for one fleeting moment. I can't breathe. There's a sudden jolt and a sickening sound of metal crunching against metal...

Sirens blare...then voices and blinding lights.

My eyes snap open.

I feel disoriented at first. I find myself lying on a bed. My heart is pounding very fast, and I am breathing rapidly, like someone who has just finished running. I realize that my neck, chest, and back are covered with sweat, so I throw back the covers. The glowing red letters of my clock tell me I've woken at 2:00 a.m. Again.

For the past two months, every time I've had this nightmare, I've struggled to go back to sleep. That's why my doctor prescribed sleeping pills. Now I have to get them, but the idea of having to walk to the bathroom makes me cringe.

I slowly get up and stand while ignoring the pain in my left side and left thigh. Then I bump into the table lamp beside my bed. Ouch. Luckily, it hit my right leg instead of my left. I look around the dark room. Once my eyes adjust, I see the minimalistic décor with elegant furniture. I know that I am on the second floor of my three-story triplex in Plateau Mont-Royal. But I haven't been living here for the past two months. I was bedridden in the hospital for a month, and I spent another month in my parents' house in Outremont. Tonight is the first night I've been back here. That's why I am so clumsy in my own place. This room used to be my library and office, but now it has been converted into a bedroom. My parents and my best friend, Jean-Luc, helped me rearrange my plex before I moved back in. Although the bedsheets, pillows, and two small table lamps on each side of the bed are the ones I used for my old bedroom on the third floor, everything feels foreign to me.

Turning on the table lamp while trying to stand steadily, I walk slowly to the window. The pain in my left leg is always worse when I wake up. I open the curtain. At 2:30 a.m., everything is dark outside. During the day, the views of Mount Royal, as well as Jeanne-Mance Park, stretch out beautifully. Although this bedroom used to be my home office, I barely used it, as I spent most of my time in my office in downtown Montreal. The view from this second-floor window is not as good as the third floor and definitely not as good as the view from my office on the 33rd floor. Well, what can I do? Before, I could have the second and third floors for myself while renting out the first floor. Now, I have to be satisfied with occupying just the second floor because my leg is still hurting me whenever I climb the stairs. I slip on my shirt and walk toward the bathroom.

At the end of the corridor, I open the bathroom door and turn on the light. I see my reflection in the mirror. A 28-year-old man with black hair and blue eyes is looking back at me. What used to be a vibrant face has become a sorrowful one. I see black shadows under my eyes, pale skin, cheeks that are a bit sunken. I look horrible. I lift up my shirt to see the surgical incision on my left side. It is a twelve-inch scar, not as red and swollen as before, but it always makes me want to look away. And there are also scars on my left thigh.

I open the cabinet to get some sleeping pills. Then I realize I have to go to the kitchen to get water. And I left my crutches in the bedroom. It's not worth it to go back to the bedroom, as I am already halfway, so I sigh and limp toward the kitchen.

I pass my combined living and dining area and turn on the lights. It actually looks cozy and bright. All the bookshelves that used to be in the library are now here in the living area. There is also a big TV. This area used to be my gym. My parents and Jean-Luc must have put all my gym equipment in storage, so I am not tempted to try them.

Finally, I arrive at the kitchen. Taking a glass from the cabinet, I fill it with water and swallow two sleeping pills. I realize I am dehydrated, especially after sweating a lot from the nightmare. I feel a bit dizzy. I cannot get dehydrated. It's not good for my kidney. Yes, kidney. Not *kidneys*. They removed one during the surgery two months ago.

In the kitchen, there is a door to the balcony. I go out and sit on the chair for a while to view the East Montreal night scene. The night is pretty quiet. I can't help but feel bitter about my new physical condition.

I had everything I needed: a good career as a valuation partner in an accounting firm, a three-story plex in the Plateau, a BMW, some expensive tailored suits, and a pretty girlfriend—Isabelle Durand. Then that incident happened.

I was driving back to my place from a friend's party at Griffintown. Isabelle and Jean-Luc were attending it, too. I decided to leave the party earlier, as I had a client meeting at 8:30 a.m. the next day. It was a good thing Isabelle and Jean-Luc stayed at the party a little bit longer. So I drove home by myself.

Then, somewhere along Sherbrooke Street, a truck hit my car from the opposite direction. It was too late for me to turn my steering wheel away. I saw blinding lights and heard loud noises. I didn't even remember when my airbag was inflated. The left side of my body was hit, but I did not feel anything. I also remember the siren from the ambulance, but I was in and out of consciousness on the way to the hospital and on a gurney to the operating room.

After the surgery, I went to the ICU, and finally, after a few days, I woke up in a hospital room. The first news I heard from the doctor was that I broke my left femur, two ribs, and I lost my left kidney.

When I heard that news, I felt nothing. Numb, to be exact. The doctors gave me a lot of morphine, so I didn't feel much pain and felt too high to process all the information. I only felt some discomfort because my left leg was elevated and there were so many tubes attached to my body. I was in a denial stage, and I didn't fully grasp my situation until a few days later.

My parents, Isabelle and Jean-Luc, took turns visiting me in the hospital. Some of my colleagues and employees from work also came to visit. But honestly, I felt ashamed of being bedridden, broken, and powerless. I hate being dependent on others. After they started removing the tubes and everything, I began to see my body more clearly. There were bruises all over, and I had lost weight. I used to be very athletic before and worked out regularly. Now I don't recognize myself.

When they started reducing my pain medication, I started to feel the pain, especially in my left thigh and left side. The surgical incision and the broken ribs also made it painful to breathe. I had to get used to breathing very slowly and shallowly. But the physical pain was nothing compared to the emotional pain. I am not the same person as before. My family, friends, colleagues, and employees used to look at me with respect. Now, they look at me with pity. I have been away from the office for two months, and I feel useless when I am not working. It also makes me feel lonely and purposeless.

I am wondering what I am supposed to do tomorrow. My next physiotherapy appointment is in two days, and my appointments with my orthopedic specialist and my internist will be next week. Since the incident, my schedule has been packed with medical appointments. I don't feel like going back to work anytime soon because everything is too much to process. Driving is still a bit risky, and I am not sure if I want to drive yet. Plus, my BMW is in the junkyard, unrepairable.

I would never have thought that my life would turn out like this. It took only a few seconds to undo all my hard work to get where I am now. Well, at least I don't have to worry about money, as I have saved enough for the rest of my life. But still, what did I ever do to deserve losing one kidney and being unable to walk?

I look up to the night sky, seeing if there is any sign of God up there. I know there isn't. I stopped believing in God a long time ago. If God existed, I would not be experiencing all of this. What's the point of living?

Chapter 2
Regina de Luca
La Maison Symphonique, Montreal
First Week of March

I know that God exists; otherwise, I wouldn't have this wonderful life.

I slide the bow across the strings of the violin tucked under my chin. My soul seems to glide above me with the beautiful notes. *Oh, my Lord, thank You for the beauty of a song and all Your gifts.*

We are in the middle of rehearsing Bach's Concerto for Two Violins in D Minor, BWV 1043. I am part of the second violin group, sitting on the left side of the first violins. The two soloists for this piece are extremely good. They communicate back and forth with their violins really well. I've always liked this piece. It is very beautiful, and it makes me want to shed tears of joy.

I would never have imagined myself being part of a world-renowned orchestra like this. I was born and raised in Sorrento, Naples, until I was fifteen years old. My childhood was filled with music, Neapolitan pizza, pasta, gelato, churches, and swimming at the beach. Both my parents are musicians. My dad is a cellist, and my mom is a vocalist. I guess I inherited their love of music. Since I was young, I have really enjoyed singing and playing the violin. Living in a peaceful and calm city like Sorrento gave me a lot of inspiration as a musician.

When I was ten years old, I visited the east coast of Canada with my parents. The first time I visited Montreal, I was fascinated by the city. Montreal combined the modern and ancient worlds, creating a beautiful, artistic vibe. There were also a lot of beautiful churches that reminded me of my hometown.

During our visit to Montreal, my parents brought me to watch an orchestra performance. Right here in *Maison Symphonique*, where I am now. At that moment, I realized that I wanted to be a professional musician and play in an orchestra.

After that visit, I was determined to go to school and to live in Montreal someday. I made a decision to be more serious with my violin lessons. I practiced more rigorously and studied French more diligently. The opportunity came five years later. A music school in Montreal called for an audition for a violin program. I grabbed this opportunity and flew to Montreal with my mom.

I was very happy when I got the acceptance letter a few weeks after; they even offered me a partial scholarship! I was so thrilled. Although, I realized that if I accepted the offer, that meant I would have to leave my hometown, my parents, and my friends, and I had to live in a new country with a new language, all by myself at fifteen years old.

I decided to take this opportunity.

The good thing was that this music school was partnering with a boarding school that offered a regular academic curriculum. Since I started at Secondary 4 (which is equivalent to Grade 10 in Italy), I had my regular academic classes in the morning and music lessons in the afternoon. The music school was adjacent to the boarding school, so it was very convenient. The school and the dorm were located in the Outremont neighborhood on the north side of Mount Royal. There was a forest path that I used to take every time I felt down. This path led to a small lookout called Belvedere Outremont, where you can see the north side of the city. I was so glad that I found this place. I usually sat on the boulder and enjoyed the view by myself.

In the beginning, of course, there was a language barrier and culture shock. The French spoken in Montreal and Quebec was apparently different from the French from Metropolitan France. When I was in Italy, I learned French from France. But over time, I managed to adapt well, even though I could never hide my Italian accent whenever I spoke French. At school, I became friends with local as well as international students. They were nice, and everybody seemed to be really serious and passionate about what they were doing. There was competition among students, obviously, but I kept telling myself to just focus and stop comparing myself to others.

The other culture shock was the weather. I did not realize that the winter in Montreal is very harsh compared to Italy. The temperature can drop to negative thirty degrees Celsius. In Sorrento, the lowest temperature was usually three degrees.

In terms of food, luckily Montreal is pretty diversified, and I can find a lot of European food here. There is even an Italian neighborhood where I can find homemade pasta that cures my homesickness.

After finishing Secondary 4, 5, and CEGEP *Collège D'enseignement Général et Professionnel* (which is the equivalent of community college in Quebec) in this music school, I enrolled at McGill Conservatory of Music to continue my violin studies. My journey to become a professional musician was not always smooth. It was extremely competitive and required a lot of work. I experienced extreme stress several times. On top of that, I also had to work part-time to pay my rent. Since my parents were aging and did not make as much money as before, I tried not to bother them with my high tuition and living costs in Montreal.

Finally, I graduated from McGill last year. And after attending several auditions, I got an offer from *Orchestre Symphonique de Mont-Royal*. I cannot believe that my twelve-year odyssey finally brought my dream to life. To this date, I thank God every day. I know that I can attribute all my success to my hard work, but I feel that God is always helping me in my journey. Since I was fifteen years old and living away from home, I had no one else to rely on other than God.

After the rehearsal is finished, I put my violin into the case. I say goodbye to my friends and walk home to my studio in the McGill ghetto area, which is only about a five-minute walk from *La Maison Symphonique*. Today is Tuesday, and I am free after my violin rehearsal. My typical schedule as an orchestra musician is:

Monday: Off
Tuesday: 10 a.m.–12:30 p.m.
Wednesday: 10 a.m.–12:30 p.m., 1:30 p.m.–3:30 p.m.
Thursday: 10 a.m.–12:30 p.m.
Friday: 8 p.m. concert
Saturday: 8 p.m. concert
Sunday: 3 p.m. concert

Being a performing artist is not as free as it seems. On top of the rehearsals with the orchestra, we also have to spend time practicing on our own to master a piece. And the pay is not that good unless you are the concertmaster. So, I usually take additional teaching jobs on Fridays. Currently, I have five students. The combined pay is enough for me to pay my rent, groceries, and bills and have additional savings.

On Tuesday and Thursday evenings, I also have choir practice in my church. I always look forward to it as I really love this community. Besides singing together, we also care about each other like a big family. Some of the choir members are immigrants like me. They came from Brazil, Haiti, the

Philippines, and South Korea. God takes care of me through my adoptive Montreal family.

I am about to open my apartment door when I see a letter has been slipped below it. I suddenly feel nervous. I take the letter and go inside, ripping the envelope and reading:

Dear Tenant,
This is to notify you that we will be raising the rent to $1,150/month effective on April 1st.
Thank you.
Your Landlord

Oh no. Currently, I am paying $1,000 per month. And this is the limit of my budget for rent. Although I can still afford $1,150 per month, I really would like to save more emergency funds. Paying an additional $150 decreases my opportunity to save.

I have considered finding a housemate before, but because I need to spend a lot of time practicing my violin at home, it is probably not a good idea. I may have to look for a new place. I sigh. What can I do?

Just when I thank God for giving me a good life, life gives me another problem. I try to remain positive.

Chapter 3
Olivier Lefebvre
Montreal General Hospital
Second Week of March

I finish my checkup earlier than expected. My dad will pick me up approximately an hour from now, as he is still playing golf with his friends. I told him I could take an Uber, but he insisted that he wanted to drive me. My disability really gets to me now. I am twenty-eight years old, but I feel like I am back to being a teenager dependent on his parents. This morning, I had to wait for my dad to pick me up and drive me to the hospital. Now I am waiting for him again.

I should be grateful that he is still willing to drive me around. But at this point, I don't have the capacity to be patient, especially with my broken body. Although my nephrologist—or kidney specialist—said that my body is recovering well and I can survive with one kidney; still, to me, that is not good news. I should not have lost my other kidney in the first place. My friend Jean-Luc, who is a lawyer, is finalizing my lawsuit against the truck driver.

On the other hand, my orthopedist said that I would still need crutches and a leg brace for another few months after he examined my X-rays. It has been two months, but every time I try to put a little bit of weight on my left leg, the pain is unbearable. Going up and down the stairs sucks my energy and sours my mood.

I look at my watch: forty-five minutes to kill. What should I do in this suffocating hospital? I don't want to sit in the corridor. Whenever people see me, their eyes will automatically be drawn to my leg brace and crutches. I don't want to be pitied by anyone.

Suddenly, I see a room that looks like a small chapel. Inside, there are pews, but no one is around. Should I go inside and sit down? I don't feel comfortable in religious places.

I was baptized in the Catholic Church when I was three years old because my grandparents were believers. My parents got me baptized just to make them happy. They think that religion is a joke. In the beginning, I enjoyed going to Sunday Mass with my grandparents, although I don't remember what I enjoyed in particular. But then, when I was about to receive my First Communion at eight years old, I witnessed something that troubles me even now. Since then, I haven't felt comfortable going to church, and I am following my parents' path. My grandparents were very disappointed, but luckily, my parents defended me.

But today, since this chapel is the only place I can be alone, I limp to one of the pews, where I close my eyes for five minutes before I hear someone entering the room. I don't bother opening my eyes until I hear my name.

"Olivier?" I open my eyes and find a man of my age in a white coat standing in front of me. He is the last person I want to see.

Have you ever had a rival? You know, someone who is always in competition with you, who always makes you want to beat him, or who makes you bitter if he wins and you lose?

I have.

I attended a French private boys' school from elementary to secondary. When I was in grade four, there was a new boy in our school. He had reddish brown hair and green eyes under his thick glasses. This boy was clearly a nerd by the way he wore his uniform. A nerdy boy usually lacks confidence, but this one was different. There was a different aura surrounding him, one of calmness and confidence. Or maybe more like serenity.

This new boy was clearly bilingual. He spoke perfect English and French without an accent, which I envied. I speak French as my first language. When I was ten years old and in Grade 4, my English was horrible. I mastered the grammar and sentence structure and everything, but my accent was still very thick. It still is.

So, this boy was already one point ahead of me. I did not know why I felt so competitive with him. I was a competitive kid from an early age, but before that new boy came, my life was easy. I was the smartest in class. Jean-Luc usually came second after me. Suddenly, I was not the smartest anymore.

Every time we got our exam results in class, the teacher would announce the highest mark, which alternated between me and this boy. It always used to be my name that was called. Whenever this boy got a higher mark than I did, I beat him on the next exam. But then he beat me on the next, and the cycle kept repeating for seven years until we finished Secondary 5.

This boy and I never really talked to each other nor became friends. I had my own friends and circle, which included Jean-Luc and several other popular kids. We were part of the school's hockey team, and we were a bit exclusive. This boy was not an athlete or anything. But he became friends with everybody—except our group. I may have earned respect from my peers, but this boy earned genuine love from the people surrounding him. Even though he was very smart, he was humble and down to earth. I admit, I was jealous of his popularity, too.

Luckily, we went to different CEGEP, and I never heard of him again until our first-year orientation at McGill University. At that time, we nodded to acknowledge each other's presence, but that was it. I was in Desautels's Faculty of Management, and I found out that he was in the Faculty of Science. We had one calculus class together. I got an A+, but then I found out that he also got an A+. After that we never had the same class again, and we barely saw each other until our undergraduate convocation day, where we both earned distinction.

I continued with my life. After graduation, I joined a big accounting firm as a staff auditor. I passed my CPA exam and earned my CPA designation. Then, I requested to be transferred to the valuation team because I wanted to do more challenging work than audit. The firm granted my request, and I started as a senior associate. I also earned my CBV (Chartered Business Valuator) designation within a year, which led to my being promoted to manager. When I was twenty-eight years old, the firm offered me a partnership. I was a partner for eight months before the accident happened.

So what happened to that boy who used to be my rival? He now stands in front of me.

"Hi, Ethan," I reply formally.

Two months ago, I did not realize that he was Ethan O'Sullivan, the boy who had been my rival since Grade 4. Except that now he is no longer a boy. Apparently, he went into medical school after completing his undergraduate. He is now doing his residency in orthopedic surgery. Coincidentally, he was part of the surgery team who fixed my femur fracture. I was on a lot of painkillers after the surgery and did not recognize him when he and his team were doing rounds.

At one point after they transferred me from the ICU to a room, Ethan visited me.

"Olivier? Do you remember me?" he asked.

It took me a while to recognize him. Somehow, the aura of calmness and confidence (or serenity, whatever you call it) brought back my memory of this boy. He is a grown man now, but his aura is still the same.

"Ethan?" I confirmed.

"Yes!" Then he dragged a chair beside my bed and sat down. "You know, I was stunned when I realized that it was you in the emergency room. I was on call, and you were badly injured. We immediately tried to ping all the trauma surgeons we could find. It was definitely a stressful moment." He looked genuinely worried.

I did not know what to say. We were not even friends. "Thank you for saving my life, Dr. O'Sullivan," I said politely.

"Hey, just call me Ethan. Listen, any time you feel sick or uncomfortable, tell the nurses to call me, okay? I know it's a tough time for you, but I am sure you will recover quickly. You are very strong."

I appreciated that he sounded encouraging instead of pitying me. "Thanks, Ethan."

"Anytime. And here is my phone number." He took a notebook from his pocket, tore off a piece of paper, and started writing his number. "I hope you recover soon and we can catch up!" He offered the paper with his number written on it.

I took it and said thanks. I was surprised by his friendliness. I never expected any kindness from him. We still saw each other when he was doing his rounds, but I never called him even after I got discharged.

"How are you feeling?" Ethan asks me as he sits beside me in the chapel.

"I am okay. Just a bit tired."

"And you are recovering okay? No complications or infections?"

"Nope."

"I am happy to hear that." He sighs with relief.

Then there is silence. I don't know what to say to him. He has been friendly so far. I feel like I should make an effort.

"My body is adjusting well with one kidney. But my leg and my ribs are still hurting."

"I see. It will probably take at least six months to walk again without crutches, but the ribs should heal faster."

"Yeah, I know."

"But how are you feeling in general? Like, do you feel depressed or anxious?" he asks with concern.

"Yes, it's hard to accept that my life will be different now. I cannot do things that I used to do before."

"I have never been in your position, but I can imagine it must be tough for you. I am assuming you still take some time off from work?"

"Yes." I nod.

"From what I read in your chart, you are an accountant?"

"More business valuator now. I don't do much accounting anymore."

"I remember when we were in elementary and secondary school, I always knew that you would become someone respected in your field." Ethan smiles.

"You, too. Congratulations on being a doctor." I think that's the first time I've given someone recognition.

"Thank you." The silence creeps between us again.

"Well, Olivier, you still have my number, right? Call me if you need someone to talk to. I can come over to your place, and we can catch up." He presses his hand on my shoulder and gets up.

"All right. I think I will. Thanks, Ethan."

After he leaves, I realize that we have known each other since Grade 4, but this is the first time we've had a real conversation.

Chapter 4
Ethan O'Sullivan
Montreal General Hospital
Second Week of March

I still have half an hour before my next operating room schedule, so I relax in my on-call room.

I did not expect to bump into Olivier in the chapel today. I never knew that he was a believer. I mean, I never really knew him to be honest.

We went to the same school from Grade 4 to Secondary 5, and we went to the same university but in different faculties. We always got the top marks at school. I wanted to be friends with him, as I felt like we may have had a lot of things in common. We studied seriously, and we had curious minds. Both of us asked a lot of questions in class, and sometimes he asked the question that I was about to ask.

The thing is, Olivier appeared aloof and unapproachable when we were in school. He was also surrounded by his close circle—one of those elite, popular boys who came from rich families, and most were athletes. I was just an Irish boy on a scholarship. But among his friends, Olivier seemed like the most decent person in his group. He played hockey very well when we were in school, and he had good grades. But he was never boastful about it.

I was surprised when I saw him in the emergency room. Even though we had not seen each other for years and we were not friends, he was still someone who had made a huge impact on my life. He motivated me to study hard at school.

When I saw him in the ER, he was not bleeding a lot on the outside. Only several visible cuts. However, when I saw that his blood pressure was dropping fast, and his left thigh and the left side of his body were bruised and swollen, I knew right away that his life was in danger from internal bleeding. I reviewed the X-ray and confirmed that his left femur was broken, as well as his two left ribs. We transferred him into the operating room immediately and called in the trauma surgeons and anesthesiologist. In the end, they had to remove his kidney because the ribs had crushed it. I have seen other devastating surgeries before, but none was as personal as this.

After his condition was stabilized, an orthopedic surgeon, my attending, was brought in to fix his left femur. We did an intramedullary nailing procedure. I helped the surgeon insert a rod into the femur. I wondered if Olivier was still playing hockey. It really broke my heart.

The surgery took almost ten hours cumulatively. We did not sleep that night, but when the surgery was over and Olivier was still alive, I was very relieved. We still had to monitor him closely for the next few days, but we had done the best we could to save him. The rest was dependent on his stamina and God's plan.

Over the next few days, I watched Olivier's recovery closely. I made sure he did not run out of fluids and the wound's dressing was changed regularly. I also monitored his temperature closely to make sure there was no sign of infection. When he regained consciousness, I ensured the pain medications were adequate, as I noticed that he had trouble breathing due to the pain from his broken ribs.

I was glad that his parents and his friend Jean-Luc took turns visiting him in the hospital. Sometimes, a blond girl came to visit. I would guess she must have been his girlfriend. Some of his colleagues also came. I thought it was a good thing that Olivier was always surrounded by his circle, especially during a time like this.

Today in the chapel was the first time Olivier and I had a real conversation. I always go to the chapel whenever I need solitude. For me, just sitting in silence can make me feel God's presence, and it gives me clarity. But I don't regret finding Olivier in the chapel. He seemed very down, and I would like to be able to help him.

People say I am an altruist. I don't know if I deserve that title or not. I believe every good thing I do is driven by God. I was born into a Catholic family. My father was a history teacher in secondary school, and my mom was a social worker. We lived humbly on the east side of Montreal. Sometimes, I think the reason my family was very devoted is because we didn't really have much. But we enjoyed a simple life. We went to Mass every Sunday. We always made time to pray together as a family. We prayed for our family, and we prayed for others, too.

God has shaped my life in a way I could never imagine. I won a scholarship to attend a good private school and received a good education through university and medical school. Had I grown up with privilege, I would probably take all the blessings in my life for granted. But I really believe in God's involvement in my life. That's why I always want to give back to my family, my friends, and my patients. God has already given me so much.

Of course, there was a phase in my life where I doubted the existence of God. Especially when I was an undergraduate. But then, when I got into medical school and learned about medicine, it confirmed my belief that God exists. I decided to stick to my Catholic faith because it gives me a lot of hope and teaches me unconditional love, although I am pretty sure that other religions teach the same things. So much depends on the person. I am someone who prefers a faith I can experience through my senses, like seeing, tasting, touching, hearing, and smelling. The Catholic Church and Catholic prayers allow me to experience all of them, like when we receive Holy Communion, smell the burning candle, listen to beautiful church music, or even touch the rosary. When I am not feeling good about myself or about other people or about a situation, I know that God will always be with me and make me feel better.

Many of my colleagues do not believe in God. And I respect their point of view. Sometimes, we can find explanations through science, and that makes us less willing to believe in God. But I can see God's greatness even more clearly in medical science. From the smallest things like childbirth to how our body regulates itself, how our brain works, or how our heart keeps pumping blood 24/7 until death. For me, it's hard to think that everything just happens on its own without God.

Aside from being a doctor, the other thing I did to give back to God was to build a solid community where people could feel a sense of belonging. In the beginning, I was not sure how to manage it. I remember that when I was in university, I took a conducting class just out of curiosity and for fun. Little did I know that this skill would bring a lot of joy and fulfillment in my life now.

Two years ago, I spoke to my church priest and said that I would like to assemble a choir team for our church. I came up with this idea because I felt sad whenever the soloist sang by herself during Mass. Nowadays, not a lot of people go to church anymore. The churches in Quebec are quite empty. Quebec used to be the most Catholic province in Canada, but because of the *Revolution Tranquille* in the 1960s, it became a secular province. I kind of understand where it was coming from. Back then, the Catholic churches abused their power, so it created resentment among my parents' generation.

Nevertheless, I told myself that there is no perfect religious institution. No perfect clergy. Nobody is perfect. Even the most religious person. Although some of the religious teachers may have been poor examples, it doesn't mean that the teaching is bad. I find that the teaching and the values of the Catholic faith help me be more positive, hopeful, and accepting. This is why I still stick to my faith.

Anyway, the priest really liked the idea of a choir and gave me permission, so I posted a call for an audition in the church bulletin. In the beginning, only five people showed up. Now we have about twenty members. I would never have expected the choir to be as established as it is now. Not only do we sing well together, but we have become like family. We do all sorts of outings– camping and retreats every year. We all come from different backgrounds, but we really care about each other. Each member feels a sense of belonging.

We usually have rehearsals every Tuesday and Thursday, and we sing during the 11 a.m. Sunday Mass. Although my residency schedule is packed, I try my best to keep this choir running smoothly. I am glad that I have found this calling.

Chapter 5
Regina de Luca
Basilica St. Augustine
Sunday, Second Week of March

On this lovely Sunday morning, I attend the Mass in English at St. Augustine Basilica downtown. Today, my choir is not scheduled to sing, so I sit in the middle of the church. Usually, we sing at the 11 a.m. Sunday Mass twice a month. Next week will be our turn.

I really like attending Mass. The music is very beautiful, and the readings, as well as the homily, can sometimes serve as reminders of our shortcomings and that there is always hope in God. Although some people think the Catholic Mass is boring and repetitive, I see the appeal. I like the familiarity and repetitiveness. It feels like home.

Being grateful for my life motivates me to go to Mass—especially for being able to live my dream life in Montreal as a violinist. I don't know how to better express my gratitude to God.

Other times, I go to church because I need strength. It is not easy living on my own in a foreign country, although I have been living here for eight years. Yes, I do have my orchestra friends and my choir friends. But sometimes, I feel lonely and isolated. Plus, I am a worrier. There are a lot of "what ifs" in my head. What if the orchestra doesn't renew my contract? What if I fail to obtain my permanent residency? Every time I feel worried, I always reach out to God.

Maybe if I lived an easy life with my family in Italy, I would not be as reliant on God as I am now. But, nevertheless, I feel like it's worth it. At least I feel like God watches over me and loves me.

Today, my concern is to find a new place to rent. Apparently, it is hard these days to find a place under $1,000. I prefer downtown because I spend most of my time in *Place des Arts* and the church. And by living downtown, I can save money on transportation, too.

So, after the Mass is over, I light a candle and pray. *God, please help me find a suitable place. Maybe I am asking too much. But I hope I can find a place close to where I work and within my budget. I trust that You will take care of me, God. Amen.*

Today, the orchestra has a concert scheduled at 3 p.m., so after Mass, I quickly return to my apartment to change clothes and practice my violin a bit more.

I admit that I am a perfectionist. Although my track record has proven that my skills are adequate—such as getting into a prestigious music school and getting an offer from a world-renowned orchestra—I still feel like I am not good enough compared to everybody else. But the more mature I become, the more I try to accept myself. I still focus on improving my technique as best as I can, but if there is nothing else I can do, I try to accept it and be kind to myself.

I don't know if I could ever become a concertmaster. The other violinists in our orchestra are much better than I am. They studied in top schools like Juilliard, Curtis, and Berklee. I admit that sometimes I suffer from impostor syndrome. Whenever I find myself not progressing as much as I want, I remind myself that God has put me in the right place and that I should be patient. My timing could be different from God's timing, but, in the end, God's timing is always better.

After I finish practicing, I put my violin in the case and change to a long black dress for the performance. I also put on some makeup and contact lenses. Then I check myself in front of the mirror.

Not bad, I think. I have long black hair down to my waist. Without my usual glasses, my eyes look bigger. I can see my black irises. Usually, I have to wear glasses. I am 165 centimeters tall and weigh fifty kilograms. Unfortunately, I have a skinny body type with an almost flat chest and butt. When I was younger, I used to be very insecure about my body. But now, I tell myself that a lot of curvy girls want to be skinny. Some skinny girls want to be curvier. The grass is always greener on the other side. So, I imagine, even if I were curvier, I might not be as happy as I thought I would be. I am more of a plain type of girl rather than beautiful or stunning. But overall, I am happy with my appearance now.

I walk toward *Place des Arts*. Montreal weather in March is still quite chilly. The temperature is about zero right now, and the snow has not all melted. Since I still have an hour to kill, I decide to sit in a coffee shop at St. Catherine Street and drink my favorite mochaccino. I listen to Bach's Air on the G String, one of the pieces that our orchestra will be performing this afternoon. This is one of my favorite activities to do by myself, drinking coffee while listening to classical music. The other things I enjoy are hunting for and reading books, and, of course, playing my violin. I think I enjoy my own company too much. Maybe that's why I am still single at twenty-three years old. I have never had a boyfriend. There were a few guys in the past who showed interest, but unfortunately, I didn't think our values aligned. So I made it clear to them.

I don't really have many criteria in terms of the type of guy I want to date. As long as he has the same values and beliefs as I do, and is loving, caring, loyal, and hardworking, that's enough for me. I don't need someone very rich or handsome or athletic.

So far, I have not found anyone. Wait, actually there is someone who caught my attention. He is our choir's conductor.

Clearly, he is very devoted to his faith and very hardworking. He also cares about us as his choir members. Many girls in our choir have a crush on him, but because he is kind to everybody, it's hard to know if he thinks of me as more than just a choir member. We've chatted quite a few times, but our conversations are only around the topic of my violin rehearsals, performances, and teaching. Sometimes, he asks me to do a solo for the choir, and I feel butterflies in my stomach.

However, I don't want to expect too much and be disappointed. And I am a shy type of girl who would not dare chase a guy. So, maybe there is no hope for me and him unless he makes a move first.

I glance at my watch, and it's time to go. I finish my mocha and walk toward *La Maison Symphonique*. At least my life as a musician keeps me busy, so I don't really have time to think about guys.

Chapter 6
Olivier Lefebvre
Plateau Mont-Royal
Tuesday, Third Week of March

"So, we should decide if we are going to continue our relationship or not. I am tired," Isabelle huffs.

Honestly, I don't understand why she brings this up now. Can't she understand that my life has turned upside down, and talking about our relationship is the least of my priorities?

"Why do you bring this up, Isabelle? I never said I wanted to break up." Exhaustion fills me.

"But you are no longer available. You have changed. You are not as responsive as before. You even ignore my text messages."

"Then why don't you call me?"

She snaps, "Why don't *you* call *me*? You are not even working. What is it that you are doing?"

"I am busy with tons of medical appointments, Isabelle! Plus, I am busy sorting out my life: talking to my personal injury lawyer, calling my insurance company, claiming my disability benefit, suing that truck driver who made my life miserable!" My patience is gone.

I still love her. I look at her beautiful face, but I'm frustrated at her lack of compassion. I expect her to be more understanding of my situation.

I remember the first time we met. It was at a party when we were in CEGEP. She is a year younger than I am. At that time, Isabelle was training to be a ballet dancer. She has blond hair and a thin figure. Like me, she is very dedicated to her work. However, back then, we were only acquaintances.

We added each other on social media and congratulated each other during birthdays, but that was it. I was not interested in a serious relationship when I was in CEGEP. After CEGEP, she joined the most prominent ballet company in Quebec as an apprentice. Not long after, she moved up the ranks from corps de ballet, to soloist, and then to principal dancer at twenty-five.

It was when I watched her performance as the swan queen during *Swan Lake* that I became captivated by her. She was still a soloist at that time, but her dancing was pure and strong. After that, I reached out to her on social media and asked her out. After she agreed, we started hanging out casually for a few months. I enjoyed her company. She was witty, elegant, ambitious, and she knew what she wanted in her life. Every time I looked at her, I was hypnotized by her beauty. She definitely has transformed since CEGEP. Moreover, she was also very good in bed. She was confident in her skin and quite sexy.

The night she got promoted to principal dancer two years ago, we celebrated her promotion by having dinner in a fancy restaurant in Old Port. We enjoyed a nice meal with a bottle of champagne. That was when I asked her to be my girlfriend. After that, we spent a beautiful night at my place.

But I have to admit that our relationship has turned cold since my accident. When I was still in the hospital, Isabelle visited me regularly. But then it became less and less often. When I was staying at my parents, our relationship turned awkward. We did not communicate or connect as much as we used to. Not to mention that we couldn't be as intimate as before due to my injury.

For some reason, I don't want to bother her too much with my problems. Maybe because I don't want to show her my vulnerability. Before the accident, our relationship was really good because my life was good. Now that my life is not as good, our relationship is not doing well.

"I am sorry if I have not been attentive lately. It is a new situation for me, too. I hope you understand." I try to reason with her.

"I think we should take a break."

I am not surprised by her response, but I admit it hurts. Yet what can I do?

"Okay then, if that's what you want." I don't know what else to say. She starts to cry. I try to hug her, but she pushes me away. She seems to be thinking while crying for a few minutes. Then she makes up her mind.

"Bye, Olivier." She gets up and leaves.

For the next few hours, I cannot feel anything. It's too much to take in. I still have not fully recovered from my injury, and now my girlfriend breaks up with me. Why does everything seem to be against me?

I think about calling Jean-Luc, but then I change my mind. Although Jean-Luc is my best friend, he has never had a serious relationship. He would not understand. Then I remember someone. I grab my wallet, pull out a piece of paper with a phone number written on it, and dial.

An hour later, Ethan shows up at my front door.

"Come in." I let him inside. I am not sure why I decided to call Ethan. Maybe because he appears very sympathetic and encouraging. "Thank you for coming on short notice," I say.

"No problem. It's perfect timing. I just finished my shift," he says, taking off his jacket. We walk toward the living and dining room area.

"Can I get you anything to drink?" I ask.

"Oh, water is fine. Thank you. But let me help you." He follows me to the kitchen and grabs two glasses. I can do it myself, even though it is a bit more tedious navigating two crutches.

"So, how are you feeling? Is everything okay?" Ethan asks after we sit down on the couch.

In the beginning, I hesitate. Why am I discussing my personal problem with someone I barely know? But for some reason, I feel I can trust him. So I tell him about Isabelle and what happened between us.

"I'm sorry that this happened to you. Especially when you're still recovering. It must be tough," Ethan says sympathetically after hearing my story.

I nod.

"But don't you think that maybe she is going through a hard time herself?"

"Oh, what do you mean?" I am curious.

"Seeing someone you love get injured is also a tough situation. And now that you are busy taking care of yourself, you take care of her less than before. Maybe she couldn't accept that."

"Yes, you could be right. But what am I supposed to do?"

"It depends on how much further you want to take this relationship. Can you imagine her in your future? Can you imagine spending the rest of your life with her? If yes, figure out a way where you can compromise with each other. Think about what she needs, and whether you are able to fulfill her needs, regardless of your own limitations. Bad things happen in life, and the purpose of having a relationship is to support each other during tough times. If both of you cannot deal with this, that's an indication that your relationship may not survive in the future. That means she may not be the one for you," Ethan explains.

I digest his words. What he said completely makes sense. He makes me reflect on why I am in a relationship with Isabelle in the first place. Yes, she is attractive and hardworking, which is why I fell for her. Whenever there was a major milestone in our lives, we enjoyed having each other. But this is the first time I am experiencing a major setback, and I don't think she is the one who can support me during tough times.

As for whether I can imagine her in my future, I don't know. So far, we only have fun—going to movies, dining out, and having sex. But I haven't really thought further than that.

"Yeah, maybe she is not the one for me. But it still hurts that we are not as close as before. Even though the relationship only lasted two years, we had a lot of fun and great memories together."

"Oh, I'm sure you did. There are no right or wrong feelings. Allow yourself to be sad." Ethan presses my shoulder.

"Thank you, Ethan."

"My pleasure." He nods.

I really like talking to him. Usually, when I discuss my problems with Isabelle or my family, I am sure they are going to be on my side, whether I am right or wrong. But Ethan is looking at it more objectively.

"Oh, it's already six-thirty. Unfortunately, I have to go now. I have choir practice." Ethan gets up from his seat.

"Choir practice? You are in a choir?" I am a bit surprised.

"Yes! I am conducting more specifically." He looks very excited. "Hey, why don't you come to watch?"

I am thinking. Since he has been so kind for coming here, then why not? "Sure."

We drive in Ethan's car. I never imagined that Ethan would also conduct a choir. I am typically more into jazz music than classical. When I was younger, I was more into classical, but since none of my peers were listening to it, over time, I learned to love pop music like they did. But jazz is something I discovered recently. I listened to my jazz playlist when I was at work.

"So you are okay living by yourself now?" Ethan asks when we are on the road.

"Yes. This is my first week alone after staying at my parents' place for a month."

"Is someone occupying your first floor?"

"Yes. He is my longtime tenant."

"How about the third floor?"

"Currently, it is empty. I used to live on the third floor before my injury. I might be looking for a tenant to occupy it soon."

"I see. I will let you know if I hear of someone who needs a place," Ethan says.

"Thank you. That would be helpful."

We enter a church complex downtown. Wait, isn't this supposed to be a choir practice? Why are we going to church? Ethan parks the car, and when he is about to enter the basilica, I stop and grab his arm.

"Is this a choir rehearsal for the church?"

"Yes, the choir is part of the church." Ethan frowns. "Is there something wrong?"

I am not sure. I don't feel comfortable in a church. I can see that it is a gigantic and gorgeous basilica with a high ceiling. But what I witnessed when I was eight years old made me feel disgusted about everything related to religion. Also, a lot of money must have been spent to build this church. It's the same thing with other beautiful churches all across Montreal. Don't they know that many people are suffering from poverty and neglect? How about the indigenous people they mistreated? Aren't people ashamed of this huge, expensive church?

"I am sorry, but church is not really my thing."

"Oh, okay." Ethan looks a bit confused. "I am sorry. I didn't know."

"No, no. I am sorry. Maybe we can catch up again some other time?" I feel a bit guilty because he has set aside his time to come over to my place to listen to my problem, but I am not willing to watch his choir rehearsal.

"Yes, no problem. How are you going to get home, though?"

"I will take an Uber. Don't worry. Sorry I cannot join you."

"It's okay. Take care, Olivier. See you around!" He looks a bit sad but still polite.

"Have fun with your choir practice!" I smile. Then he disappears into the church.

I take out my phone and open my Uber app. The driver will be here in five minutes. Phew.

Chapter 7
Regina de Luca
Basilica St. Augustine
Tuesday, Third Week of March

"So you are looking for a new place?" Christie Lim, one of my fellow sopranos, asks me while we are waiting for the choir rehearsal to begin. It is 7:40 p.m., and the rehearsal usually starts at 8 p.m. The rehearsal is on the third-floor balcony, where the organ is located. The Mass itself is usually on the main floor, so the people on the main floor can hear our voices, but they aren't able to see us unless they sit on the third floor.

"Yes. Possibly in downtown and within walking distance from *Place des Arts*," I answer.

"And your budget is?" Christie asks.

"A thousand dollars." Christie frowns. "I know it's kind of hard," I say.

"I pay twelve hundred in Rosemont." Christie is working as a computer programmer. Her office is downtown, but she can work from home three days per week.

"Yeah, we'll see. Maybe I will be lucky."

Then people start coming in. There are seven sopranos, five altos, three tenors, four basses, and one organist in our choir group. We are all close to each other. But the people I hang out with outside of the rehearsal are Christie, Genevieve, and Carla from alto, as well as Samuel and Luiz from tenor. We are a pretty diverse group here. Christie came to Canada from South Korea when she was eighteen years old; Genevieve is a local Franco-Quebecer; Carla is of Filipino descent and was born here; Samuel came to Canada two years ago from Haiti; and Luiz immigrated from Brazil when he was five years old. All of us relate well because we are around the same age range, which is twenty-two to twenty-five. We are all in the beginning of our adult lives. Genevieve is an elementary school teacher, Carla is an accountant, Samuel is pursuing his master's degree in history, and Luiz manages his family's restaurant.

Some choir members, university students, are younger. Others are in the age range of twenty-five to thirty, including our conductor, Ethan O'Sullivan. If I am not mistaken, he is twenty-eight years old and currently working as an orthopedic surgery resident.

"Hey, how are you guys doing?" Luiz greets us with a big smile, as usual. Maybe because he serves customers every day, he always has a lively and fun personality. He brings such a positive vibe. Luiz and Samuel take a seat behind Genevieve and Carla. Christie and I sit beside Genevieve and Carla.

"Good, good. How are you?" Genevieve asks.

"Terrific! Our restaurant is getting busier and busier. Which is a good sign," Luiz says. We speak in French to each other because that's the language we are more comfortable with compared to English. We listen to see what everybody is up to.

At 7:55 p.m., Ethan comes in. Christie brushes her arm against mine to tease me. She knows I used to have a crush on Ethan. Even though I try to convince her it's all in the past, she keeps teasing me. Luckily, only she knows about my feelings toward Ethan. I give Christie a warning look.

"Okay, thanks for coming in on time, everyone." Ethan is looking at all of us with approval. He speaks in English because not all the choir members understand French. Some of them are not originally from Montreal and are here only to study at the university.

"This Sunday, we are scheduled to sing at 11 a.m. So, today is our second to last rehearsal before the big day. Let's polish everything today, if possible. And on Thursday, we will be in good shape for the final rehearsal."

Although Ethan is very warm and kind, he can be quite strict and a perfectionist when it comes to rehearsal. Sometimes if he is not satisfied with the sound, he will ask us to repeat by group—soprano, alto, tenor, or bass—separately. That can be intimidating.

We start with a prayer and then we start rehearsing with the opening song for the Mass, "Gather the People," by Daniel Schutte. At least the opening song went pretty well. Ethan only asked the altos to repeat the refrain part once. I like the hymns that we sing during Mass. They are very simple. Usually there is a typical refrain and then several verses. The fact that it is repetitive and predictable is what I like. It allows people to pay attention to the meaning, not just the melody. This particular song makes me more joyful and reminds me to treat the Mass like an invitation from God to be united with people and to share the joy.

Then we continue with the offertory song, Communion, and the closing song. There are still the ordinary songs, psalms, and alleluia that we have not had a chance to practice. But it's already almost 9:30 p.m. As I said, due to Ethan's perfectionism, we will not move on to the next song until he is satisfied with the current song.

"All right, I think we have enough for today. You guys have done a good job. There is still some room for improvement, and we will try that next Thursday. And please, when you sing, try to understand the meaning instead of just singing the melody and following the rhythm. Even though we sing for God, not for entertaining an audience, I still want you to sing well. The better you sing, the more people will be touched and inspired by the message of the song. Understand?"

"Yes!" We all nod in agreement. I am glad that Ethan also has the same thoughts as I do.

We start to collect our belongings to leave. While we descend the stairs, Christie catches up with me.

"I really hope that you will find a place soon. Keep me updated, and I will keep looking for you." I like that Christie is always supportive and caring.

"Yes, I will. Thank you so much!" I say with a smile.

"Okay, I have to rush now. See you on Thursday!" She hurries out the door.

"See ya!" I shout back.

Then a voice from behind startles me a bit.

"You are looking for a place, Regina?"

It's Ethan.

"Um, yes. I am trying to find a place because my current landlord is increasing my rent."

He descends the stairs with me.

"You live in McGill Ghetto, right? What is your budget per month?"

I am surprised that he still remembers where I live. I think I told him quite a while ago. "A thousand dollars. They are increasing it to eleven-fifty," I say with disappointment.

"I know someone who is looking for a tenant. He lives near Mont-Royal and Esplanade Avenue. Right on the northeast corner of Jeanne-Mance Park. Are you interested? I don't know how much he charges, though."

I am calculating in my head how far it is to walk from Jeanne-Mance Park to *Place des Arts*. It will probably take about thirty minutes. During the summer it's fun. Especially in the Plateau area. On the way to *Place des Arts*, I can drink coffee on St. Laurent Street, where there are unique local restaurants and coffee shops. How about in the winter, though? But since it's

March now and spring is almost here, maybe staying there temporarily is fine. The thing is it's almost two weeks before April 1st, and I have to find a place before then.

"Yeah, I'm interested if it is less than eleven-fifty," I say enthusiastically.

"Perfect. I'll ask him and text you." Ethan smiles.

"Thank you so much, Ethan!"

"My pleasure."

On the way out, we continue talking about my upcoming violin performance as well as his residency. I always find him easy to talk to. But he is friendly and very approachable to everybody, not just to me, so I remind myself to not be too hopeful.

Chapter 8
Olivier Lefebvre
Plateau Mont-Royal
Wednesday, Fourth Week of March

I am in the middle of cleaning my place when I receive a text from Ethan. Since I have not gone back to work yet, I want to do something useful even with my limited capacity, such as cooking and cleaning.

Hey Olivier, how much do you charge to rent the third floor at your place? A friend of mine is interested. Please let me know.

How much should I charge? Good question. The tenant who occupies the first floor pays $1,000. So I think it would be fair to charge $1,100 for the third floor. I reply to Ethan:

$1,100 all included (wi-fi, electricity, and furnished). What is your friend's occupation?

It takes longer for Ethan to reply:

She is a violinist with the Orchestre Symphonique de Mont-Royal. She asks if it is possible to reduce the price to $1,000.

Hmm. A violinist, doesn't that mean that she is going to make loud noises when she is practicing? But if she is with the *Orchestre Symphonique de Mont-Royal*, she must be good, no? Also, as a professional musician with the best orchestra in town, I don't think she would fail to pay rent in a timely manner.

Okay. Let me know when she wants to schedule a visit.

In the end, we agree that she will come tomorrow to see the place. That means I have to clean the upper floor as well, which is great. I haven't cleaned the upper floor since I moved back to my plex.

I quickly finish cleaning my floor and go to the upper floor. I still have to use crutches, so it takes quite a lot of effort to go up. I rely on both my hands and my uninjured right leg. Halfway up, I have to stop to take a breath. Sometimes my side still feels painful when I take a deep breath.

When I finally arrive at the third floor, all my memories about my life before the incident come back. The floor plan is similar to the second floor. I walk to the bedroom where I used to sleep. Isabelle used to sleep over almost every weekend. I miss her now. We have not contacted each other since she decided to take a break from me. I feel sad.

The living room and the dining room on the third floor are combined, and there is my old kitchen at the back. I am not into cooking that much. I only cook basic stuff for my survival. I used to dine out a lot with Isabelle.

The third-floor plex also has its own balcony. The view is stunning; you can see Stade Olympique and the east view of Montreal from here.

I start cleaning the third floor. It's not that bad, but the dust is thick because I haven't lived here for three and a half months now. I change the sheets in the bedroom, wipe all the dust from every table and countertop. Once I finish that, I sweep and mop the floor.

Cleaning the bathroom will be a little bit challenging. I will have to bend my body and my knee, and that will put pressure on my ribs and femur. But if I don't push myself to move more, I feel like I am not going to make progress in my recovery.

So, I take a spray cleaner and a sponge, slowly put my crutches against the wall, and only rely on my right leg to stand. I kneel beside the bathtub but only put weight on my right knee. I spray the cleaner all over the bathtub and let the soap soak for a while. Damn, my right leg starts to cramp.

I lean forward to start scrubbing the bathtub, although my ribs hurt. I try not to twist my body much. But after five minutes, I give up. I am out of breath already.

I sit on the floor and lean against the bathtub while keeping both legs straight. I close my eyes, trying to catch my breath. *Welcome to a new reality,* I tell myself.

Chapter 9
Regina de Luca
Plateau Mont-Royal
Thursday, Fourth Week of March

I check the address that Ethan gave me one more time to make sure I am in front of the right house. I look at the plex. It is such a gorgeous and big triplex made from red brick. The outdoor staircase to the second floor is made from metal, and it's beautifully angled.

According to Ethan, the vacant unit is on the third floor, but the owner is living on the second floor. So I knock on the second floor door.

I climb the stairs carefully because it's pretty steep. Luckily, there is no more snow on the stairs. I arrive at the balcony on the second floor. In front of me there are two doors: one door is to enter the second-floor unit, and the other is for the third-floor unit.

I take a deep breath and knock on the door to the second-floor unit. In less than a minute, a man opens the door.

I have never seen a man so beautiful but so heartbreaking at the same time. How would I describe him? A man in his late twenties or early thirties. He is very handsome and polished with his neat black hair and blue eyes. He looks very classy in a dress shirt tucked into his jeans. But at the same time, he looks…broken. He has crutches and wears a leg brace on his left leg. It seems like he is still recovering from his injury. His face looks gaunt although still very handsome. There is an aura of royalty surrounding him.

"Hi. You must be Ethan's friend." The man speaks in French. He sounds very formal and a bit cold.

I reply in French, too. "Yes. My name is Regina. I am here to look at the rental unit."

"I am Olivier. Nice to meet you." We shake hands. He is polite, but he doesn't smile. "We'll go to the third floor."

He slowly locks the door to the second-floor unit and unlocks the door to the third-floor unit. After that, he stands back a bit to let me go up first. So, I climb the stairs while he is climbing behind me.

Poor guy. He must be struggling with his crutches.

By the time we arrive on the third floor, he is already panting hard. I feel bad for him. It makes me wonder what happened to him. Perhaps he sustained injuries other than his leg.

I look around. The unit looks spacious despite being in a triplex. It is also very cozy and antique. The furniture is old but very elegant.

"I will show you the bedroom." Now, he takes the lead, and I follow him. The bedroom has a king-size bed and small tables on each side with table lamps. The view from the window overlooks Mount Royal and a glimpse of the downtown skyline. He also shows me the closet, which is bigger than what I need.

Then we continue to the living/dining room, which is designed elegantly. There is natural light from the big window that offers an east view of Montreal. Aside from that, most of the lighting is yellow, which is my preference. I imagine that living here must be very comfortable. Everything looks classy and serene.

Olivier shows me the bathroom. It is much brighter and bigger than my current bathroom.

"Sorry, I didn't have a chance to clean the bathtub because of my condition." He points toward his left leg.

"No worries at all. It all looks good to me," I reply with an encouraging smile.

Then he shows me the kitchen, which I really like. It is quite big and has a lot of storage. I cook a lot, especially Italian food. I also like to try new recipes.

After the kitchen, we go to the balcony at the back. The view is stunning. I can see other plexes, Mont-Royal Avenue, and Stade Olympic from afar. Montreal seems very calm and European from here.

"This is gorgeous," I say.

"I agree." He nods and smiles. He looks more relaxed when he smiles.

After the tour, I know my decision already. Although it's a bit far from *Place des Arts*, it is such a nice place. A place like this can give me a lot of inspiration as a musician. Plus our orchestra usually plays baroque, classical, and romantic music. This place has the perfect ambiance.

We go back to the stairs to go down. I notice that he is a bit hesitant. Going upstairs with crutches is one thing. Going down them without a handrail is another.

"Do you need help?" I offer my right arm for him to hold. He hesitates a bit, but then he moves his left crutch to his right hand and holds my arm with his left hand. His hand feels cold on my skin.

"Thank you," he says. Then we go down slowly. He winces every time he has to put weight on his left thigh.

"So what happened to you, if you don't mind me asking?"

"Car accident."

"I am sorry."

"That's okay."

After we arrive at the second-floor balcony, he releases my arm.

"Thank you for helping me."

"No worries. I am interested in the place," I reply. He turns to me with a bit of surprise. Maybe he doesn't expect that I will make the decision that quickly. The thing is, April 1st is approaching, and finding a new apartment is a bit stressful. And this one is very good for its price.

"Great. I will send you the paperwork by email." Then we exchange email addresses and phone numbers.

"Okay. I don't know if Ethan has told you or not, but I am a violinist, so I have to practice every day. Would the noise be a problem for you? I will not practice after nine p.m., though, I promise."

"No, it won't be a problem. As long as you play well," he says with a smile. A bigger smile this time.

I feel hopeful that we will get along as neighbors.

Chapter 10
Olivier Lefebvre
Plateau Mont-Royal
Thursday, Fourth Week of March

I close the door after Regina leaves. I have a good feeling about her. I think she will be a good tenant. She looks like a modest girl by the way she dresses and talks. She wears thick glasses and no makeup. Probably a bit nerdy, but in a good way, like Ethan. I would assume she is just a diligent girl who likes to play violin and is not a troublemaker. In case you are wondering, I am not attracted to Regina physically, as my heart is still for Isabelle.

I am so sick of not being able to walk properly, and it irritates me. I was a bit embarrassed when I had to hold on to Regina to go downstairs. Yesterday, I went down the stairs on my butt. Obviously, I don't want to do that in front of other people.

I made a decision to stop complaining about my pain and just start working. The managing partner has asked about my return to work. He is also giving me a work-from-home option. I initially thought that I was not going to start working until mid-April. But I think working will make me feel normal again, gain a sense of accomplishment, and distract me from the pain.

So, I start setting up a workstation in the living room by the window with my laptop, two monitors, and a printer/scanner. I add some stationery and papers.

Up until now, I have been replying to some work emails through my phone. I typically receive about 300 emails per day. During my absence, I handed over all my client engagements to Alex, one of the senior managers whom I trust. I think in the next few weeks, I will be busy reviewing and signing some valuation reports that he has completed.

I prefer doing valuation much more than audit. I have found it more fulfilling. Our clients typically consist of large companies in Canada who are looking to buy other companies through mergers and acquisitions. Our team provides a valuation assessment of how much the potential company is worth. I started as a senior associate who crunched the numbers, performed financial modeling, and did market research analysis.

I have always believed in myself. I know my strengths and how to leverage them. Although I am confident, I don't think I appear pretentious or anything. I treat other people with respect. And if I appear harsh to other people, I am also hard on myself. If I don't know something, I try to figure out the answer. *Lazy* is not in my dictionary. When I was a junior at the firm, I never pointed out problems without proposing the solution to my boss, even if it meant that I had to take extra steps. But because of that, I learned new things and gained new experiences that have benefited me in the long run. I also position myself in my boss' shoes. What is it that he wants to know? How can I deliver it to him in the best possible way so that he can save time when reviewing it? Because of this mentality, my boss and my junior always relied on me. I have to go back to work as soon as possible so that I can feel I am doing something useful again.

Since it's already 4 p.m. and the sky is turning dark blue, I decide that I will start work tomorrow instead. In the meantime, I am sending Regina a copy of the tenant agreement that she can sign. I'm slowly putting my life together again.

At night, I make myself an herbal tea and drink it on my balcony at the back. I enjoy listening to the wind and feeling the breeze. I realize that I am lonely and purposeless without my job and without someone by my side.

Chapter 11
Regina de Luca
Plateau Mont-Royal
Monday, First Week of April

Today is moving day. My choir friends—Christie, Genevieve, Carla, Sam, and Luiz—have agreed to help me out. Although I don't have that many belongings, I still appreciate their kindness.

Apparently, I only need two cars to fit all my belongings. We use Luiz and Genevieve's cars to transport my belongings from McGill Ghetto to the Plateau, while Carla, Sam, and I drive with Christie to the Plateau. It is a really fun time together.

It is 6 p.m. by the time we finish moving everything to the third-floor unit. It was challenging and tiring to climb two giant staircases while carrying stuff—quite a workout.

Ethan joined during the last hour. Honestly, I don't know how to thank him. If it wasn't for him, I would probably still be struggling to find a place. Or maybe I would have found one but not as comfortable and beautiful.

After the moving is finished, we order pizza and hang out in my new apartment. My friends agree that the place is very beautiful and elegantly designed. I sometimes glance at Ethan, excited that he is able to join us today.

"So, I am curious about your landlord. Ethan, I heard that he is your friend?" Genevieve asks.

"Yes. We went to the same school since Grade 4."

"Wow, that's such a long friendship. He must be very well off to own a plex like this," Genevieve waves as if to encompass the whole place.

"What does he do for a living?" Christie asks. Everybody is curious about my landlord now.

"He used to be an accountant and is now a business valuator and partner at a big accounting firm," Ethan replies.

"Wow, that's impressive. Becoming a partner before thirty is not easy," Carla adds. She is also an accountant but in a smaller firm. Right now she is pursuing her CPA designation.

"Yeah, when we were in school, he was extremely smart," Ethan says.

"Smarter than you?" I ask him, half curious, half teasing.

"Hmm…depends on which subjects. Sometimes, he achieved higher grades; sometimes, I did."

"So what does he look like?" Genevieve asks.

I look at Ethan, and he looks at me. I am not sure how to describe him.

"He is very polished and formal. I feel like he is upper class, you know," I say.

"Haha, are you intimidated by him, Regina? You're such an accomplished musician yourself," Ethan reminds me.

My heart leaps with joy. Ethan is always very encouraging.

"Thank you, Ethan." I blush.

"You should invite him to join our choir. We need more tenors, assuming he is one," Luiz says.

"Yeah, that would be a good idea. Does he sing, Ethan?" Sam asks.

"Hmm. Good question. I have never heard him sing."

"Do you think he is downstairs now? Why don't we sing so that he may be persuaded to join when he hears us?" Luiz says.

"I don't think he would be interested. Good attempt though, Luiz," Ethan says.

"Regardless, why don't we practice while we are together now? It would be fun, no?" Sam proposes.

"Yeah, I am in. What song should we sing?" Genevieve is now enthusiastic.

"How about 'You Are My Hiding Place' by Michael Ledner?" Carla asks.

We all nod enthusiastically.

"Yeah, let's do it!" Christie says.

"Ethan, are you ready?" Sam asks.

Now Ethan seems to be moved by our enthusiasm. "Okay, let's all stand." Ethan gets up, and so do we.

We warm up our voices a little bit and then start singing. This is one of our choir's favorite songs and my favorite, too. Every time I sing this, I believe that I can always rely on God, and I don't have to be afraid. Last month, I was so worried about finding a new place. But in the end, my move went well. God has guided me multiple times, but I still have worries. I hope I can just trust Him more and live lighter with fewer burdens.

I really enjoy singing together with my friends. It enhances teamwork. We're all trying to make a unity of the sound instead of trying to make our own voices stand out.

I truly enjoy my evening.

***

I thank all my friends who have come and helped me move. I look at them one by one going down the stairs and wave one last time. I notice Ethan doesn't go down.

"I think I am going to say hi to Olivier. Do you want to come?" he asks. I look at my watch. It's almost 9 p.m. I am not sure if he would welcome visitors.

"Yeah, I hope he doesn't mind," I say.

We knock on his door and wait. Then Olivier appears behind the door. Good thing he doesn't look surprised to see us. He looks really good in his black polo shirt and khaki shorts. His complexion is also much better than the last time I saw him.

"Hey, Olivier, are you busy? Would you mind if we come in? I just want to catch up. It's not going to take long," Ethan says.

"Yes, of course, no problem. Come on in." He also throws a smile at me while letting us in.

This is the first time I've seen his place. The layout is identical to mine. The difference is his unit has a longer hallway while mine is more open space.

He serves us water, and we sit in his living room. I notice he has his office set up by the window.

"You look much better, Olivier. How are you feeling?" Ethan asks.

"Much better. I have started working from home. Only four or five hours per day, though. I take it easy. But it definitely makes me focus on something other than the pain."

"I am glad to hear that. You are also walking better."

"True. My left thigh still hurts, but it's getting better. My ribs are also healing fine. Although I feel like they are still fragile, I can breathe easier now."

"Oh, you broke your ribs as well?" I ask. I thought he only hurt his leg. I didn't realize that he may have injured other parts of his body during the accident.

"Yes, two lower ribs and…" Olivier seems to want to say more but hesitates. "Yeah, it sucks."

"I am very sorry."

"That's okay. Things happen in life."

"Don't forget your medications, medical appointments, and the physiotherapy, though. They are very important," Ethan says.

"Yes. Thanks for the reminder."

They chat a bit more, and after that, Ethan decides to let Olivier rest.

"All right, call me any time you have questions or if you feel uncomfortable," Ethan says.

"I will. Thank you."

"You can let me know if you need help with anything, too. We are neighbors now," I say with a smile.

"For sure. Thanks, Regina. I hope you are settling in well. Let me know if you need anything, too." Olivier smiles back.

Chapter 12
Olivier Lefebvre
Le Plateau Mont-Royal
Second Week of April

This week, I start working full-time. Even overtime some days. There are a lot of things to catch up on. We are actually very far behind in our client engagements due to my absence.

I usually wake up at seven, eat breakfast, shower, and start working at eight. When it's 8 a.m. sharp, aside from logging into my computer, there is something else. I am waiting for a violin melody to float down from my neighbor above.

The first time I heard Regina playing violin was the day after she moved in. It was so beautiful. She was playing "Swan Lake," if I was not mistaken. The sound from her violin truly gave me goosebumps. The music melted my heart and made me calmer. I also had fewer nightmares about my incident this week. Plus, I could concentrate better at work while she was playing her violin.

I hope today she is going to play something good as usual. I drink my coffee and log in to my computer. When I am about to open my email, she starts playing.

I don't recognize the song this time—maybe a piece by Bach. She makes me want to go back to playing piano again. When I was younger, I took piano lessons until I was in secondary, but after that, I focused on hockey instead. Now that I can no longer play hockey, maybe I can go back to piano.

Instead of going through my email, I look up *Orchestre-Symphonique de Mont-Royal*. Apparently, April is a busy season for them. This weekend, they will perform at *La Maison Symphonique* for Bach repertoires.

Interesting. I check the ticket prices, and they're not expensive at all, so I buy a ticket for a main floor seat on Saturday evening. I don't book the VIP seat because usually VIP seats are in the front rows, and who knows, maybe the musicians can recognize the faces in those rows. I don't want Regina to discover that I will be attending her concert. That would be creepy.

At 9 a.m., the house becomes quiet again. I think Regina might be getting ready to work. After she leaves, I usually open my YouTube or Spotify playlist to continue to listen to classical music. Sometimes I listen to violin solos, sometimes orchestra, and sometimes piano, depending on my mood.

Regina is usually home at around 4 p.m., except for the weekends, when she practices later in the afternoon, leaves her place, and comes back at night. I know her schedule, not because I have a crush on her but because I enjoy her music.

Suddenly, I have an idea. Why don't I buy a musical instrument myself and start playing again? I obviously cannot play violin, but what if I buy a piano? There is still a lot of space in this living and dining area. Yeah. That's a good idea.

***

Olivier Levebvre

Archambault

Friday, Second Week of April

On Friday, I go to Archambault near Berri Uqam station. Since yesterday, I have started using an elbow crutch instead of my regular underarm crutches. The pain is still there, but it's much better these days. My new work routine and the live violin music make me feel so much better.

I go up to the top floor where they sell pianos. As much as the grand piano is tempting me, I don't think I need it. First of all, my place is not that big, and secondly, I don't play that well. I think the last level I completed was Level 8.

So, I try some upright pianos. Each brand has a different sound. I like the sound that is not too ringing. I prefer ones that are more subdued. Since I don't remember any songs, I just play the C major scale to try the piano. Finally, after trying six or seven different brands, I decide to buy the Steinway upright piano. I pay the cashier and ask the salesperson to deliver the piano to my address.

I don't know what has gotten into me. But the music that Regina plays is really inspiring and makes me want to play my music, too. I cannot wait until the piano arrives, which is in two business days. I can't stop smiling when I leave Archambault.

***

Olivier Levebvre
La Maison Symphonique
Saturday, Second Week of April

My Uber stops in front of *La Maison Symphonique* at *Place des Arts* complex. It looks like a lot of people are going to this concert hall to watch *Orchestre Symphonique de Mont-Royal.*

I used to go to Salle Wilfrid-Pelletier to watch Isabelle's ballet performances. It is also right beside *La Maison Symphonique.* This reminds me of Isabelle and makes me sad.

I walk inside the concert hall and go to the main floor hall. I am still self-conscious about my crutch and feel a bit insecure about my appearance. There are some older people using crutches in the hall, but I am the only young person who does.

Inside, the performance hall is almost full of people. The seating capacity is 1,900, and there are three balconies. The stage is still empty, with only chairs and music stands. The orchestra members must be backstage getting ready. It's still fifteen minutes before the concert starts.

My seat is in the middle. I sit down and skim the concert program for tonight:

Bach—Air, Suite No. 3 in D Major BWV 1068
Bach—Violin Concerto in A Minor BWV 1041
Allegro moderato
Andante
Allegro assai
Bach—Badinerie Orchestral Suite no. 7 BWV 1067
~Intermezzo~
Bach—Brandenburg Concerto no. 3 in G Major, BWV 1048
Allegro
Adagio
Allegro
Bach—Violin Concerto for Two Violins in D Minor, BWV 1043
Vivace
Largo ma non-Tanto
Allegro

So today they focus on Bach. I am familiar with half of the pieces and am really excited for the concert to start.

A few minutes later, the orchestra members start to appear one by one. I see Regina right away. She is with the second violin group. She looks nice in the long black dress and without glasses.

I did my research about orchestra before coming here, including the orchestra types, the instruments, the seating positions, and particularly *Orchestre Symphonique de Mont-Royal.* The orchestra was established in 1960 in Montreal. Currently, it has about ninety musicians. The instruments include strings, woodwinds, brass, and percussion. However, for tonight, there will be a harpsichord as well since Bach is from the Baroque era.

I also read a little bit about the musicians' backgrounds. You know who in particular. I found out that Regina was born in Sorrento, Italy. I knew from her accent that she was not from here and that she has an Italian last name. Nevertheless, I am still very impressed that she graduated from McGill and was able to join the best orchestra in the province. Even for the locals, it is pretty challenging.

Today is not the first time I've watched an orchestra performance. I have attended many times before, but usually to accompany my parents, not of my own volition. This time, I am the one who chose to go.

Then, the orchestra starts.

I honestly forgot how beautiful live orchestral performances can be. Listening on YouTube is not the same as listening live. Here, you can really feel the emotion of the music, and the musicians are all cohesive. When the orchestra finishes "Air," the audience applauds vigorously. It was very beautiful.

In the beginning, I thought I only knew half of the pieces on the program, but apparently, I've heard all these compositions when I was young. It's just I don't know the names. Despite hearing Regina practice every day, it's a whole new experience to hear her with the full orchestra.

Regina looks immersed in her music. Although she is not a soloist, she seems to be enjoying what she is doing and giving 100 percent. She also looks calm and peaceful when she plays. She is very comfortable with her violin and plays it with strength and beauty.

I am glad that I came to this concert tonight.

Chapter 13
Regina de Luca
La Maison Symphonique
Saturday, Second Week of April

My heart swells with joy when we finish the last piece, the third movement of the Violin Concerto for Two Violins in D minor. Although I was only part of the second violin group, not the soloist, I still feel fulfilled. Of course, everybody wants to be noticed; however, I realize that being a good musician sometimes means being okay in the background as a supporting role without losing the motivation to produce good, wholehearted music.

The audience gives us standing applause, and we bow. Today was such a good concert. It went smoothly and better than the rehearsals. I am proud to be part of this talented group.

Tomorrow will be our last concert, so I am going to take it easy tonight. Next week is going to be brutal because it's Easter week and our choir has to sing during the Easter Vigil.

I quickly go backstage and put my violin in the case, say goodbye to my friends, and walk to the bus stop to catch number 55. I know I can walk, but it's already almost 10:00 p.m., and I don't want to get exhausted.

Luckily, the bus arrives on time. It's only a ten-minute bus ride plus a five-minute walk to where I live now. I cannot wait to go to bed. I am happy but tired at the same time.

***

Regina de Luca
Plateau Mont-Royal

By the time I approach the plex, a car stops right in front of it. I am surprised to see Olivier exit the car. What a coincidence. It's been a week since I last saw him. Although we live in the same building, we don't really hang out, and I barely see him outside the house, not even in the backyard. However, he looks so much better now. Instead of using underarm crutches, now he only uses an elbow crutch.

"Hi, Olivier."

He turns to me and looks very surprised. Even more surprised than I am.

"Oh. Hi, Regina." He seems a bit more nervous than usual. He's dressed up tonight, with a white shirt and black dress pants. He's also slicked back his hair with gel. It looks like he has just had an important meeting or something, even though it's Saturday night.

"How are you?" I ask.

"I am good. How are you?"

"I am good, too. I see that you are using a new crutch now. Are you feeling better?"

"Yes, I am. Thanks for asking."

I have an impression that he is avoiding my gaze for some reason, and he doesn't look comfortable. It's weird. "Are you just coming back from somewhere?" I try to make him comfortable, although, I still feel a bit nervous around him. He is a bit intimidating with his formality and politeness.

"Yes, I just went to eat. How about you?"

Ah, that makes sense. Maybe he had an important dinner. "I just had a concert." I point at my violin.

"Oh, how did it go?"

"I think it went well. Better than expected." I smile.

"Good for you. What did you guys play tonight?" he asks while we start climbing the stairs. He lets me climb first as usual.

"This month is specifically dedicated to Bach, so we play a lot of his violin concertos and the Brandenburg Concertos as well as his other popular pieces. Do you know a lot about classical or baroque music?"

"Yeah, actually I am quite familiar with some of them. It's good that you play in an orchestra. It's not easy to get in, I am assuming."

We finally arrive in front of his door.

"Yeah, not easy. I think I am just lucky."

"I am sure you are good." He looks at the floor when he says it.

"Thank you." I smile at him.

"How do you like your new place, by the way? Are you settling in well?"

"Yes, I am. Thank you for asking. It's a very nice place."

"I'm glad."

"By the way, can you hear when I practice the violin?" I ask cautiously. "I am afraid it bothers you and the neighbor."

"Yes, I can hear you, but it doesn't bother me at all. You can continue practicing the way you do. I don't know about the neighbor, but I haven't heard any complaints yet," Olivier says.

"Okay. I will continue practicing then. Thank you for being accommodating."

"No problem. Goodnight, Regina."

"Goodnight, Olivier."

I walk up to my floor and enter my bedroom to change.

I replay my conversation with Olivier just now. I wonder why he looked a bit nervous earlier. Maybe it's just my imagination.

Maybe Olivier is not as cold, unapproachable, and intimidating as I thought he was. I also realize that that was the first time the two of us had a real conversation.

***

Olivier Lefebvre
Plateau Mont-Royal

I didn't expect that Regina would arrive home at the same time as I did. I should have considered that may happen. But I didn't.

I guess there is nothing wrong with going to a concert on Saturday night, right? Yes, Regina gave me the idea, but I don't think I went to the *Orchestre Symphonique de Mont-Royal* tonight specifically to watch her, did I?

With Isabelle not talking to me, I can't picture myself having feelings for another woman. At first glance, Regina is not my type. She is different from Isabelle. But when she wore a dress, didn't wear her usual glasses, and played violin on the stage, she showed me the other side of her today. However, I realize this is shallow. Maybe I put too much emphasis on physical appearance.

But Regina is a very nice and polite girl. In addition to that, she is very hardworking, practicing her violin diligently every day. She joined the best orchestra in the province. She came all the way from Italy and had to speak a foreign language and adapt to the culture. I wonder where her family is. It shows a lot of courage if she is, indeed, living in Montreal by herself.

Anyway, I try not to think about her.

I shower to clear my head and then climb into bed.

Chapter 14
Olivier Lefebvre
Plateau Mont-Royal
Thursday, Third Week of April

This week, I heard Regina practice singing. In the beginning, I didn't really pay attention to her singing as much as her playing the violin. Don't get me wrong, I think her voice is beautiful, even when I only hear it faintly from the second floor. The thing is, the songs she sings are more church music than popular music. It's not that I don't like church music; it's just not my genre.

I remember when Regina moved in, her choir members, including Ethan, helped her move, and at one point, they were singing together. It was beautiful, but it's just not something I usually listen to. Apparently, Regina is part of Ethan's choir. That's how they knew each other, and that's how Ethan knew she needed a place and recommended my place to her.

I also see Ethan in a new way. Before, when we were in school, I always assumed that he was just a kind boy who got along with everybody, except for my social circle. I was never really interested in venturing out of my circle. Now that I think about it, maybe we were a bit pretentious and exclusive. And now I can see why everybody likes Ethan. He is very kind and caring. Even his choir friends seem caring and supportive toward each other.

I wonder about my own circle. When I was still in the hospital, recovering from my injuries, they expressed a lot of sympathy. But over time, I feel like they have stopped asking how I am doing or how I am feeling. Only my parents check in on me. Not even Isabelle. She only cares about when I will go back to work.

Even my colleagues at work expressed sympathy in the beginning but now less and less. It's not that I want them to pity me all the time. It's just that I feel like nobody cares about me really. The firm probably only cares if I bring in revenue or not. The managing partners are probably wondering if I injured my brain during the incident. They want to make sure I am still able to ensure the quality of my valuation reports before signing them.

Anyway, maybe I became more sensitive and more self-conscious after the incident.

I go over to my new piano, a K-52 traditional upright Steinway, in the living room. It arrived two days ago, and I have started playing the pieces I played in secondary. It's been such a long time, but I am surprised that I still remember how to play the scales and even some of Bach's toccatas and fugues and Beethoven's piano sonatas—not with a perfect technique or anything. I made plenty of mistakes the first time, and I don't think I played with the right rhythm. But it helps to distract me from my daily frustration due to my physical pain and limitations. I also find myself pretty good at sight-reading.

When I am in the middle of playing a C major scale, my phone beeps with a text. I am surprised and excited when I read the sender's name—Isabelle.

Hey Olivier, would you like to have dinner tonight at Chez Victoire? There is something I need to talk to you about. Let me know.

My heart leaps with joy. From the tone of the text, it looks like we may continue our relationship. I reply right away:

Sure. What time?

Isabelle replies almost instantly.
Does 7 work for you?
Right now, it is 5 p.m. I still have two hours to get ready. I reply:
Yes, it works. See you.

It's been almost a month since she decided to take a break. I think a month is enough to make up our minds. Being away from her makes me realize that I miss her so much, and I need her presence in my life. I quickly shower and put gel in my hair. For our dinner, I wear my gray Massimo Dutti shirt and dress pants.

I am glad that now I am only using an elbow crutch. Last time Isabelle saw me, I was still using my underarm crutches. I want to look strong in front of her.

By 6:30 p.m., I am ready and leave the house.

***

Olivier Lefebvre

Chez Victoire

Isabelle is already at the restaurant, although I arrive ten minutes early. She is wearing an elegant black dress and looks stunning as usual.

"Hey." I sit in front of her.

"Hey."

I am not sure how our conversation is going to turn out. We order our food and catch up a bit about my work and her upcoming ballet performances. Apparently, she is going to be the lead role in *Cinderella*. We talk like normal. Maybe a bit more formal than before, but I take it as a good sign.

"So what is it that you want to talk about? Is it about our relationship?" I ask.

She drinks her wine slowly before taking a deep breath and saying, "Yes. I don't think we can continue our relationship."

My heart skips a beat. I expected this kind of conversation. My world is falling apart, and I want to cling to her, so why does she keep drifting away? And now our relationship is hanging on by a thread. It's painful to hear. I am not going to give up, though.

"What makes you want to break up?" I ask calmly.

"I just don't feel the same anymore. I am sorry."

"Is it because of my injury?"

"No."

"Then what is it?"

She keeps silent for a few minutes. I wait patiently. Maybe there is something else I don't know, and I don't want to push her too much.

"I fell in love with someone else. I am sorry," Isabelle admits.

I don't know how to describe my feelings. I feel numb in the beginning. This is something I didn't expect. If she wants to break up because of my behavior or something, then I can make a compromise. But this is something I cannot control or change. She fell in love with someone else? It's not fair at all. What did I do wrong?

I have had a lot of self-esteem issues since my accident, and this situation makes it even worse. I want to scream out of frustration, but I try to keep my composure.

"Who is this guy?" I ask.

"Do you really want to know?"

"Yes."

"Jean-Luc."

I freeze for a few seconds. *Jean-Luc*? My best friend since elementary school?

Jean-Luc is definitely more social than I am. He is more a charming type of guy, and I am more the "cool" guy. Jean-Luc is like me in that we never had to study hard, but we managed to get good grades. He studied sociology and then continued to law school at McGill University. Now he is working as a senior associate in one of the big law firms in Montreal.

He dated a lot of women, but none of them were serious relationships. He lives in the present moment, taking a lot of recreational drugs and partying, but he still manages to function really well at work.

I know that Jean-Luc and Isabelle are very close. They tease each other often. But I would never have suspected that they were having an affair. The Jean-Luc I knew was always beside me. He was the one who helped my parents take care of me after the incident. He helped them reorganize my place. His easygoing nature cheered me up tremendously during this difficult time. When I expressed my dissatisfaction about losing one kidney, he said, "Man, at least it's your kidney. Not your eyes or one of your limbs."

I never thought he would betray me. But I have noticed that he has been a bit distant lately. We haven't spoken that much since I returned to my place last month.

"Does he reciprocate your feelings?" I ask.

"Yes."

"Did you guys sleep together?" I know I am just hurting myself, but I need to know.

"Yes. I am sorry, Olivier."

"When did this happen?"

"When you were in the hospital. Sometimes, he drove me home. We both were devastated, you know. And then it just happened."

I don't know what else to say or to feel. This is too much for me to absorb. I want to punch something. Especially Jean-Luc's face. But I don't want Isabelle to see me broken.

"Okay. Good luck to the two of you then."

"I am sorry, Olivier. I really am. Jean-Luc, too. He feels so bad." She looks genuinely sad, but I don't trust her anymore. She is a ballerina after all. All she does is dance and act.

"Goodbye, Isabelle." I put some cash on the table and leave half of my steak uneaten. I cannot bear being in the same room with her even one more second. This is too much to take.

***

Olivier Lefebvre
Plateau Mont-Royal

My heart is beating fast on the way home. I feel like I am in flight or fight mode now.

I need some time to digest this change in my life. My best friend and my girlfriend are having an affair. The two people I love the most. Why? What's wrong with me?

That night, I cannot sleep. I cannot cry. I just stare at the ceiling in agony.

Chapter 15
Olivier Lefebvre
Plateau Mont-Royal
Friday, Third Week of April

The next day, reality starts to kick in. *Isabelle broke up with me. She is having an affair with Jean-Luc.* This means the future I imagined with her no longer exists. She is gone from my life. So is Jean-Luc.

I thought getting into a car accident was bad. This is worse. If I could choose, I would rather have another car accident but still be with Isabelle.

I cannot concentrate at work. I don't have any appetite. It is hard to keep taking care of myself. I keep asking myself what I could have done differently. Had the accident not happened, would we still be together? It feels like my life has no meaning now. I've never felt this empty and lonely.

Then, suddenly, I hear singing from above.

When you are alone, I am with you
When you suffer, I suffer with you
When your burden is too heavy
Trust Me and carry it with Me
Don't be afraid as things will get better
My child, I love you forever.

I wish I could believe there was someone who could share the burden with me like the God in the song. Or someone who could tell me not to be afraid of the future and that he or she loves me.

I feel tears in my eyes and a lump in my throat. Last time I cried was when I was in the hospital, when I realized that I had only one kidney. But that wasn't a cry like this. Today, I feel more broken than ever.

Suddenly, I have an idea. I text Ethan.

Hey, when is your next choir performance?

Ethan replies almost right away.

Tomorrow night during Easter Vigil.

I am not sure why I am doing this. Maybe because I want to hear more singing from Regina and the choir. It is kind of comforting. Or maybe it is because I just want to add some discomfort to my life. The more overall pain and discomfort you have, the less you focus on each of them.

***

Olivier Lefebvre

Basilica St. Augustine

Saturday, Third Week of April

The last time I was inside the church was when I was eight years old. Today I sit in one of the pews on the main floor. I thought I would feel uncomfortable because of what I witnessed when I was young, but surprisingly, I feel quite comfortable. I feel like I am at home. There is a sense of familiarity.

Most of the Masses in this church are in English. I guess this church is mostly for the Anglophone community. There are quite a lot of people here today for the Easter Vigil. If I remember correctly, this is the night when people celebrate the Resurrection of Jesus.

I don't know if I believe that someone can be resurrected from the dead. But regardless, I just need a good distraction from my breakup with Isabelle. At this point, I don't care if this celebration is superstitious or not.

In the past, when I was stressed, I usually called Jean-Luc or Isabelle and went to a bar and partied until late at night. Now, thinking about them makes my heart ache. Also, I felt empty going to the bar and getting drunk. Though I liked it on some levels, it never solved my problems.

I am not saying going to church will solve my problem either. But I feel a comforting vibe from the people who go to this church, like Ethan and Regina. I still feel guilty that the last time Ethan invited me to the church, I refused, so now I would like to listen to their performance.

Suddenly, the lights go off, and people start distributing candles. I take a candle from the man sitting beside me. He also shares his lighter and we all light our candles.

Then the procession begins, and the choir starts singing. I read the Mass guide that was distributed earlier. The song that they are singing right now is "Christ Be Our Light" by Bernadette Farrell.

It seems like the choir is on the third floor. I am actually very touched by their singing, even though I am not a believer. It represents how I feel right now—I am in the dark. I need some guidance and light, although I am not sure that Christ is the light I need.

I envy these believers, though. They must be very optimistic and hopeful in life because they have their God and Jesus. Who can I rely on when I am at the rock bottom of my life?

The Mass continues with some readings from the Bible. I only listen to 50 percent of it. The other half of me is still thinking about Isabelle and Jean-Luc. At least I am not as bitter and heartbroken as when I was at home by myself.

After the readings, there is a baptism ceremony. I forgot that older children and adults are baptized during the Easter Vigil. One by one, they come in front of the altar wearing white robes. There are five of them. Some of them seem older than I am, and some of them are my age and younger. Each of them has a godparent. Then the priest asks them a series of questions to confirm their faith.

After the baptism, the choir sings. The male soloist starts the first verse. I heard this song the night when Regina moved in. I read the Mass guide again and read the title: "You Are My Hiding Place" by Michael Ledner. Then I hear a female soloist singing the next verse. After that, the choir sings together.

Suddenly, I feel tears in my eyes again. With all these tragedies in my life and listening to this beautiful singing, I just want to surrender my life and hope that things will be all right for me in the end. At that instant, I experience an emotional breakdown and cry. It is so embarrassing. I have never cried in public before.

But then suddenly, the man beside me who shared the candle light offers me a Kleenex and puts his hand on my shoulder. He smiles sympathetically, even though we don't speak to each other.

I receive the Kleenex and whisper thanks to him. I feel extremely tired and drained of energy. But at least I feel something different. I feel sad but less bitter and more at peace.

Chapter 16
Ethan O'Sullivan
Basilica St. Augustine
Saturday, Third Week of April

It's already past midnight by the time we finish the Easter Vigil Mass. I thank all my choir members. They must be extremely tired, but I am sure we all feel satisfied to be able to sacrifice our time, energy, and effort to serve God.

They leave one by one while I am still gathering all the music sheets to put them in my bag. I thank again Luiz and Christie, who sang the solo parts for today's songs. I can see that they have practiced hard, and they delivered the song very well.

Then Linda, our organist, approaches me. She is a very kind lady and extremely dedicated.

"Hi, Linda. Great job today. Thank you very much for your service," I tell her.

"Thank you, Ethan. You are always very dedicated. I enjoy working with you."

"Thanks for saying that, Linda."

"However, Ethan, I am afraid it is time for me to retire from being the organist," she says.

I freeze for a second. What? No way. Without Linda, who will be playing the organ? What are we going to do without her?

"Oh, no. Why, Linda? Is it because of the schedule?" We usually have to sing twice a month, sometimes three times when other singers are not available. However, we usually practice twice a week every week, and I am aware that it is a big commitment.

"Not really. I would love to play as often as possible; however, my body does not allow me. I am seventy years old, Ethan." Linda's eyes look sad.

"Ah, okay. I understand. Thank you for letting me know, Linda. I hope you know how much you have helped us for the past two years. And for the past twenty years for this church."

"Of course. I am very happy to be a service to you all. I will keep playing until you find a new organist, and I will help train him or her. How does that sound?"

"That would be greatly appreciated. Thank you, Linda." I hug her and watch as she leaves and descends the stairs carefully, as fast as her frail body allows. I feel sad for her. Maybe I pushed her too much these past two years.

As I am the only person left on the balcony, I zip my bag and descend the stairs. This week was brutal. I didn't get enough sleep. I have to wake up at 4:30 a.m. to do rounds at 5 a.m. every morning. Plus, spending almost all my day in the OR. Today, I was on call all day before the Mass. I feel extremely tired, and I just want to go home.

I am about to exit the church when I see a man sitting in the middle of the pew. He is the only person left in the church. I walk carefully toward him. Then I realize that it's Olivier!

He looks like he is sleeping with his head tilted backward and his eyes closed. I didn't expect to find him here. I remember him texting me, asking about my next choir performance, but he didn't confirm that he would come.

"Olivier?" I shake his shoulder gently to wake him up.

He opens his eyes suddenly and looks disoriented for a while.

"Ethan?" I notice that his eyes are red. His pallor doesn't look good either.

"Are you okay?"

"Oh yeah, I am. I fell asleep after the Mass." He sits straighter now.

"What brings you here?" I sit beside him.

"I wanted to listen to your choir. I heard Regina's practice, and it was beautiful."

"Oh, yes. I am glad that you came."

I look at the high ceiling of the basilica. It is very beautiful. I am tired, but I am happy that Olivier decided to come here on his own, even though he is not a believer. We sit in the middle of the pew for a while.

"Are you sure you are okay? Your color doesn't look good," I say.

"Yeah, I am good. Thank you for asking. Maybe we should go." He rises from the seat.

I rise, too. "Do you want to come over to my place?" I know something is troubling him right now. I have interacted with many patients since I was in medical school, and I have a gut feeling when something is not right. Plus, tomorrow is my day off.

He seems a bit hesitant in the beginning. "It's already late. I don't want to bother you."

"You won't bother me. We can have a drink, and you can sleep over."

He thinks for a few seconds and says, "Okay."

***

Olivier Lefebvre
Le Solano, Old Port

Ethan lives in one of the upper-end condos near the Old Port. His unit is on the seventh floor facing south, which means that we can see the old port and the St. Lawrence River. I can see the clock tower and the Jacques Cartier Bridge from here.

At night, the light makes the view even more beautiful.

"This is such a nice place!" I say to Ethan.

"Thanks. I bought it last year." Ethan takes off his jacket and walks to the fridge to get a nonalcoholic beer for me. He knows that I better not drink alcohol with only one kidney.

"Thanks." We sit in his living room while enjoying the beer.

"I broke up with Isabelle," I blurt it out.

Ethan looks surprised. He doesn't say anything for a minute.

"I am sorry. How did that happen?" Ethan's voice drops to a sympathetic tone.

"Apparently, she had an affair with my friend Jean-Luc. Do you remember him?"

"I recognized him when he was visiting you in the hospital."

I feel the sadness again. Isabelle and Jean-Luc have been my biggest supporters. Now they are gone. I try not to cry in front of Ethan, but the lump in my throat feels unbearable.

"It's gonna be okay. Give yourself some time. You are entitled to be sad." Ethan puts his hand on my shoulder.

I put my face in my hands and start to break down. "You believe in God, right? Why do I have to experience all these things? I got into a car accident, lost my kidney, and now my girlfriend betrayed me with my best friend." I am hoping that he can give me the answer.

"It is indeed hard to understand God's plan. But later on, we will eventually understand. We just have to be patient," Ethan explains.

"I am not even sure if God exists."

"Some years ago, I felt the same thing. I didn't believe that He cared about me. Maybe He invented the universe, but He was not involved in my destiny."

"What makes you believe in Him now?"

"Well, it's a long story."

"I have all night to listen."

Ethan leans back, gets comfortable, and takes a sip of his drink. "When I was younger, I believed in Him because He somehow always made the things that seemed impossible to me become possible. For example, you know that my family is not as rich as your family. But luckily, I was able to attend good schools and get a good education from elementary school until university.

"But then, during my undergraduate, I became too cocky. Like I stopped attributing all my success to God and refused to give Him credit. I started to think that all my achievements were due to my own hard work instead of His guidance.

"Then, after obtaining my bachelor's degree, I had to take a one-year gap before entering medical school because my MCAT score was not good enough, and I did not have enough volunteering experience. During that gap year, I reached out to God again to help me.

"Finally, I started medical school, and I felt closer to God again because everything I learned about human life feels impossible to just happen by itself, you know. This was a real turning point. I became more serious about my faith." Ethan sits straightener and speaks more enthusiastically. "God is actually very involved in my life, and not just as a provider or someone who could grant my wishes. Now I feel that God is involved in all aspects of my life, especially through guiding my thoughts. He turns me into a better person. For example, before, I was very ambitious. I wanted to be a surgeon because it is a very respectable field in medicine. But because of my faith, I feel like God always reminds me to be humble and let go of my pride. As a result, when I study and work, it's not about my pride; it's about doing something good for other people.

"So what makes me believe in Him? Before, it was because God had provided everything that I needed. Now, in addition to that, I feel His guidance in my day-to-day life."

"But how do you know what is truly His involvement and guidance and what is not?" I ask.

"It's very simple. Don't imagine God as an old man in the sky. God is closer than you think. God is love. Everything that comes out of love—it's God's involvement."

"I still don't understand."

"Think about it. When you love your parents, that's God. When you love your friends, that's God. Right now, you feel hurt by Isabelle and Jean-Luc because you love them very much. Now that they hurt you, it's your choice whether you want to take revenge or forgive them and wish them to be happy. If you let God guide you, then you will learn how to forgive and be at peace with them and with yourself. Because God is love. Unconditional love. Only when you love someone unconditionally can you forgive them. No matter how cruel what they did to you was. I know it's easy to say but hard to do. So, that's how you can let God be involved in your life."

I need some time to digest his words. This is something new for me. Nobody ever explained the concept of God like Ethan just did.

"Back to your questions. If God exists, why did He let you get into a car accident and let Isabelle betray you? Maybe this will be a turning point for you. Like during my gap year before entering medical school. Maybe this experience will transform who you are as a person. Maybe through this experience, you will meet new people who can show you unconditional love. Your life may seem like a misery now, but

I am sure later on, you will find new happiness that you would have never imagined before. But you have to be patient," Ethan says.

I nod. Although I wouldn't say I am a believer like him yet, I still appreciate what Ethan said. It gives me hope. It's better than nothing. "Thank you very much, Ethan."

"My pleasure."

"Sorry, can I ask you another question?"

"Yes, of course, shoot."

"After you really get to know God, is life always free of worry, and do you feel at peace all the time?"

"No. That's the thing. I am still worried all the time—about my residency, my future, my love life, my family, et cetera. And I am a planner, too. I like to take control of my life. I think you do, too, right? So, sometimes it's hard for me to let God decide what would be the best for me. But the more I surrender to Him, the less worried I am. However, it's a lifetime learning process. I have to remind myself of that all the time. I cannot be free of worries right away, even though I am a believer.

"For example, earlier today, my organist said that she is retiring. Now, I don't know what to do, you know. Our choir is really dependent on her. That still worries me, even though I have God."

I know how much the choir means to Ethan. I am sad that his organist is retiring. But suddenly, I have an idea.

"Maybe I can help." I like his choir, and I don't want them to stop singing because they have no organist. Although I am not yet comfortable being associated with the church, this is something on which I can compromise. After Ethan's explanation about God and everything He has done, the

Catholic faith does not seem as hypocritical as I thought it would be.

"Oh, you know someone who can play the organ? Who?" Ethan's eyes light up.

"Well, I was going to offer myself. I am not good at playing the organ, but I know the basics of piano. I can read sheet music."

Ethan suddenly becomes very enthusiastic, taking out his briefcase and showing me all the sheet music for the choir. We discuss if this is something I can do. I tell him I will let him know after I try playing some of the pieces.

We go over the music until 3 a.m., and I end up sleeping on his couch until morning.

Chapter 17
Regina de Luca
Mont-Royal
Saturday, Fourth Week of April

I take a week off from my orchestra practice. I haven't taken any days off since I joined last year, and my schedule for the past two weeks has been hectic, so I thought it may be a good idea to take it easy.

There is no choir practice this week as we practiced a lot for the Easter Vigil, so this is a good time for me to relax.

On Saturday, I have decided to hike Mont-Royal. It's been a while. I prepare two sandwiches for lunch and some snacks. I always bring extra food just in case.

I put on my jacket and shoes, and I am ready to go. When I'm locking my door, Olivier appears from his apartment. It seems he is ready to go out, too. I haven't seen him since the last time we bumped into each other when I came back from my orchestra performance. It has been almost a month since I've moved to his plex. We don't really talk that much.

He is still using his elbow crutch, but he is moving with more ease every time I see him. I am glad that he is recovering well.

"Hi, Regina. How are you doing?"

"I am good. How are you?"

"I am good, too. Are you going somewhere?"

"Yes. I am going to take a walk to Mont-Royal. How about you?"

"I am going to take a walk, too, although I am not sure where. Mont-Royal seems like a good idea, though."

I am not sure if I should invite him. I like to walk by myself. However, it doesn't hurt to get to know my landlord better. We stand awkwardly for a few seconds.

"You can join me if you want."

"Okay. Why not? Thank you for the invite." He smiles. He looks really handsome when he smiles. Today, he is wearing a dark-blue polo shirt and jeans and jacket. Very casual but still classy. His hair is slicked back as usual. Even for just taking a walk.

We carefully climb down the steep stairs. The weather is nice today. The temperature is only ten degrees. In Montreal, a ten-degree temperature is considered warm.

We walk to the east side of Mont-Royal and follow the Olmstead Trail from there.

For the first ten minutes, we just walk in silence. Honestly, I like that. Olivier also seems to enjoy his surroundings.

"So, how's your violin and singing practice?" Olivier asks.

"It's going well. Last week and the week before, my performance schedule was pretty brutal. So, this week, I am taking some time off. Ethan also allows us to have a week off from choir rehearsal."

"Okay. That explains why I haven't heard your violin and singing as often this week."

"Oh, you noticed that?"

"Yes, of course. I like it when you practice the violin. The melody is very soothing. Also your singing."

"Thank you. It's very nice of you to say that." I start to like him. He is very genuine when giving compliments.

"How long have you been playing violin and singing?" Olivier asks.

"Since I was little. My mom was a soprano, and my dad was a cellist. They always shared their music with me."

"So, what made you choose the violin?"

"I listened to a lot of beautiful violin concertos when I was little. I dreamt of someday being one of the musicians who plays the beautiful melody."

"So, you have already achieved your dream."

"Not really. I auditioned for the first violin position, but I was placed in the second violin. Normally, it's the first violins that play the main melody. The second violins play the harmony."

"Oh, I see. But I usually heard you playing the melody when you were practicing."

A warmth spreads on my cheeks as I stare at the ground. "That's because I dream of being in the first violin group, if not the soloist. That's how I keep motivating myself, by practicing the melody part in addition to my own part. A lot of musicians get discouraged because they never have a chance to play the melody. Also, if someday I can play the first violin, I want to be ready." I hope that does not sound desperate or too eager.

"That's a very good mentality, Regina."

"Do you think so?"

"Yes. You create your own opportunities instead of waiting for them. You find a way to enjoy the music regardless of your position and rank. A lot of people would blame the situation for not being able to advance their careers, and they end up losing interest in the music itself. But by doing what you are doing, you will be less affected by external motivations such as position and rank. You are motivated internally by the music itself."

I would never have expected these encouraging words coming from Olivier. Ethan says kind things all the time, but I thought Olivier would be more formal.

"Thank you, Olivier. Do you play any musical instruments?"

"I play a bit of piano."

I understand something now. "Oh, I've recently heard a piano melody, too. But I wasn't sure where the sound came from. Was it you playing?"

"Yes." He doesn't look at me when he answers.

"You bought a piano recently? Because last time I visited your place with Ethan, I didn't see one."

"I just bought it last week."

"Ah, okay. That explains it." I smile. Apparently, we have something in common. I play violin, and he plays piano. At least I don't have to feel bad practicing loudly if he is also a musical person.

"How long have you been playing piano?"

"Since I was little until secondary. But then I stopped. I haven't played for more than ten years. I may sound a bit rusty."

"Actually, no. You sound quite good. I heard some famous pieces from Bach and Beethoven." Sometimes, I recognized the songs we sing in the church. However, he didn't play them from beginning to end. He was still focusing on one part at a time. "What made you decide to play piano again?" I continue.

He appears hesitant before answering. "Because I cannot do things that I usually did before the accident, like going to the gym, running, skating, and playing hockey. So, I have to find a new hobby, such as playing piano again."

"I see. That's also a good mentality. Rather than blaming your situation, you look at what is within your capacity to have a fulfilling life again." I copy his words.

"Thank you, Regina."

We don't realize that we have walked quite a ways. Now I can see the city laid out below from the path we walk on.

Then we arrive at a point where we can choose to climb the grand staircases or continue on the path, but it will take longer to reach the lookout point.

"Which one do you prefer?" I am not sure if climbing the stairs will be okay for him. Even for people in good shape, climbing these stairs is not easy.

"Let's take the stairs. I would like to push myself," Olivier says.

I let him climb first so that I will be able to help right away in case he is having difficulties. He starts to climb the stairs slowly. Luckily, there are not as many people as in the summer.

For the first half of the stairs, he is still doing okay. But for the second half, he starts running out of breath. So do I.

We sometimes take a break on the side of the stairs. Olivier forgot to bring a water bottle, so I share mine with him.

"I'm sorry to bother you," he says after drinking from my water bottle.

"Don't worry at all. We can refill it when we reach the top," I say with a smile.

Then we continue again. I am impressed with his determination. It must be quite challenging for him to climb with his crutch.

Relief fills me when we reach the lookout, called the Belvedere Kondiaronk. It really feels like we are in Europe as there is a terrace where people can admire the south view of the city. I can see the downtown skyline, the St. Lawrence River, and some bridges that connect Montreal to the south shore, including Pont Victoria and Pont Samuel de Champlain. There is also a beautiful chalet on this lookout.

I have been to this place more than twenty times since I've lived here, and the view never fails to take my breath away. I stand there for ten minutes just to admire the city that I have come to love so very much.

Luckily, Olivier seems to be enjoying the view too, although he still seems a bit pale. He was out of breath for five minutes after we reached the lookout.

"Are you hungry? I made two sandwiches, and I brought some snacks."

"Oh, wow! You are so prepared."

"Let's sit over there." I point out a semicircle in front of the chalet.

We eat the sandwiches in silence. Today is such a beautiful day. Spending time with Olivier is also surprisingly fun. I thought it was going to be more awkward than this.

"Would you like a hot chocolate?" Olivier asks when he has finished the sandwich.

"Oh yeah, good idea."

"You can wait here and finish eating. I will go buy them," he says with a smile and then disappears into the chalet.

I continue to eat my sandwich. I am a slow eater.

Five minutes later, Olivier comes back with two cups of hot chocolate.

"Thank you very much. How much do I owe you?"

"It's me who owes you. Thank you for the sandwich and the encouragement when I was struggling to climb the stairs."

"It's my pleasure." I smile at him.

The friendship starts to blossom between us. I feel strong compassion for Olivier, especially when he is showing his warm side. What I feel may not necessarily be a romantic feeling, but it is definitely a strong connection and maybe affection.

On the way down, we don't talk a lot because I know he is tired. But today, we had such a beautiful walk.

Chapter 18
Olivier Lefebvre
Plateau Mont-Royal
Tuesday, First Week of May

Today will be the first time I join the choir rehearsal. I am excited to try this new activity as well as meeting new friends, especially Ethan and Regina. I am probably doing this because I am lonely, not because I am searching for God or anything. I like the speech that Ethan gave me about his perspective on God; however, I don't think my faith is going to grow as deep as his.

I still think a lot about the walk at Mont-Royal with Regina. It was really fun. I was a bit tired on the way back, but we still had a good time.

I texted her once that same night: *Thank you for today. I had fun.*

She replied: *Me, too. I really enjoyed it.*

I definitely want to get to know Regina more. I want to be her friend because she has such a good attitude and positive vibes.

I still think about Isabelle a lot. Part of me still cannot accept what she has done. What did I do wrong? What could I have done differently? I gave everything I could to her. Sometimes, I feel extremely empty. I miss talking to her and spending time with her. Unfortunately, it's going to take some time before I can open my heart to another woman.

In the meantime, work is going well, although I am not as enthusiastic as before. I am still working from home and haven't spent any hours on business development. All partners and senior managers are expected to spend time networking with potential clients. But most of our clients are referred by our audit or merger and acquisition departments anyway. According to my secretary, who receives all the mail coming to my office, there are some social invitations from clients that I have to attend. I have sent my senior manager, Alex, to attend them. He will be more than happy to do that.

At 7 p.m., I start to get ready for my first choir rehearsal as the organist. Since last week, I have practiced some pieces that Ethan suggested. Linda, the current organist, will still help me out. She will play half of the pieces, and I will play the other half.

I haven't told Regina I will be joining their choir, because during our hike last Saturday, I hadn't made up my mind. I just told Ethan on Sunday. Ethan seemed very relieved and enthusiastic. I hope I will not let him down.

***

Olivier Lefebvre
Basilica St. Augustine

I arrive at the church fifteen minutes in advance and go up to the third floor, where they usually hold the choir rehearsal. There are some people there already. I feel out of place. Most of them seem to be younger than I am.

I see the old lady behind the organ. She must be Linda. I walk toward her. I can see people are looking at me while I am walking. Maybe they are concerned because I am using a crutch or because I am new.

"Hi. You must be Linda."

"Hi, you must be Olivier. Ethan told me about you."

"Yes. Nice meeting you."

We chat a bit about my musical background; I have to admit that I have no experience with piano accompaniment at all. But Linda is very supportive and encouraging. Ethan has chosen the songs that I will be playing. I will play four songs, and Linda will play the rest. Since I am not a churchgoer, Linda has to explain the order of the songs. She uses a lot of church terms that I don't understand like *ordinarium* or *Communion*. Also, because this is an English-speaking church, she uses a lot of English words (or maybe Latin words), even though she is speaking French with me.

"Olivier?" A female voice comes from behind me. I turn and find Regina. She seems surprised to see me here.

"Hey."

"What are you doing here?"

"I am learning to become an organist for the choir. Ethan needs someone to replace Linda, as she is retiring. So, I volunteered to help."

"Oh, wow. That's very noble of you."

"Thanks."

"And are you retiring, Linda? Why?" Regina asks. She appears surprised and sad at the same time.

"Oh, dear, I am seventy years old. What can you expect from me," Linda says.

"But your spirit is not near seventy. More like forty," Regina replies. That seems to make Linda happy.

Five minutes to 8 p.m., around twenty people start arriving. Then I see Ethan. His face lights up when he sees me.

"Olivier! Thank you very much for coming." He puts his bag on the floor.

"My pleasure."

"I will make the announcement shortly, and then we can start," Ethan says. I nod and turn to face the crowd. "Okay, everyone, thanks for coming today. I have an announcement," he says in English. Now everybody is silent.

"I am sad to announce that our dedicated organist, Linda, will be retiring next month."

People groan in unison. Everybody appears to be reluctant to let Linda go.

"At the same time, I am delighted to announce that our new member, Olivier Lefebvre, has agreed to replace Linda. Let's give him a warm welcome." Ethan starts to clap.

Everybody claps enthusiastically. Now, they look at me with bright faces.

"Linda will still help Olivier for the first few weeks. Olivier, do you want to introduce yourself?" Ethan nods and smiles at me.

I wish he hadn't put me on the spot like this, but I find myself standing up. "Hi, everyone. Thank you for your warm welcome. When Ethan told me that this choir needed an organist, I decided to join because I know how much this choir means to him. I played piano when I was younger, but this will be my first time being an organist. Thank you for your support," I say in English.

Everybody applauds again. I look at Regina, who is sitting in the front row and smiling at me. The others also give me warm, welcoming smiles. I start to feel at home.

"Okay. Let us begin in prayer. In the name of the Father, and the Son, and the Holy Spirit. Amen." Ethan and everybody in the room make the sign of a cross.

I follow their example awkwardly.

"Lord, thank You for gathering all of us here for our rehearsal. We would like to sing together to glorify You and to give thanks to You for all Your blessings in our lives. Lord, although we are going to sing, please let us stay away from vanity. Let the glory be for You and not for us. Thank You,

Lord. Amen." Ethan and the others make the sign of a cross again.

They start by warming up their voices. Then we begin our opening song, "This Is the Day" by John Rutter.

I take a deep breath before I begin, then start the intro.

It feels magical. I never do things like this. Usually, when I play the piano, I play the pieces for piano solo, not as accompaniment. While piano solos focus on you, piano accompaniment is more like playing to support the singers. There is a joy that I cannot explain through words.

Although playing an organ is completely different from playing a piano, I try to adapt. I also try my best not to make mistakes when playing. But since I practiced four songs within a week or so, I haven't really made them perfect. Sometimes, I make little errors, but I keep going.

By the end of the first song, Ethan gives me an approving nod. Then he wants each group—soprano, alto, tenor, and bass—to sing separately by group. The singers appear a bit intimidated. I find it becomes easier once I play the song for the fifth time.

Then we move on to the Communion song, "You Are My Hiding Place." Apparently, Ethan is not rehearsing the songs in the order Linda explained.

"For the Communion song, I need one female and one male soloist. Does anybody want to volunteer?" Ethan asks. Nobody is volunteering. Everybody looks very shy.

"Okay then, how about Regina and Sam this time? Last time Christie and Luiz sang the solo part."

"Okay." Regina and a guy who must be Sam answer at the same time. I notice Regina looks very happy. I am happy for her, too, so I try to play the song as perfectly as I can. I have heard them sing this song before.

Sam apparently has a really good voice, too. I can tell that he sings from the heart. By the time Regina's solo part begins, her voice melts my heart as always. I try to focus on playing my part without mistakes so that I don't ruin her beautiful singing.

Time flies during the rehearsal. We only have a chance to rehearse the offertory song, "Here I Am, Lord," once, and then it's already 9:30 p.m. Linda hasn't even played her songs!

"I think we have had enough for today; let's continue on Thursday," Ethan says. He looks very tired but overall satisfied. They close the rehearsal in prayer again and then the choir is dismissed.

I collect my stuff. It wasn't bad for my first rehearsal, I think.

Linda comes up to me after the rehearsal. "Olivier, you did very well!"

"Thank you, Linda. Do you have any feedback?"

"Not much. For your first time doing this, I was actually quite impressed. The only thing is, maybe after you feel comfortable with the notes, you can play it with more emotion. Sing the melody in your head when you are playing it."

I think deeply about what she says, and she is right. So far I have only focused on hitting the right notes. Not so much on the melody.

"That's true. Thank you, Linda. I will keep this in mind next time."

Ethan joins us. "Hey, how did you enjoy your first rehearsal?"

"Surprisingly, I enjoyed it more than I thought I would. It was tough, but overall, it was fun."

"Great. I think you did it very well for the first time. I hope you can continue."

"Yes, I will," I reassure him.

"Sorry, Linda, we didn't get a chance to practice your part. On Thursday, we will, for sure," he says.

"Oh, no problem at all. I am happy to just sit in and listen. You young people really have a good spirit. Keep it up!" Linda says.

"Thanks, Linda." Ethan smiles.

This is the first time I've seen Ethan leading and conducting the choir, and I am actually very impressed. He is dedicated and strict but kind to all the members.

***

Regina de Luca
Basilica St. Augustine

I glance toward Olivier, Ethan, and Linda. They are all discussing something serious beside the organ. I feel sad that Linda is retiring, but I am surprised that Olivier is willing to step up and help out.

"So, Regina, tell us about Olivier. How do you know him? How did he end up here?" Genevieve asks with intense curiosity in her voice. Christie, Carla, Luiz, and Sam also surround me to shower me with questions. We keep our voices down so that Olivier doesn't hear us talking about him.

"He is actually the landlord that you asked me about last time."

"What?" Genevieve seems very surprised.

"Yeah. He is Ethan's friend. I didn't even know that he was joining us today. I am as surprised as everybody else," I explain.

"Is there something going on between the two of you?" Carla asks with a teasing voice.

"No. Not at all. We are just neighbors. That's all."

"Hmm…but by the way he looks at you, I feel like there is something more," Christie adds.

Luiz leans in, joining the gossip. "Yeah, I feel the same."

"Well, think whatever you want. But nothing is going on between us."

"What happened to his leg?" Sam asks. Now everybody is looking at Olivier's leg. I hope they are not that obvious. It seems like Olivier doesn't notice, as he is still talking with Ethan and Linda.

"Car accident." I don't actually know the details.

"Poor guy," Christie says.

We catch up a bit more until, suddenly, Olivier is standing behind me. All my friends suddenly become quiet and just stare at him.

"Hey." I feel a bit awkward.

"Hey."

"Oh, let me introduce you guys. Olivier, this is Christie, Genevieve, Carla, Luiz, and Sam." I point to them when calling their names.

Olivier shakes hands with each of them. "Nice to meet you all."

We all chat a bit but not too long, as it's already 10 p.m.

"Okay. I have to leave now. See you guys on Thursday!" Luiz says.

"See ya!" we all reply.

Then, one by one, everyone leaves.

"See you both on Thursday!" Ethan heads toward the door.

Now, it's just the two of us. Olivier and I.

"Shall we go?" I say.

"Yes, sure," Olivier says.

Although I said to my friends that nothing is going on between us, I have to admit that now I feel a bit nervous around Olivier. I also feel butterflies in my stomach, and I am excited that we are going to go home together. I would like to get to know him better.

Chapter 19
Regina de Luca
Plateau Mont-Royal
Tuesday, First Week of May

It's 10 p.m., and Olivier and I decide to walk home. It will take more than half an hour, but we discover that we both like walking. Plus it's good for his leg. So we cross René Lévesque Street and walk along *Rue de Bleury* and enjoy Montreal's night.

"So how do you like the choir rehearsal?" I ask curiously. He is definitely not someone I pictured to be our organist. I am not sure why. Maybe because he seems to be from a different world than us.

"I really like it, although it's pretty challenging. I've never done something like this, so it's a good learning experience."

"You did very well. Thanks for helping us." I smile.

"You sing very well, too. I am impressed."

"Thank you."

Now we walk to the north along Avenue du Parc. This is one of my favorite streets in Montreal. On the left side, I can see Mount Royal, and on the right side is Jeanne Mance Park.

At night, there are not a lot of people on the street. If I were by myself, I would probably feel a bit unsafe, even though Montreal is considered a very safe city. However, because I am with Olivier, I feel perfectly secure.

Olivier suddenly asks, "Regina, I hope you don't mind me asking. Do your parents live here?"

"I don't mind you asking. No. They live in Italy. In Sorrento near Naples."

"That's where you are from, right?"

"Yes."

"When did you move to Canada?"

"I came here when I was fifteen." I start telling him about my experience visiting Montreal with my parents when I was ten years old and watching the *Orchestre Symphonique de Mont-Royal,* which inspired me to study music in Montreal and to become who I am now.

"Wow, that's very brave of you. To move here by yourself when you were so young, speak a new language, adapt to a new culture, and pursue your music career, all by yourself."

"It's not as scary as you imagine. But, yeah, in the end, I feel it's worth it. It's like an adventure."

"Do you miss home? How often do you go back?"

"Yes, sometimes I miss home. When I was still in school, I returned every other summer. And my parents came to visit me in the summer when I didn't go back home. So it was not that bad."

"And what made you join this choir aside from your love of singing?" Olivier asks.

"I have been going to St. Augustine Basilica since I moved here," I explain. "Initially, I just went to church without knowing anyone. Then, two years ago, I was reading our church bulletin and found out they were looking for choir members. So I decided to audition and got in. Then I got to know Ethan and the other members. I am so glad I found this community. I mean, I have friends from school and orchestra, but with these friends, I can connect on a deeper level. I can be myself, and I can talk about my faith freely. I feel at home."

"Yes. It must be good to have a group of friends who support each other." He nods.

"True. It's all thanks to Ethan. He brought people together." Then I remember something. "Speaking about Ethan, I heard that you guys have known each other since you were young?"

"Yes, we went to the same elementary school since Grade 4," Olivier says.

"Oh, wow. It must be nice to have such a longtime friend."

He looks a bit hesitant.

"Err…honestly, no. We only became friends recently."

"Oh?"

"So, we went to the same school until secondary and then we went to the same university. However, we never really talked. Maybe because I saw him as a rival. He and I were always alternating between the first and second rank in class. Ethan literally was friends with everybody, while I had my own circle." There is a hint of jealousy in his voice.

"But how did you guys end up being friends now?"

"He was one of the surgeons who operated on my leg. He saved my life. "

"Oh, wow." Although I wish he had never had the accident, I am glad something fruitful came from this unfortunate experience. Ethan and Olivier have become friends, and they can support each other.

"I regret that I never talked to him while we were in school. Apparently, he is a very loyal friend who will always be there for you. I had another childhood friend whom I thought was my real friend, but apparently, he's been cheating with my ex-girlfriend."

"What?" I can hardly imagine everything he has been through. "I am so sorry."

"Thank you. But this experience really opened my eyes. I discovered who my real friends are."

"Yes. It may seem very hard in the beginning, but later on, you will understand."

"Yeah. Ethan has been a big support for me since that accident. That's why I decided to help him by joining the choir, although I am not a churchgoer nor a believer myself."

"That's very kind of you." I don't want to comment about him not being a churchgoer. I respect everybody's faith, and not going to church does not necessarily make someone a bad person. I feel like being a Catholic means I have easier access to becoming a good and hopeful person.

We continue to chat until we arrive home.

Chapter 20
Regina de Luca
Basilica St. Augustine
Thursday, First Week of May

When I arrive at the church for our choir rehearsal the following Thursday, I don't feel very well. After the orchestra practice this afternoon, I started to feel feverish and a bit chilled. Then I decided to go back home to rest. Usually, in between orchestra practice and choir rehearsal, I either keep practicing with my orchestra friends or read a book in a coffee shop.

Olivier arrives at the church ten minutes before the rehearsal. He smiles at me, and I smile back at him. He joins Linda behind the organ. I am happy that he is committed to our rehearsal.

Not long after that, Christie arrives.

"Hey, how is it going?" she asks.

"I am good. You?"

"Good, too." She studies my face for a few seconds. "Are you okay, Regina? You don't look well."

"I am just a bit tired. Thanks for your concern, though." I smile at her.

Then the rest of the group arrives, including Ethan. We open with a prayer as usual and then continue on with the offertory song, "Here I Am, Lord."

Olivier plays with more confidence compared to the last rehearsal. His playing sounds more melodious, too. After the offertory, we rehearse the closing song, "A Clare Benediction" by John Rutter. This is such a beautiful song. I really like the selections this time. I cannot wait to sing during the Mass next week.

Ethan wants us to rehearse the Communion song again, which is "You Are My Hiding Place." I feel very honored to sing the solo part for this song, even though I feel like I don't deserve it. Christie would make a much better soloist, but I try to be more confident in myself.

Olivier starts the melodious intro, and Sam sings his solo part beautifully. I try to gather my energy.

My solo part begins. I close my eyes, try to forget everything else and focus on delivering the message through singing. I probably would sing better if I didn't feel sick, but I try my best.

For the rest of the rehearsal, we practice the ordinary songs, psalm, and alleluia. By the end of the rehearsal, I feel extremely tired. I probably will take a bus home instead of walking.

"Get rest, Regina, you don't look well at all. Are you going home with Olivier?" Christie asks me with concern after we finish the rehearsal. I am not sure how Olivier is going to get home, though.

"Maybe. Thanks for your concern, Christie."

"As long as you don't walk home by yourself. I feel like you can faint at any time. Get well soon, okay?" Christie says.

I nod and smile at her.

A moment later, Olivier is standing in front of me.

"Hey."

"Hey," I greet him back. He studies my face just like Christie.

"Are you okay, Regina?"

"I feel a bit unwell. But it's okay."

"Okay. Let's go home together. I will call an Uber." He takes out his phone.

"Okay. Thanks." Is it really obvious that I am not feeling well? Just by looking at my face?

"Hey, Regina." This time, it's Ethan.

"Hey, Ethan."

"You don't look well." That's a statement. Not a question.

"Yeah. I just feel tired."

He puts his hand on my forehead. "Oh, no. You have a high fever. Since when?"

"This afternoon, I think. Yesterday, I felt okay."

"You need to rest."

"I know." I smile weakly.

Olivier finishes booking the Uber. "Okay. The Uber will be here in three minutes."

"Great. Regina has a fever. Please take care of her," Ethan says to him.

I feel surprised. I didn't expect that Ethan would care that much. I feel supported, but I am also embarrassed. I feel like a five-year-old kid who needs to be taken care of.

"Yes, I will. Don't worry, Ethan," Olivier says.

I am even more surprised by his answer. Although Olivier and I have started to become friends recently, we are not close enough to take care of each other when one is sick.

***

Regina de Luca
Plateau Mont Royal

It takes about ten minutes to get to our place. My energy is fading fast, and I need to get to bed.

Olivier puts his hand around my waist when we climb up the stairs, as I am so wobbly. Now my head starts to ache as well.

"You can lean on me," Olivier says gently.

"Thanks."

"I will walk you in," he says when we are in front of my door. I don't complain. My body feels so weak. It's good that I have somebody to rely on.

Olivier takes me straight to my room. I realize that it is the first time I have been alone with a guy, in my bedroom, at night. I tell myself that this is a special circumstance.

"I will leave you to get changed. In the meantime, I will get you a glass of water and medication. Do you need anything else?"

"I think I am good. Thank you very much, Olivier," I say to him gratefully. He seems to know what he needs to do more than I do.

After he closes the door, I change into my pajamas. I keep my bra on as Olivier is still here. I also feel reluctant to lie down on the bed. I know he will not do anything, but he is still technically a stranger, even though we have recently become friendly.

Then I hear a knock at the door.

"Regina, can I come in?"

"Yes." I sit on my bed when he opens the door. He has a glass of water, TYLENOL, and a cool cloth. I wonder how he could find everything so fast, and then I realize that this is his place, too. I notice that he leaves his crutch and is limping.

"Thank you so much. You don't have to do this."

"It's okay. Let me help you. I know how it feels to be sick and powerless," he says sympathetically and offers me a glass of water and TYLENOL.

I drink it quickly.

Then he carefully puts the cool cloth on my head. I feel touched by this simple but caring gesture.

"Are you going to be okay by yourself now?" he asks.

"Yes, I am. Sorry for bothering you."

"If you are worse tomorrow, maybe we could call Ethan or another doctor."

"Oh no, don't worry. I am sure I will be okay by tomorrow. Thanks for all your help."

"I will leave now. Call me if there is any problem, okay?"

I nod.

He gives me a quick but gentle hug before he leaves. It gives me butterflies in my stomach.

Chapter 21
Olivier Lefebvre
Plateau Mont-Royal
Thursday, First Week of May

I am still worried about Regina when I get home. I don't want to leave her by herself when she is sick like that. But I know she doesn't have any family to take care of her.

When I was bedridden after my accident, at least there was always someone who helped me. I cannot imagine if I was by myself. I would be scared and discouraged.

I hear my phone beep. It's a text from Ethan.

Hey Olivier, how's Regina?
I reply quickly.
She is still very sick. But I gave her a TYLENOL and a compress. Are you available to come tomorrow in case she gets worse?
I will be in the OR the whole day tomorrow. But I can come after. Please keep me updated.
I will. Thanks, Ethan.

I remove my clothes and go to bed. Today was a long day for me. After five months of being absent, I decided to go to the office, as we are in the middle of doing a valuation for a big client who owns a hotel chain. I assembled the team who will be working on this engagement: Alex, the senior manager; Brad, the manager; one senior consultant; and a junior consultant. This will be a very time-consuming engagement with a big budget.

They threw me a surprise party when I arrived. I was not expecting that at all. It was probably Alex who set it up.

I had mixed feelings about going back to the office. On one hand, it felt good to do my normal routine again and to see my colleagues in person. I also feel more confident as I can rely less on my crutch now, even though I am still limping.

On the other hand, I was used to working from home. I can work more than ten hours in my home office and don't really feel it. Half of the people in the office have also adopted hybrid working arrangements. It's up to us where we want to work, as long as we are online and available. I haven't decided yet whether I will work from home or from the main office or both.

After work, I had a quick supper before going to choir rehearsal, which was better than last Tuesday as I am getting used to playing the organ. Also, today, Linda finally got a chance to practice her songs as well.

I kept glancing at Regina throughout the choir rehearsal. I noticed that she appeared a bit pale and quieter than usual. I could tell she tried her best, especially during her solo, although she didn't seem to be feeling very well. I really admire her dedication.

The more time I spend with her, the more I like her. She is very different from Isabelle. Isabelle always demanded attention from me, while Regina seems to be the opposite. She doesn't want to bother other people, even when she needs help.

I know that I care about Regina. I just haven't figured out whether I just want to be friends or I want more. She also doesn't give me any hint that she is interested in me more than a friend. Furthermore, I don't want to rush into a new relationship. I want to enjoy getting to know her and take care of her as I would take care of a friend.

I am definitely attracted to her personality. I especially like it when she is playing the violin and singing. The more I look at her, the more I realize she is actually pretty. Especially when she does not wear glasses. Before, my taste in women may have been a bit shallow. The older I get, the more I realize that personality is more important than looks. Regina may not be someone who can make all men turn heads, but she has a big and brave heart that is more meaningful to a relationship than looks.

Thanks to my new routine—working, practicing piano, choir rehearsal, and my new friendship with Ethan and Regina—I think less and less often of Isabelle and Jean-Luc.

I turn off the light, and for the first time, I pray. I ask God to take care of Regina so that she feels better tomorrow. I haven't become a believer yet, but there is nothing wrong with praying to the God that Regina believes in.

Chapter 22
Regina de Luca
Plateau Mont-Royal
Friday, First Week of May

The next day, I feel worse. I have extreme chills, and all my joints hurt. Then my throat starts to get irritated as well. I know what I have to do.

These past few years, the world has been hit by a new coronavirus. I have gotten complete doses of the vaccine, but it does not guarantee that I won't get the virus.

When I try to get out of bed, I almost lose my balance. I feel so sick. I go to the kitchen to get the rapid test, swab both of my nostrils, and follow the instructions.

While waiting for the test result, I text my orchestra leader that I cannot attend this week's concert as I am not feeling well. I also receive text messages from Christie, Ethan, and Olivier asking how I am.

Fifteen minutes later, my results are in.

It's positive for COVID.

I sigh. I should have known. But then, I must have endangered everybody else. *No way.*

I quickly text Ethan:

Ethan, I tested positive for Covid. All the choir members should probably get tested, too, since they were in contact with me yesterday. I am so sorry.

I also text my orchestra leader, apologizing because I didn't realize that I had the virus. I may have spread it already. I hope they can still perform the concert.

Ethan texts me back:

Don't feel bad at all. It's not your fault. I will let everybody know. Please rest and get well soon. Let me know if you need any help.

Then I reply to Christie and Olivier, and they reply similarly.

After texting people back and forth, I finally break down and start crying. I don't know if it's because of COVID, because I am feeling guilty that I endangered everybody's health, or because I am afraid this virus will hit me hard.

Even though I am usually pretty self-sufficient, this is the first time I have been really sick and nobody is going to take care of me. This makes me miss my parents a lot. I wonder if I should tell them that I have COVID.

I feel lonely and isolated now. I know a lot of people died because of the virus. What if I die by myself and nobody knows until it's too late? I try to get rid of these thoughts.

I drink another glass of water, take some TYLENOL, and stumble back to bed. I will just sleep all day.

I have almost fallen asleep when I hear my phone ring.

It's Olivier.

"Hey. I am outside your door. Would you mind letting me in?"

"Did you receive my text? I have COVID."

"I know. That's why I'm here. I will take care of you. Please let me in. I am wearing a mask. Don't worry." His tone is not something you can debate. I put on my own mask to greet him.

It's 9 a.m., and I am still in my pajamas. But who cares about that at this point?

I open the door, and I find him standing there, very polished, unlike me. He wears a dress shirt and dress pants. He has his work bag hanging on his shoulder. His hair is slicked back as usual.

"Do you know that I am very contagious?" I ask while letting him in.

"I know. But you cannot do this by yourself, Regina."

I have no energy to argue with him.

"Aren't you supposed to go to work?" I ask.

"Yes. But I can work from here today if you don't mind. You can just sleep and pretend I am not here. I will sit in the living room."

"Okay. Thank you for coming." I realize that he is making a big sacrifice for me. It's extremely risky to be near me now. What if he gets the virus as well? But I feel lucky that he is here with me right now. We are not even a couple.

We walk to my bedroom, and he takes the cloth and the empty glass while I lie down under the blanket. The chills and the muscle pain are really killing me.

Then Olivier comes back with a fresh cool cloth, a glass full of water, and more TYLENOL. I feel very grateful that I don't need to leave my bed.

"Have you eaten breakfast yet?" he asks while placing the cool cloth on my forehead.

"Not yet."

"Okay. I will come back in an hour or so. By the way, you should remove your mask while you are sleeping," he says, and then he leaves me to rest.

I must have fallen asleep for quite some time. Olivier wakes me up gently. I see a bowl of chicken noodle soup on a tray. He must have made it while I was asleep.

"You need to eat," he says.

I sit up. "Thank you. What time is it?"

"Eleven thirty." He removes the cloth from my forehead and checks my fever. "I am not sure why your fever is not going down much. Here, eat this, and I will be back soon." He passes the tray to me and leaves.

I try the soup, but I cannot smell or taste it. I don't have any appetite either, but I don't want to hurt his feelings. It was thoughtful of him, so I try to finish it.

Olivier comes back with a digital thermometer, places it on my forehead, and presses the button.

"Thirty-nine point eight degrees. It's too hot. How do you feel right now?"

"Awful. I cannot taste the soup either," I say weakly.

"I feel bad for you. But I am here if you need any help. If you are getting worse, I will take you to the hospital. Be strong, Regina."

"Thank you very much, Olivier."

Then I sleep all day after that.

***

Regina de Luca
Plateau Mont Royal

When I wake up, it's already dark outside. I've lost track of the time. The phone beside my bed shows that it's 7 p.m., and I have a lot of missed calls and texts.

I read the first text from Ethan:

Hi, Regina, how are you feeling now? Just wanted to let you know that all other members tested negative including me. I hope that will make you feel better.

He also called me at around 6 p.m. The next text is from my orchestra leader, who says that two other members tested positive. Two out of eighty to ninety members. So that's kind of good news. And those two who tested positive may or may not have contracted the virus from me.

Then Olivier shows up at my bedroom door. I left it open in case he needed to enter while I was sleeping. He looks as tired as I am.

"Have you been here all day, Olivier?"

"Yes. How are you feeling?"

"Slightly better I think." I touch my forehead. It doesn't feel as hot as before. However, I still feel extreme chills and muscle pain.

Olivier walks toward the bed and checks my temperature. "Thirty-eight point nine. It's still hot, but at least it's going down a bit. I will bring your dinner. Hang on one second." He leaves the room.

He comes back with a tray. This time the bowl is filled with Chinese congee. It looks delicious.

"Thank you. Did you make this yourself?"

"No. I ordered from Uber Eats." He seems a bit embarrassed.

"Regardless, I really appreciate it." I smile at him.

"Ethan wanted to know if we needed his help."

"Hmm…no. I don't think so. There is nothing he can do. He will be risking himself coming here."

"Okay. I will let him know then." He pulls out his phone and starts texting.

I also reply to Ethan while eating the congee. Then my throat feels irritated, and I start coughing.

"Are you okay?" Olivier asks. His eyes look worried.

"Yes. I think the virus is starting to get to my throat."

"Let me get you more water and medications," he says and leaves the room. I feel bad for him. I could have gotten up to get them myself. I don't deserve to be spoiled.

Olivier comes back with more water, throat candy, and cough syrup. I cannot stop thanking him.

"Do you need help with cleaning yourself up?" he asks. I am a bit surprised by his question. He seems to notice it. "Please don't get me wrong. I am not that type of guy. You know, when I was bedridden after my incident, the nurse cleaned me up in a professional way. I know how it feels when you are sick and powerless. I spent a month in hospital and a month in my parents' house not being able to take care of myself." He looks at the ground when he says it.

"Thanks for explaining. I know that you genuinely want to help," I say.

I am contemplating if I am strong enough to take a shower. With the chills and muscle pain, it's going to be uncomfortable to take a shower in a regular way. Even going to the bathroom to pee takes a lot of effort. So, I tell Olivier that he can help me.

He leaves the room and comes back with a towel and a stainless steel bowl full of water. He hands me the towel and turns his back to me so that I can remove my clothes.

I remove my pajama top and my bra. Then I place the towel in front of my body and cover it with the blanket. I have never been naked in front of a man before.

"Are you done?" Olivier says, still not looking.

"Yes. I am done now."

I cannot believe that I'm letting him bathe me. He washes my face first. He does it so gently, I feel very touched. Then he washes my arms, shoulders, and back, too.

Nobody ever sees this much skin except for my mom. But Olivier does it very politely. He never touches nor stares inappropriately.

"Now, I think you can wash your front while I get you clean clothes. Then I will help you with your legs."

Again I just follow his lead.

He brings me a new set of pajamas as well as underwear. I can feel that my face is turning red. He turns around again while I put on my pajama top and bra. Then I remove my pajama pants but keep my underwear.

Olivier washes both my legs. After that, I wash my private parts and put on clean underwear and pajama pants. He takes all my dirty clothes and the bowl without speaking. I am wondering what's on his mind after he has done this big service to me.

With him being here, feeding me, and bathing me, I don't feel scared anymore.

Chapter 23
Olivier Lefebvre
Plateau Mont-Royal
Monday, Second Week of May

While Regina has been recovering over the weekend, it's me who starts not feeling well on Monday.

So I take the rapid test. And I test positive.

I knew when I was taking care of Regina that there was a big chance that I would get the virus, too. It was the risk I accepted. I couldn't leave her alone like that.

I have never taken care of anyone before. Although I didn't like seeing her getting sick, I felt happy to be there for her when she needed someone. In the past, when I was being kind to a girl, it was usually because I wanted to date her, and I wanted the desire to be reciprocated. But now, I want to be kind to Regina, not because I want to date her, but because I feel genuine compassion for her.

On Monday morning, I only have a mild fever, headache, and sore throat. But at least I can still work from home as the valuation report for the hotel chain needs to be done by Friday.

For Regina, her worst days were three days, from Thursday to Saturday. By Saturday night, she had no more fever, and she could continue her daily activities as usual without my help, even though she still tested positive. I know everybody has a different immune system, but if I get really sick in the next two days, I still have Thursday and Friday to finish reviewing this valuation report.

Unfortunately, I will not be able to make it on Sunday for our choir performance at the church because I will still be under self-quarantine. A sad feeling pummels my chest. I really want to be able to help out, but unfortunately, I can't. So, I decide to text Ethan.

Hey Ethan, I tested positive for Covid. So I don't think I can make it to the rehearsals and to the Mass on Sunday. I am sorry.

A few minutes later, he replies back:

Oh, no. Before it was Regina. Now, it's you. Take care of yourself and keep me updated. Let me know if you need any help. I will let Linda know.

Without the choir rehearsals, now my life is only work, work, and work. I don't remember how I managed it before. Oh, yeah, before, I had Isabelle and Jean-Luc. Usually, we met up two or three times per week. I realize that I feel less hurt by them now. Maybe because I am occupied with the choir and I feel a greater sense of purpose. Maybe some sense of belonging, too, although I haven't talked much with the other choir members other than Ethan, Regina, and Linda.

I work nonstop until 3 p.m. By this time, I start to feel that my body is defeated by the virus. The fever and headache are getting unbearable. I feel chills and muscle pain. Also, I start to cough a lot. Damn. I haven't finished what I need to finish today. But the headache is killing me. I decide to take a nap for a few minutes.

Right when I'm about to lie down on my bed, I receive a text from Regina:

Hi, Olivier, do you mind if I come over to return your Tupperware? Thank you so much for the meal!

Oh, I forgot that she still has my Tupperware. On Saturday morning, I cooked soup for her in my kitchen and then brought her additional food that would last two or three days so that she didn't need to cook while she was sick.

I quickly reply to her text:

You can keep it for a while. Unfortunately, I tested positive for Covid, too.

I don't know how this virus works. If Regina has recovered and then she is in contact with me, is it going to delay her recovery, or would it not make a difference, as she is already immune to it? I would say better not to take a chance.

My phone rings. It's Regina.

"Hey."

"Hey. How bad is it? Should I come over?" she asks.

"No, please don't. It's a bit messy over here. And you are just recovering. What if you get sick again?"

"I don't care. How bad is it?" she asks again.

"Not bad at all. Just a mild fever and sore throat."

She probably detects the lie because she says, "I'll come over now," and then hangs up.

When Olivier opens the door, I know that he was lying earlier. His face does not look good at all, even though he is wearing a mask. He looks very sick, just like I was a few days ago. Thankfully, I am feeling better now, aside from the fatigue and a very mild cough. I also haven't recovered my senses of smell and taste, but other than that, I am pretty much capable of taking care of myself and other people. Plus, I am still under self-quarantine. Other than practicing the violin, I am kind of bored at home.

"You look awful. Sorry. It was because of me," I say when he lets me in.

"No. I was the one who wanted to take care of you. Don't feel bad. I knew the risk."

I still feel bad. He was so helpful when I was sick, and now I will do the same.

Olivier is lying down on his bed when I start to cook for him. His kitchen has pretty much the same layout as my unit, so it's easy to find things that I need.

Then his computer starts ringing. It looks like he is in the middle of working on something. I hear Olivier walking from the bedroom toward the living room. He picks up the headset and starts talking. I feel bad for him having to work while not feeling well. His voice is getting hoarse the more he talks.

It looks like he is having a very serious conversation about business valuation. He brings up discount rates, market risks, company-specific risks, debt, equity, CAPM, whatever it stands for, etc. This is the first time I've heard him at work. He sounds very knowledgeable and authoritative. I can tell that he is someone who is in a high position as well as the decision maker.

After the phone conversation, he continues looking at the spreadsheet on his screens. Yes, he has two big screens, and they all look very sophisticated.

Twenty minutes later, the computer rings again. He answers it again. This time they are debating about the sales projection. He is also coughing a lot. I hope the other person on the line lets him rest.

I finish making the soup, which contains chicken, macaroni, carrots, and other vegetables. I put the soup in a bowl for him and bring cough syrup, too.

"You better eat this while it's still hot," I say.

He looks at the bowl with gratitude. "Thank you so much." And he starts eating.

"Can you taste it?"

"Yes, I can. This is very good!"

I am happy that he likes the soup.

"I shouldn't drink this now." He points out the cough syrup. "I still have to work, and this will make me sleepy."

"Okay, then. It's already almost five, though. What time are you going to finish work?" I ask.

"I don't know. There is still much to do, and the deadline is Friday."

I look at his face closely. His cheeks are flushed from fever, and his eyes are a bit watery. I put my hand on his forehead automatically. It feels very hot.

"I cannot understand how you can keep working when you are sick like this," I say.

"I just have to. No other choice." He sighs weakly.

At least when I was sick, I could just sleep all day. But he still has to work.

He gets up from his seat, but then he almost loses his balance. I rush forward to steady him and grab his arms. "Tell me what you need."

"I am going to take a quick bath. I think it will help."

"Okay. Wait here, and I will fill the bathtub for you."

"Thanks." He sits down again and puts his head on his arms against the table.

I walk to the bathroom to fill the bathtub with warm water and soap. When I come back to the living room, he is still in the same position. I pat him gently to wake him up. Every time I leave him alone, he seems to get worse and worse.

I help him walk to the bathroom. I put my arm around his waist, and he puts his arm around my shoulder. Once we are in the bathroom, I ask him whether I should help him or leave him.

"Stay, will you?" he says with a weak voice.

I notice that he is out of breath.

"Okay." I sit him on the edge of the tub and start unbuttoning his shirt. Then I am stunned when I see a long scar on his side. I remember he said that he broke two ribs from his car accident, but this surgery scar is…?

"It's nasty, isn't it?" Olivier asks me while his eyes are still closed.

"This is from your car accident?"

"Yes, the accident. They had to remove my kidney because my ribs crushed it during my accident."

"I am sorry to hear that." So it's not only his leg but also his kidney that got damaged. I can't imagine how hard it must have been for him.

Now reality starts to kick in for me. He only has one kidney. Will this virus endanger his life? After looking at his scar, I just want him to quickly recover. I will do my best to support him.

I continue freeing him from his pants. Then I see other scars on his left hip and thighs. Oh, poor him. I almost cannot face it. He has been through a lot in his life. Now I feel guilty for making him sick like this.

The last part is the most challenging. I have never seen a man naked in front of me. I am not sure if I can do this. I help him stand while he is holding on to me. His skin is extremely hot, and he is shaking almost convulsively.

Olivier seems to notice my hesitation. "I can do the rest on my own. Thank you, Regina," Olivier says breathlessly.

I'm relieved, although I'm a bit worried about leaving him alone. "Okay. I'll leave the door unlocked and just call me if you need anything." I say.

He nods weakly.

15 minutes later, Olivier comes out from the bathroom in his bathrobe. He leans against the wall to catch his breath. He looks like he can pass out at any time.

I let him lean on me while walking him toward the bedroom. Once we are in the bedroom, I help him into comfortable clothes. The virus seems to hit him really hard as simple activities make him breathless.

After giving him some TYLENOL, I put him in bed and cover him with a blanket. I also put a cool cloth on his burning forehead and watch him fall asleep.

Chapter 25
Olivier Lefebvre
Plateau Mont-Royal
Tuesday, Second Week of May

The next day, I feel slightly better. My fever has gone down a bit, and I don't feel the chills as much. However, the cough is getting worse, and I have a runny nose. At least I can do normal activities without having to rely on Regina all the time.

I continue working on the valuation report with the team remotely. I need to spend more time on this than usual. Ideally, as a partner, you want to spend the least amount of time possible because your hourly rate is extremely expensive. But the good news is we are still way under budget on this file.

Regina arrives at 9 a.m. I am happy to see her. She made everything more bearable, especially when I felt so sick yesterday.

"How are you feeling today?" she asks.

"Better. Thank you for yesterday, and thank you for coming today." My voice sounds nasally and raspy.

"My pleasure."

Then she starts to cook while I am working. At least I don't have to worry about food. Her cooking is so much healthier than most restaurant food, especially since I am sick. She makes a tasty, warm soup to relieve my throat.

Today goes really well. We are making so much progress at work. In the middle of the day, I tell Regina that she can practice her violin here in my place if she wants. And she agrees.

So, I have live music when working. Great.

Regina plays "Swan Lake" and "Ave Maria." It really warms my heart. She plays it with full emotion. The melody is beautiful and makes me forget about my sickness. During my break, I ask her to sing "You Are My Hiding Place" while I accompany her with the piano. I know she is sad that she will not be able to sing her solo part on Sunday as she is still under self-quarantine.

As always, she sings beautifully. Her voice is crystal clear, and her face looks peaceful.

Although I have been coughing a lot throughout the day, and my nose is very stuffy, I don't feel bothered. I don't want tonight to end.

***

Olivier Lefebvre
Plateau Mont-Royal
Sunday, Second Week of May

By Sunday, I am pretty much back in shape. No more fever, headache, chills, muscle pain, or runny nose. Only a lingering cough. I still test positive, though. Regina has tested negative, but she decided not to do the solo that she is supposed to do today because she hasn't practiced enough.

I keep thinking about Regina this whole week.

I realize that she is someone special. She is always there for me when I need her. She inspires me through her music and her kindness. She is someone I am comfortable spending time with and even showing my vulnerability to. With Isabelle, I was more reluctant to be vulnerable.

I am wondering why she is still single. She has such a great personality. Do other men know what a gem she is? Or maybe she is selective about the men she dates. Maybe I can ask Ethan.

But if I decide to pursue her, the only concern is her faith. I am not sure I will be as devoted as she is, and I am wondering if it's going to be a deal breaker for her if I am not Catholic. And do I really want to have a Catholic girlfriend? What is her point of view about sexual relationships and contraception?

I am 99 percent sure that Regina is still a virgin by how nervous she was when she helped me dress. It was clear to me that she had never seen a man naked before. But I really appreciated that she helped me out when I felt extremely sick and had no energy, even to take care of myself.

With regard to work, we finally finalize the valuation report on Friday. We have decided for the hotel chain how much its worth is. Then the buyer will come up with their own valuation to see if they agree with our number. Most of the time, they don't. Sometimes, we have to meet in the middle, or we have to bring a third party for another independent valuation.

Now that work is slowing down, I have more time to practice piano, especially for the choir rehearsals. Ethan has advised that on Sunday, two weeks from now, the choir is going to sing the same songs as the ones they sing today. So I don't have to practice a new set of songs. However, Linda asked me if I would like to try to practice the ordinary songs as well as the psalm and alleluia. And I said yes. So, two weeks from now, I will play all the songs on my own.

Being an organist in a church teaches me to suppress my ego. You still have to practice as hard as if you were playing solo. However, when you perform, the attention is not supposed to be on you but on the choir. A good organist will give the spotlight to the choir and not to himself. This is something I have never learned before, and now I am glad that I am experiencing it.

Chapter 26
Ethan O'Sullivan
Montreal General Hospital
Tuesday, Third Week of May

I come out from the OR feeling very tired. Today's case was an ankle surgery. It went pretty well. The reason I chose orthopedic surgery is because I imagined it would feel so good to see my patients recovered and able to resume their normal activities.

However, now I am not sure anymore.

In reality, I don't spend that much time with my patients as a surgeon. The only time I have one-on-one meetings with the patients is in the clinic when they do pre-op or follow-up visits. The rest of the time, I only see them in the OR when they are unconscious under anesthesia or during rounds.

I am wondering if this is the right career path for me. Sometimes I feel a bit jealous of the nurse who gets more time with the patients.

Last week, Olivier got really sick from the coronavirus. Two weeks ago, it was Regina who was really sick. Although I texted them every day to check how they were doing, I wish I could have taken care of my friends more, but I was stuck at work. What is the point of being a doctor if I cannot even take care of my friends?

I go to the shower room and take off my scrubs. I take a quick shower and change to my street clothes. Today is in the third week of May, and my second year of residency will end in June. Between now and June, I am supposed to register for my third year of residency, which will start in July. The thing is, I am not sure if I want to register.

There is no choir rehearsal tonight as we were scheduled to sing at the Mass last Sunday. I always give them a break after we sing at the Mass. So I have plenty of time tonight. I call Olivier.

"Hey, Ethan."

I am glad that his voice sounds much better now. Last week, he sounded very hoarse and stuffed.

"How's it going?"

"Great. I finally tested negative yesterday."

"Nice. Do you want to come over to my place and have a drink?" I ask.

"Sure. What time?"

"How about an hour from now?"

"Okay. See you."

***

Ethan O'Sullivan
Le Solano

Olivier arrives an hour later with my favorite six-pack of beer. He is wearing a mask.

"Are you still having symptoms?" I ask.

"Just the cough."

We sit in my living room. I take one of the beers. I make him a cup of hot tea to soothe his throat.

"Did you work today?" I ask him.

"I worked half the day. This afternoon, I had an appointment with my family doctor. You know, after catching the virus, I just want to make sure my only kidney is not affected."

"And what did he say?"

"So far, no problem, but he wants me to do some more tests tomorrow."

"This year has been really crazy for you, right? Going to the hospital back and forth." I feel like he has been through a lot. From the accident, breaking up with his ex-girlfriend, and catching the coronavirus.

"I know. But there are new things I have enjoyed this year— like getting involved with your choir and going to the church."

"I'm glad that you enjoy it. I wish you and Regina were there last Sunday. Christie stepped up for the solo part, and Linda ended up playing your songs, too. But I missed the other two important members in my choir."

We talk a bit about the choir and also catch up about other things in life.

"So why did you call me today, Ethan? Is there anything I can help you with?" he asks.

I am not sure how to ask. There is a reason I called him. I need a devil's advocate. I know that he is very rational. I want to hear a logical argument instead of an emotional one.

"I am thinking about quitting my residency." I finally say it. Olivier looks surprised. He doesn't say anything in the beginning.

"What's the reason?" he finally asks.

"I just don't feel fulfilled anymore. I don't interact with the patients as often as I want. I feel like I see them more and more as case studies rather than human beings. This is not what I want."

"What are you going to do otherwise then? I think there are pros and cons in every job. There is no perfect job."

"I feel like I have another calling in my life. It's been in my mind for a while. I thought the idea was crazy, and I kept avoiding it. But the more I ignore it, the more vivid it becomes."

"And what is this calling?"

"I think my calling is to serve God by becoming a priest."

Olivier chokes on his tea. I pat his back and get him a glass of water.

"Okay, let's examine the practicality of this profession—if you can call it a profession. How much do you get paid by becoming a priest? Can you pay your mortgage and the bills?"

"I think you get a very small salary, and you live in the rectory with other priests. Although depending on the diocese, some may maintain their primary residence," I say.

"And you cannot get married and have kids, right?"

"Correct."

"Then you know the answer."

"I wish it was that simple."

"Ethan, you are one of the smartest people I have ever met. Why would you do this?"

"That's why I haven't really done anything about it. That's why I am still doing my current job. And that's why I called you. I knew you would be against it."

"Okay. Tell me, what's so fulfilling about being a priest? What is more fulfilling and more honorable than saving lives?"

"You know that I always enjoy being in the Church and attending the Mass. It's refreshing to talk to people, like when you called me about your problems. There is nothing quite so powerful as sharing my understanding of God with others. And it would give me inexplicable joy if I could help people find God Himself through the sacraments, prayers, and teachings of the Church. And you know, nowadays in Quebec, there are very few people who want to be a priest. Perhaps I am more needed in the Church."

"But the hospital also needs you, no?"

"Yeah. But I feel that my calling in the Church is stronger than in the hospital."

"What will happen to your residency? What will happen if you quit your job and find out that being a priest is not the right calling for you?"

"Then I can continue my residency."

"Can you finish your residency first before becoming a priest?"

"It's going to take three more years. I don't know if I can wait another three years to discover where my true calling is."

"Have you ever talked to an actual priest about this?"

"Yes. So many times. The more I talked to them, the more convinced I was. They don't even try to lure me in. They are very upfront about the pros and cons."

Olivier seems to think hard about how to convince me that this is a bad idea. This is what I need—someone who will force me to consider all sides.

"If I decide to enroll in the seminary, which will start in August, I am not going to register for my third-year residency."

Olivier thinks hard again. "How long have you been thinking about becoming a priest?"

"Since I was a child until secondary. But then it stopped. And for the past few months, it has come back again. I am thinking about it more often every day."

"A few months are not enough to make a life-changing decision. How about this, find a way to love your current job, stay for another year, and see if you still have this calling about being a priest a year from now. After all, your current job is also God's calling, right? Being a priest could just be a different calling. But it's important to make a decision about entering the seminary when you are at peace with your current job. That will make you certain that this calling to be a priest is not to avoid your current problem or dissatisfaction. And while waiting for another year, you are still fulfilling God's other calling. It's a win-win situation."

Olivier's wisdom makes me speechless for a second. Why didn't I think about it like this before? Due to the hectic stress of my daily schedule, I forgot that my current job is also God's calling. I just need to step back and see how I can add more value to my patients. How could I forget that? Surprisingly, Olivier, who is a nonbeliever, is the one who reminds me about this.

"Wow, I think you are right. Thank you very much for your input. I think I will register for my third-year residency then." I look at him with gratitude, glad I called him today.

"No problem. There is another thing I need to tell you, though. This may change your perception about priests," Olivier says.

"What's that?"

"Do you remember when we became friends, I was so hesitant to go to church?"

"Yes. Why?"

Olivier starts his story.

"I was only eight years old and excited for my first Communion preparation class. I liked being in the church because people smiled a lot. Everybody appeared very calm and peaceful, especially my grandfather.

That day, I had just finished my class and was walking along the long hallway in the building behind the church. Suddenly, I heard a muffled scream behind one of the rooms in the hallway. I traced the voice and stood in front of the door where the scream was coming from. I opened the door and found a priest and a boy. The boy was about the same age as me. The priest stood behind the boy. The boy was bending over the table. His pants were down on the floor. What I saw haunted me for the rest of my life.

I was not sure what happened between the priest and the boy at that time, but I instantly felt nauseated. I ran away as fast as possible. I heard a quick footstep. I knew that the priest was following me. I ran quicker and saw a wardrobe. I opened the door and found a lot of priests' robes inside. I hid there, my breathing quickened. I was horribly afraid and my whole body was shaking.

Then I could feel that the footsteps were getting closer. I held my breath.

After that, the footsteps stopped, and the wardrobe door opened.

The same priest was standing there looking at me. His eyes were very cold, and they gave me chills. Then with a threatening voice, he said, "If you tell anyone what you have just seen, I will do the same thing to you."

Trembling, I said, "I will not say anything."

"Then go."

I ran out of the room and never wanted to go back."

After Olivier finishes his story, I don't say anything at first. This is not the first time I have heard a story like this, but it doesn't discourage me from becoming a priest. Instead, it gives me more reason to stand up for my faith.

"Olivier, if I ever become a priest, do you think I will be like the priest that you have just described?"

He draws a sharp breath and looks at me. "No, of course not. That's not what I meant. I just wanted you to know what you are getting yourself into."

"Thanks, Olivier. And trust me, I know."

Christie and I decided to jog along the Lachine Canal after work today. After almost two weeks of self-quarantine, I need some fresh air. I am happy that I don't have any symptoms anymore.

After jogging, we enjoy hot chocolate at *Marche* Atwater to catch up.

"So tomorrow, Olivier and you will be able to join the choir practice, right?" Christie asks.

"Yes. I no longer have symptoms. Olivier told me he still has a mild cough, but he has tested negative."

"Great. It was so dull without both of you last Sunday. We were excited to hear your solo and to hear the new organist, but then you guys got sick."

"Yeah, it was terrible for both of us. I would never want to get the virus again."

"So, how is it going between you and Olivier?"

My face heats up. I don't know how to describe my feelings toward him, but I admit that I keep thinking about him these days. And it gives me butterflies. "Hmm…I don't know. I think we started to get closer when we took care of each other when we both were sick. I like him. But I am not even sure how he feels toward me."

"Hmm… I think you have a crush on him. How about him? Do you think he has a crush on you?"

"I am pretty sure he doesn't. Look at me. I am too skinny, too nerdy, and have no boobs."

"Stop saying that. You are pretty. And you have a great personality. Appearance is not the only thing. Does he text you often?"

"Yes, when we don't see each other during the day, he asks me how things are going. And I ask about his day, and that's it. He does not flirt at all."

"Does he like to compliment you?"

"Only when necessary. Never out of the blue. There is still distance between us. We still act a bit formal to each other. Aside from when we took care of each other when we were sick, I guess."

"It looks like your relationship has developed more deeply than I thought. I think if you guys only saw each other as friends, you wouldn't go as far as taking care of each other when sick, especially with something as highly contagious as COVID.

"Anyway, I hope you guys will discover your feelings toward each other soon. So you no longer have feelings for Ethan?" she asks.

I have to think about her questions. I admit that I have thought less and less about Ethan and more about Olivier these days. I gave up on Ethan a long time ago since he didn't seem to be interested. So, I tell Christie that.

Christie asks another hard question. "Okay. If Olivier asks you to be his girlfriend, what would you say?"

"Good question, although I don't think it will happen. The thing is, he is not a believer, even though he is the organist at our church."

"He isn't? I didn't know that. Would you be open to dating a nonbeliever?"

"I'm not sure. I always imagined dating a man who has the same faith. I never thought that Olivier would fall for me, so I never really thought about his faith."

"Okay. Fair enough."

"Okay, now it is your turn."

"My turn for what?"

"How about you and Luiz?" I tease her. I know that Luiz has feelings for her, as they both are the best soloists in our choir, and Luiz likes to invite Christie to his place to practice together. In the beginning, I was a bit jealous of Christie. She is prettier than I am. She gets more attention from other guys in the choir. She sings better, and Ethan gives her more solos. But over time, I realized that I could not be the main character all the time. I may never be. In my orchestra, I am a second violinist. In the choir, although I am a soprano, I am not always the soloist. But when I step back, I should be grateful that I can join an orchestra and a choir, which are the two things I really like. And I have decided that I would like Christie to get what she wants. After all her achievements, she is still a very kind and caring girl. She is not pretentious at all, even though she is our main soloist and she is very attractive. So, I am happy to support her.

Christie furrows her brow, deep in thought, but is not very enthusiastic. "I am not sure. He is fun and charming, but I'd really like to date someone more mature."

"Okay. How old is he? Twenty-four? Twenty-five? Maybe wait until he turns thirty or something?"

"Yeah, maybe."

"How about Ethan? He is mature. You don't consider him because I used to have a crush on him, right?"

"No. Ethan isn't someone to date but someone to admire. He is too busy taking care of everyone."

"Yeah. That's true," I say.

I enjoy having a girl talk with Christie. It is so fun to genuinely open up to someone about how I feel and find support. We finish our hot chocolate and return home.

Chapter 28
Olivier Lefebvre
Basilica St. Augustine
Sunday, Fourth Week of May

Today is finally the day I officially become the choir's organist. I try to memorize the liturgy order. The Catholic Church has a lot of traditions to follow. In the beginning, I didn't see the value of repeating the same thing every week. But now, I realize that the tradition has some remarkable benefits. For example, wherever you go in the world, Mass will follow the same order, just in different languages. If people start to change the tradition according to what the individual wants, then there won't be unity. At least that's what Ethan told me.

Five minutes before the Mass begins, I review my notes for the order of the songs we will play today:

- Opening—"This Is the Day" by John Rutter
- *Kyrie* (Lord Have Mercy)
- *Gloria* (Glory)
- Psalm
- Alleluia
- Offertory—"Here I Am, Lord" by Dan Schutte
- *Sanctus* (Holy)
- *Agnus Dei* (Lamb of God)
- Communion—"You Are My Hiding Place" by Michael Ledner
- Closing—"A Clare Benediction" by John Rutter

I have to admit that I am a bit nervous since this is my first time going solo. I keep reminding myself, that as long as I try my best, it's okay. I play not for perfect performance and appreciation, but to help the choir.

The procession is about to start, and Ethan gives a sign to the choir to stand and motions for me to start.

I never imagined being part of a church service like this. Although I cannot see what's going on below, I know that once I start the song, people will rise from their seats, and the procession will begin. It makes me feel important and useful.

After the procession, the priest recites some prayers, and we continue with *Kyrie* and then *Gloria.* Then, another prayer and we are allowed to sit.

The next thing is the first reading from the Bible, the Old Testament. After the first reading, we sing the psalm. There is a church soloist who sings the psalm outside of our choir. But I still have to accompany the soloist. Then, we continue with the second reading from the New Testament, which is from one of St. Paul's letters. After the second reading, we sing the alleluia. Next, the priest reads the third reading, which is the Gospel, a story of Jesus Christ. And finally, I can take a break.

Now comes the homily session. The priest tries to explain the connection between the first and second reading as well as the Gospel. Initially, I didn't see that they were all related. But now I understand. However, I can imagine that for some people, the homily may sound dry and uninspiring. The other day, Ethan explained that Catholic priests usually don't want to draw attention to themselves. They want the people to focus on the ceremony and the Eucharist. That's why the homily sometimes may sound dull.

After that, the Mass continues with the offertory. I only give ten dollars since I also donate to other charities. Also, I still disagree with the Church using people's money to build such an extravagant church building while there are so many poor and hungry people. Maybe Ethan can give me an explanation on this later on.

I admit that every time I discuss my dislike regarding the Church's practices with Ethan, he always gives a satisfactory answer, and I become more understanding. I was so surprised that Ethan told me he was thinking about becoming a priest. After I told him what I witnessed as a child, Ethan responded by saying that there will always be good and bad examples everywhere. Good and bad teachers. Good and bad doctors. Good and bad accountants. Good and bad priests. I cannot judge the Church just by looking at one bad representative. Pedophilia exists everywhere and can be committed by anybody. Being a member of the Church doesn't automatically make a man holy, even if he is a priest. At the end of the day, we are all human, and we make mistakes.

Then what's the point of going to church if we are still sinning? It's like asking what's the point of eating if we are going to be hungry again? What is the point of taking a shower if we are going to be dirty again? Apparently, for Ethan, going to church is a manifestation of his faith. A way for him to feel God's presence with other believers. A way to be connected with God and to strengthen his relationship with God. For me, this part is still hard to understand. A relationship with God. He said it was really a relationship with love that I need to experience myself. Unfortunately, I haven't experienced it yet.

After the offertory, we continue with some more prayers and then we sing *Sanctus*. After that, we all kneel for the Eucharistic prayer. According to Ethan, who gave me a short course about the Mass, this is the most important part. It is when the priest turns the host into the Body of Christ and the wine into the Blood of Christ. I was too little to understand this back then. All I know is that throughout my life, *hosti* and *chalice* were profanities in Quebec. A lot of my friends used these words when they were swearing.

We all pray the Lord's Prayer and give everybody the sign of peace. Apparently, the Lord's Prayer is the complete prayer that Jesus taught. It teaches us to let God rule the world according to His will, which is much better than human will; to ask for daily food and necessities; to ask for God's forgiveness and to forgive others; and to ask for protection from bad things. Also, the sign of peace gives people a chance to interact with each other.

We continue with the song *Agnus Dei* and then an individual prayer to prepare ourselves to receive the consecrated bread and wine. Since I did not complete my first Communion preparation, I cannot take the Body and Blood of Christ. At this point, I am totally fine with it because I don't consider myself a believer yet. However, the more I learn about the Catholic faith, the more curious I am and the more I see its merits.

During Communion, all the choir members line up. I am not sure what to do since I am not going to receive the host and the wine. But then Ethan encourages me to line up to get a blessing from the priest. He tells me to cross my arms in front of my chest as a sign that I will not receive Communion. I do as he tells me.

Once I arrive in front of the priest, he looks me in the eyes and gives me a blessing by drawing a cross on my forehead with his thumb. At that point, I remember my early childhood experiences at Mass and how I enjoyed it so much. Strangely enough, I felt so protected when the priest drew a cross on my forehead. I look at the priest in the eyes. He smiles at me and looks genuine. Maybe I shouldn't feel scared of priests anymore, especially if my best friend becomes one in the future.

Then I go back to the organ and start the intro for the Communion song, "You Are My Hiding Place." I practiced more on this piece because I wanted to make it perfect for Sam and Regina. They have practiced very hard, too, so I don't want to let them down.

Sam starts his solo beautifully. I can see how he takes it to heart. Then Regina starts. As usual, her soft and beautiful voice always touches my heart. The song gives me hope that I can always hide in God whenever I am afraid and that I can trust Him. When the song finishes, I experience an inexplicable peace.

After Communion, there are some announcements before the closing prayer and blessings. I continue with the last song, "A Clare Benediction," when the procession walks out.

***

Olivier Lefebvre
Cycle Action Sports

I stop at a bicycle shop. After the Mass earlier, I overheard Christie talking to Regina. Apparently, Regina's birthday is coming up. I really want to give her a birthday gift.

What can I give her? What would she need? I know she likes to sing and play the violin, but she already has everything she needs for that. But then I remember that she usually has to walk to *Place des Arts*, thirty minutes every day, for orchestra practice. I know what to give her.

Now, here I am in front of Cycle Action Sports on Papineau Avenue and Ontario Street. This bicycle shop has good reviews on Google. I enter the shop and see many bicycles on display—city bikes, hybrid bikes, and mountain bikes. In addition to bicycles, this store also sells bicycle parts and accessories. Their inventory is up to the ceiling. I am very impressed.

A guy with a blue uniform greets me right away. "Good afternoon. How may I help you?"

"I am looking for a woman's bicycle."

Then he asks me several questions about the type of bike that my friend needs, how often she will ride it, her height, and so on. The guy is very thorough.

He shows me all the bicycles that are suitable for Regina. I look at them one by one. Then, I finally find it. A silver hybrid bicycle with twenty-one gears and a medium frame. I know that Regina will mostly use it to go to work. However, I also know that she really likes going up Mount Royal. A hybrid bike with a lot of gears will make the ride more enjoyable for her.

Smiling at the guy in the uniform, I say, "I will take this one."

Unfortunately, the store doesn't provide a delivery service. So, either I have to pay someone to deliver the bike to my place or I carry it myself. I decide to just carry it myself.

It takes approximately forty minutes to walk from the store to my place. I don't want to ride the bike that I have just bought because I want Regina to be the first one who rides it. So I walk with the bike.

I don't know what got into me. I have never done anything like this before, not even for Isabelle. While I am walking, it makes me happy to imagine that Regina will ride it to work and that she will save time and energy. I smile to myself.

Chapter 29
Regina de Luca
Plateau Mont-Royal
Tuesday, First Week of June

The morning of my birthday, I wake up with enthusiasm. I do a quick prayer to God to say thanks that I am turning twenty-four years old today.

I only have orchestra practice in the morning. In the afternoon, I will be free. I may go to a coffee shop and read a book. Tonight, we will have a birthday party at my place. Ethan and Christie have set it up. Usually, we have a choir rehearsal on Tuesday night, but because we were just singing at the Mass last Sunday, we have the day off. I really cannot wait for the party.

When I exit my apartment, I am surprised to see a silver bicycle on the balcony. At first, I think Olivier may have a guest. But then I see that a card with a pink ribbon is attached to the bicycle. My name is written on the card.

Wow. Who would give me a bicycle for my birthday? I take out the card from the ribbon and read:

Happy birthday, Regina. I hope you have a good one. I figure that this bicycle will be useful for you to go to work and other places. I hope you like it. Olivier.

I am speechless. A bike like this must cost at least $1,000! It has twenty-one gears, and it will be very useful in Montreal, especially where the streets are sometimes hilly.

What have I done to deserve this? This is such a unique and useful gift—it's *very Olivier.* I smile to myself. I decide to thank him in person and call his cell first to see if I can come by.

Olivier picks up. "*Allô.*"

"Hey, Olivier, are you at home? Can I come in?"

"Hey, Regina. I am actually already in the office now. I left home half an hour ago."

"Ah, okay. I just wanted to tell you that I received the bike. Thank you very much, Olivier! I really like the bike. This is very useful, and it means a lot to me."

"I am glad you like it! Also, I wanted to ask, are you free this afternoon?"

I think for a second. I don't have anything scheduled after my orchestra rehearsal. "Yes. My rehearsal finishes at twelve-thirty. What's up?"

"Ethan and Christie invited me to your birthday party tonight. Unfortunately, I will not be able to make it. I have a company event. Do you want to have lunch together?"

I am surprised by his request. My heart skips a beat, and I feel butterflies in my stomach. Is this a date?

"That would be a great idea. Where?"

"There is a rooftop restaurant in my office building. We can enjoy Montreal's view from there. What do you think?"

Okay. This sounds like a date.

"I can't wait. Would you mind texting me the address?"

"I will. So, see you at one o'clock?" Olivier says.

"See you!"

"And, Regina?"

"Yes?"

"Happy birthday."

***

Regina de Luca

La Maison Symphonique—Olivier's office

I cannot concentrate throughout the orchestra practice. This is the first time I've wished time could pass by faster. A lunch with Olivier? I know this is not the first time we've eaten together, but this is different. We planned it. I don't want to have too many expectations. Maybe this is just a casual lunch. Maybe he feels guilty because he will not be able to make it to my birthday party tonight. Regardless, I am still excited to meet him.

Right after the rehearsal finishes, I ride my new bike to Olivier's office. Apparently, his office is very close to our church. It is on *René Lévesque Boulevard* and only takes eight minutes by bike from *La Maison Symphonique*.

Once I arrive in front of his office, I park my bike and enter the lobby. The lobby intimidates me right away. It has a high ceiling and is very luxurious. I am glad that I dressed up nicely this morning because it is my birthday. The security guard in reception glances at me curiously, maybe because I have my violin on my back and I appear out of place.

I am about to text Olivier when he finally shows up. I almost don't recognize him at first.

Olivier is walking toward me in a full business suit. He wears a white dress shirt, black dress pants, a tie, and a black suit jacket. His hair is gelled neatly, and he looks professional, mature, and extremely handsome, like a CEO. I am almost speechless. It's not that he is not handsome day to day. In fact, he is. During our choir practice, he doesn't usually wear his full suit. Just a white shirt and jeans or dress pants. But today, he looks exceptional.

"Hi." I greet him nervously, a bit intimidated by his handsomeness.

"Hi, Regina. Happy birthday again." He smiles.

"Thank you."

Then he leads me into the elevator and presses the button for the 33rd floor.

"How's work today?" I ask him.

"It's okay. It's been a busy morning. Since I will have a company event tonight, I want to finish as much as I can. I regret that I cannot come tonight. I am really sorry, Regina."

"Don't worry. All good." I smile at him.

"We'll go to my office first so that you can put your violin inside." He points at my violin.

"That would be great. Thank you."

Then the elevator door opens and we step out. The hallway to his office is very well decorated, and the floor is covered with brown carpet. We walk into the office. I have never been to a large accounting firm like this. Olivier gives me a quick tour. He says the firm actually occupies seven floors in this building. Right now we are on the valuation floor.

We pass the cubicles where many staff nod at Olivier respectfully. I know that he is a partner, which is a very high position in the firm. Some of them throw a curious look at me.

Then we stop in front of his office. I see the nameplate on his door: Olivier Lefebvre, CPA, CBV. Once inside, I find that his office is very elegant and comfortable. There is an oak wood desk with two computer screens. Behind the desk is a huge bookshelf with thick books. It's probably his accounting or valuation handbooks. There are also big leather couches around a glass coffee table.

But, most impressive, is definitely the view. From the 33rd floor facing south, we can see other office towers, St. Lawrence River, Champlain Bridge, and even the famous Farine Five Roses sign.

"Wow. You have a nice view from here."

"Thanks. Let me take you to the rooftop. It's a 360-degree view. Even better," Olivier says.

We walk toward the elevator again, and this time we go up to the 50th floor—the rooftop. Olivier was right. The view is gorgeous. I can see all of Montreal. I see many churches from here, especially St. Joseph's Oratory, *Mont-Royal,* Old Port, bridges, the river, and even Longueuil and the mountains across the river.

"Olivier, this is so beautiful. Thank you for bringing me here."

"You are welcome. I knew you would like it." He smiles.

Then we sit in a rooftop restaurant and order food. All the food on the menu is very expensive. I decide to order fish and chips, but Olivier orders me a steak instead.

"The food will be on me. We get a discount here," he says.

"You are so kind. Thank you."

"No problem. So, how was your violin practice today?"

"It was good. We practiced some of Tchaikovsky's pieces. It was very challenging but rewarding."

We talk about music for quite some time. I have noticed that his playing is getting better and better and not only in church. These days he is also playing some Beethoven sonatas, Chopin etudes, and other advanced compositions. I tell him I really like his new music and how sophisticated it sounds.

"You really think my playing is good? Wow. I play purely for fun, though. Not as a professional like you. But thank you."

"Honestly, you should be proud of yourself, Olivier. You are a very accomplished individual. You have a great career, you are serving as an organist in our church, and you even play the piano very well." I am genuinely impressed by him.

"Thanks for thinking that highly of me. But, first of all, I am already twenty-eight years old. Career-wise, this is what I expect of myself. Also, to get where I am now, it was not only because of hard work but also family background."

"How so?"

"Because my father had a lot of connections, I managed to bring in many clients. That's why they promoted me to be a partner."

"But if you had a lot of connections but you did sloppy work, they wouldn't have promoted you, right?"

"I am not sure."

"I think you should give more credit to your hard work than family background. I saw you working the other day; you seemed to know what you were doing."

"Thank you. I used to think that I was so good and accomplished. But after my accident, I realized that I shouldn't be too cocky and think that all my accomplishments are because of me. There are external factors that contribute to my success, my family background, for example."

"And God, at least for me."

"Yes, and God," he adds. "Anyway, you, too, Regina, are such an accomplished musician. And I listen to you practice almost every day. You are very dedicated and thorough. I am sure you will be successful, too."

"Thank you. It means a lot to hear you say that." I smile.

***

Regina de Luca
Plateau Mont-Royal

That night, my friends arrive one by one. Christie, Genevieve, Carla, Luiz, Sam, and Ethan. I am sad that Olivier could not join us, but at least we had a really nice time this afternoon. He walked me to my bike and seemed very happy to see that I was riding it. I was very happy, too.

150

Yesterday, I cooked spaghetti and prepared a pizza for tonight's event. Now I am presenting them on the dining table for my friends to try.

"Your pasta is really good, Regina," Christie says.

"I agree, you are truly an Italian, Regina! I wish I could include this in my restaurant's menu," Luiz says.

"Haha. Thank you! I can give you the recipe if you want."

"Me, I like this Neapolitan pizza," Sam adds.

"Take as much as you want. We still have plenty here," I say.

I am happy when my friends enjoy the food that I made. Although it's a lot of work, it's worth it when I see their happy faces.

Then we go to the balcony at the back to enjoy the night and the view, although it's crowded with seven people.

"Oh, you bought a new bicycle, Regina?" Ethan points at my new bike.

"Oh, that's from Olivier," I answer shyly.

"Olivier? Are you guys dating?" Genevieve looks a bit jealous.

"We are not," I reply quickly.

"But he gave this bicycle to you?"

"Yes. For my birthday. He is a really good friend."

"Why isn't he coming tonight?" Carla asks.

"He has a company event that he cannot avoid." I don't tell them that Olivier and I had lunch this afternoon. I think Genevieve would be more jealous.

It looks like Genevieve has a strong crush on Olivier. Whenever Olivier was around during our practice, she always tried to get his attention. They spoke in informal Quebec French that Christie and I could not understand. Sometimes they joked around.

I noticed that sometimes I got jealous, too. But I tried not to get affected. First of all, Olivier is not my boyfriend. He is free to date any girls he likes. It's hard not to be jealous of Genevieve, though. She is very beautiful with her thick brown hair and hourglass figure, unlike me. She is full of confidence, too.

I hope we all can just be good friends and there is no competition amongst each other. I am back to enjoying the night with my friends.

Chapter 30
Olivier Lefebvre
Plateau Mont-Royal
Wednesday, First Week of June

I came home today with my new bike.

After buying a bike for Regina, I was tempted to buy one for myself, too. First of all, I imagined I would ride home with her every time we came home after choir practice. Honestly, before, I wouldn't even think about biking or walking or using public transport. In the past, I always drove or took an Uber. Since I met Regina, I have become more down-to-earth.

Secondly, my limping is pretty much unnoticeable now. Only sometimes do I feel weird in my femur, but I think it's normal. I leave the rod there because I don't see the need to take it out. So, I thought I might as well start riding a bike for exercise.

However, when I try my new bike, I can't enjoy it as much as before, unfortunately. My left thigh feels very strange and a bit painful every time I pedal. I have to go extremely slow and in the lowest gear, which is the lightest and slowest. And whenever there is an incline, I really can't bear it, and I have to get off my bike and walk with it instead.

It's been almost six months since my accident. When will I be fully recovered and back to normal? But then I tell myself, I am almost normal except when I ride a bike. Rather than focusing on what has gone wrong, I focus on what has gotten better. I have gone back to work; my kidney and ribs are now okay. Also, with my new friends and choir practice, I don't really miss going to the gym or playing hockey.

I have started to jog a little every morning but not too fast and not too long. I am more out of breath than before, but everything else is okay. I also cook more often because I have to limit my salt intake for my kidney. If I order food from restaurants, I am afraid that they will put too much salt in it. Overall, this does not bother me that much, and I try to stay positive. I don't know if it's because of my new friendship with Ethan and Regina, or because I listen to positive messages at the church every time I play the organ during Mass, but I feel like I have become more positive than before.

I want to put my new bike on the balcony at the back of my unit. So I have to carry the heavy bike all the way up the stairs. I did this yesterday morning for Regina's bike, too. For some reason, it's more burdensome when I have to do it for my own bike. When I did this for her, it felt light and not burdensome at all.

After that, I open a can of non-alcoholic beer and sit behind my desk. I still have to do some work. Last night and today, I was busy attending client events. At least I've started business development again. Now it's time to do more technical work, which is reviewing valuation reports prepared by the managers.

While reviewing a report, I realize that I feel very hungry. I didn't eat much today at the client events because of my dietary restriction. Without much enthusiasm, I walk to the kitchen to find something decent and quick to eat.

When I am about to open the refrigerator, my phone beeps. A text message from Regina! I read it quickly:

Hi, Olivier, I have some pizza and pasta for you. These are some leftovers from yesterday. Please let me know when I can drop it by your place. Regina.

I quickly send her a reply:

Right now would be great, please, if you don't mind. I am starving. Thank you very much!

I check my watch; it's already 8 p.m. I still have a lot of work to do, but I hope I can spend time with Regina.

A few minutes later, I hear the doorbell ring. I quickly open the door.

Regina is standing there with a big plastic bag. She is wearing a cute knee-length peach dress. What a beautiful sight!

"Hey, Regina." I suddenly feel nervous and a bit self-conscious in front of her. I hope my hair looks okay.

"Hey, Olivier." She blushes a little bit.

"Come on in. Thank you very much for bringing food. I am starving now."

"Oh, what did you eat today?"

"Nothing much really. I have been attending a lot of clients' events that didn't provide decent food for my dietary restrictions."

"Oh, I see. Good news for you, I didn't put much salt on the pasta and pizza. When I made it, I separated the ones that belong to you versus the ones that belong to the group. I hope you find it okay," Regina says.

I almost kiss her. "Thank you, Regina. You didn't have to do that, but I really appreciate it."

"My pleasure! Since you missed my birthday party yesterday, and you treated me to a steak lunch at the restaurant, this is the least I can do." She smiles.

This is what I like about Regina. She is always grateful and appreciative of the kind things that people do for her. She also makes me feel good about myself.

"Have you eaten yet? Let's eat together," I say.

"Oh, don't worry. I have eaten dinner. I had too much pasta and pizza yesterday and today. It's okay, Olivier. It's all yours."

"Do you want something to drink?"

"Hmm… No, I am okay."

"What is your favorite drink?"

"Err… I love bubble tea. You must find it weird, right? Haha."

"Not at all," says Olivier. "Although, I have never tried it myself. Let's order." I take out my phone and scroll through the food delivery application that I usually use.

"Wait, no. You don't have to." She seems uncomfortable and is looking down at the ground.

"Why not? Here, make your selection and recommend one for me, too, please." I give her my phone.

"Are you sure?"

"Yes."

So, she ends up ordering regular milk tea with tapioca for both of us. Apparently, we can order drinks with less sugar, too. Ordering drinks is also a way to make Regina stay here longer.

I eat my pasta and pizza while Regina is drinking her bubble tea. She made chicken Alfredo pasta with spinach and Neapolitan pizza. The bubble tea also tastes good, although I don't think it's that healthy. But yesterday and today are still cheat days for her birthday.

"Thanks for the food, Regina. I really enjoyed it. It tasted like authentic Italian pasta and pizza."

"Thank you! And thanks for the bubble tea, too!" She looks very excited.

"Are you busy after this?" I ask.

I check my watch. It's 9 p.m. I still need another hour to review the valuation reports. And I wish Regina could stay until I finish. For some reason, I feel more motivated when she is with me.

"Do you want to stay until I finish? I will be done at around ten. You can play music or read books. Here, I have a lot of selections." I point out my giant bookshelf. I remember at one point she told me she likes to read in addition to playing violin and singing.

"Umm…sure. I think I am done with my music for today. So I'll just read a book."

"Sure. Feel free to read whatever you like." I smile. Although my book collection mostly consists of accounting and finance books, there are some personal development books, spy novels, and non-fiction about technology, business, and economics. I hope she finds what she likes.

She looks around and takes out a Bible. "Oh, how come you have a Bible here?"

I look at the Bible in her hands. "My grandfather gave it to me."

"I see. Have you ever read it?"

"Truth? Not really, no. Sorry. But we all read it in the church, no?"

"Yes. Why sorry? That's completely fine." She laughs. Then she takes the Bible and reads it on the couch.

I continue working while playing classical music pieces from my laptop.

I like this. We don't need to talk, and we do our own things while being physically there for each other.

When I finish at ten, I find that Regina has fallen asleep on the couch with my Bible. I like watching her sleep. The last time I watched her sleep was when she was sick. But at that time, I had only started to get to know her. My feelings are much stronger now.

I carefully lift her up from the couch without waking her up. Her body is so small in my arms. I walk toward my bedroom and put her on my bed and cover her with the blanket. As much as I want to kiss her forehead, I restrain myself. I sleep on the couch that night, but it is the most exciting but calming night for me as Regina is sleeping close by. I wish I could hug her in my sleep.

Chapter 31
Regina de Luca
Third Week of June
Old Port

Today is St. Jean Baptiste Day in Quebec, which means a day off. Olivier, Ethan, Christie, and I go on a bike ride. It is now summer, and everybody is looking forward to spending time outside as much as possible.

For the past few weeks, my friendship with Olivier has grown very close. We've started to be more comfortable around each other. We visit each other's unit and play music together. We always ride our bikes home together after choir practices. Sometimes we watch movies in his apartment, and I let him taste my cooking. I find myself confiding in him about my concerns as a career musician. He also confides in me about the pressure from his job. I feel so grateful to have a friend to share things with. Although I am still not used to having someone as handsome and sophisticated as he is as a friend.

Last week, we invited each of our best friends to go with us on a bike ride. He picked Ethan and I picked Christie. I am happy to see his friendship with Ethan is developing, especially after ignoring each other for many years.

Today, we met at Olivier's place in the morning and packed our lunch. Then from the Plateau, we rode to Jacques Cartier Bridge and rode along the bridge while enjoying the beautiful city views and St. Lawrence River below the bridge. After that, we continued to *Parc Jean-Drapeau* at *Île St. Helene.* We ate our lunch there while chatting and enjoying Montreal's downtown view from the island. I really enjoy spending time with friends like this while surrounded by the green trees, enjoying the sun, and looking at the water.

After lunch, we continue to *Circuit Gilles Villeneuve* at *Île Notre Dame.* This is where the Formula 1 Grand Prix is held every summer. The next Formula 1 race in Montreal will be next month. Unfortunately, even after living in Montreal for eight years, I haven't watched the race in person. Apparently, Olivier and Ethan have watched it multiple times.

Biking in Circuit Gilles Villeneuve is the best. We can ride our bikes as fast as possible because the lane is very smooth and wide. By the time we finish, we are tired and decide to go back.

We pass the bridge again, but after that, we get a drink in one of the bars in the Old Port area. So now, here we are, enjoying our drinks.

"What an intense workout," Ethan says.

"I know, right? I haven't been biking for the past few months. My legs will be so sore tomorrow," Christie says.

"We should do this more often," Olivier says.

"Is your left leg really okay? It's been just over six months since your injury," I ask him. He was struggling earlier, especially when we were going up the Jacques Cartier Bridge.

"In the beginning, it hurt a bit. But after that, I got used to it. When we went up the bridge, though, it was quite painful, but I think Ethan did a great job fixing my leg." Olivier raises his glass to Ethan.

"Thanks, man. Although, it was my attending who was doing the hard job. I was only assisting. But I am happy to take the credit." Ethan raises his glass as well.

We continue to chat until a group of four men approaches. Although it is only 5 p.m., they seem a bit drunk and high already. Two men stop close to me, and the other two are standing close to Christie. They try to make a conversation with us, but their body language feels a bit intrusive. That makes me and Christie uncomfortable.

Olivier moves close to me, and Ethan gets closer to Christie. They both realize that Christie and I may need some protection.

"Hey, do you want some more drinks? We can buy you some," one of the guys says to me.

I decline politely. "No, thank you. We are leaving soon."

"Hey, where are you from? *Ni hao ma?*" Another guy who has blond hair starts talking to Christie in Chinese because Christie is Asian.

"I am not Chinese," Christie says coldly.

"So, where are you from?" The blond guy almost touches Christie's hair before Ethan stops him.

"Hey, guys, would you mind leaving us alone?" Ethan says.

The blond-haired guy looks a bit offended, and now he takes a step closer to Ethan to intimidate him.

"Hey, man, take it easy. Is she your girlfriend?" Now his face is only inches from Ethan's face. Olivier and I step in between Ethan and the blond guy.

"Sorry, guys, we really need to go," I say firmly.

"C'mon, hang out with us first." The blond guy suddenly grabs my waist. What happens next is just like in the movies. Olivier steps in and yanks the guy's arm off me. I try to release myself.

"Back off, please," Olivier says.

The blond guy pushes him, and Olivier pushes him back. Then his friends start to join him. One of them tries to punch Olivier in the face, but Olivier ducks out of the way. But then the other friend uses the opportunity to kick Olivier in the stomach really hard, knocking him to the ground.

Now, Ethan steps in between Olivier and these guys. Christie and I try to help Olivier get up.

"Are you okay?" I ask him. Olivier nods even though he winces. Every breath seems to cause him pain. We finally help him get back on his feet.

Then another guy hits Ethan on the jaw. This pisses Olivier off, so he grabs the guy from behind to stop him from punching further. But the guy is too strong. He ends up thrusting his elbow into Olivier's chest to free himself. I feel terrified when I hear a *dug* sound, and I can feel the pain as if it was me who was elbowed. Olivier almost falls again, but this time he regains his balance quickly and locks both of the guy's arms.

Luckily, two security guards rush in. Somebody must have called them. The security guards drive the drunken guys out of the bar. The blond guy spits on the floor, and the other guy gives Ethan and Olivier his middle finger before they leave.

After the drunken guys leave, Ethan turns to Olivier. "Did you get hurt?" he asks with a panicked voice, even though Ethan himself seems to not be able to move his jaw properly.

"Not really. How about you? I think he broke your jaw," Olivier says while panting.

"I don't know. I don't think so." Ethan touches his jaw. Then he lifts Olivier's shirt to examine the spot where he got hit. "Did they hit your right side?" he asks with concern. As Olivier only has one kidney remaining, he has to ensure that his right kidney is unharmed.

"Fortunately, no," Olivier says.

"Good to know. Let's get out of here." Ethan sighs.

***

Regina de Luca
Le Solano

After the bar, we stop by Ethan's place near Old Port. Christie and I are sitting in the living room while Ethan is with Olivier in the bedroom to examine him further. We are worried about Ethan and Olivier. They must be in a lot of pain, but they are trying not to show it.

"Do you think they will be okay?" Christie asks me.

"I hope so," I say.

"I didn't know that Olivier had a surgery scar on his left side too. Was it also from the car accident?" Christie must have noticed the scar when Ethan examined him.

"Yes. They had to remove his left kidney."

"I didn't know this. I thought it was only his left leg. Poor him."

"Yeah, he has been through a lot."

Then Ethan and Olivier come out from the bedroom. Christie and I bombard them with questions right away.

"How are you?" Christie asks.

"Are you guys okay?" I ask.

"Yes, we both are fine. No broken bones at least," Ethan says while walking to the fridge to get an ice pack for his jaw.

"Yeah, they were too drunk; they could not really kick that hard," Olivier says while taking a seat beside me on the couch. He doesn't seem to be in as much pain as before.

"Thank you guys for protecting us. But sorry to drag you into trouble," I say.

"Yeah, imagine if it was only me and Regina in the bar," Christie adds.

"Don't worry at all. We are glad that you are safe," Olivier says.

"Yeah, all good," Ethan says.

Christie helps Ethan hold the ice pack against his jaw. Now his jaw has started to swell. Both Christie and I keep apologizing, and they keep insisting that we don't blame ourselves.

Regardless, today was still a good day. We all enjoyed our bike ride. We got some exercise. We had a good time with each other. I am also relieved that Ethan and Olivier are not badly injured

.

Chapter 32
Olivier Lefebvre
Plateau Mont-Royal - La Maison Symphonique
Saturday, Second Week of July

I look at myself in the mirror while putting gel in my hair. I wear my usual white shirt and dress pants. Today, Ethan, Christie, and I are going to watch Regina's concert. The program for today is mostly Beethoven. I am super excited to watch, as Beethoven is one of my favorite composers.

Since the bike ride the other day, the four of us have become closer. We have started spending time together outside of choir rehearsals and performances. Sometimes, we just chill out at my place or Ethan's place. We haven't gone to that bar again, as we do not want to bump into those drunk guys again.

I am starting to care for Ethan like my big brother and Christie as my little sister. I am happy that they welcome me, even though I am not a believer—yet. I often listen to them talking about their faith. Although sometimes I cannot relate, I still respect their points of view and enjoy their friendship. One thing I notice is that they are always expressing their gratitude about life and are very positive and optimistic. When I was spending time with Jean-Luc and Isabelle, we were mostly joking about other people, making fun of their stupidity, which was not very kind. But I did not realize it until I met this new group of people. I realize how much I have changed since I became friends with this choir and church group, went to church with them, and performed with them.

My friendship with Regina also brings a lot of joy into my life. I am very sure of my feelings toward her now, and I would like to share them with her. The only reason I haven't is because I still need some time by myself. I only broke up with Isabelle three months ago. I don't want to rush into a new relationship, as there is part of me that is still hurt and needs to heal. Also, I am not sure if Regina is okay with dating a nonbeliever. This is something I would like to discuss with her as well.

I take an Uber to *Place des Arts* as I don't feel like taking the bus or riding my bike. By the time I arrive at the concert hall at *La Maison Symphonique*, Christie is already sitting there. Ethan's seat is still empty. He hasn't arrived yet. There are twenty minutes before the concert starts, but 80 percent of the seats are already full.

"Hey, Christie, how are you doing?" I take a seat beside her and take off my jacket.

"I am good. How are you?"

"I am good, too. Thanks."

We chat a bit about life. Christie is an immigrant from South Korea. She is currently working as a computer programmer. I enjoy talking to her, as programming is really not my forte, and I learn a lot from her. For people who immigrated here, Christie and Regina have been doing very well. They both are strong women and survivors in a foreign country.

"Is this the first time you've watched Regina's concert?" Christie suddenly asks.

I hesitate. Should I confess that this is my second time? But Regina herself is not aware that I watched her concert some time ago.

I tell Christie the truth. "Actually, this is my second time. But the first time was a secret, okay? Regina didn't know."

"Okay. I won't tell Regina." Christie smiles to herself. "So, how is it going with her?" she asks in a teasing tone. I can feel my face blushing. I have never told her that I have a crush on Regina. But she probably has guessed.

"It's good. She is a good tenant and a good friend. I enjoy listening to her violin and singing every day."

"Hmm…is she just a friend? I think the attraction between the two of you is obvious." Christie says with a meaningful smile.

"I wish it could be more than friends. Do you think she is willing to date someone who is a non-Catholic?" Christie is Regina's best friend; she would know the answer.

"I am not sure. I know that she is very devoted. But to not pursue a genuine relationship just because of the faith difference is, I think, a waste. I can see that both of you have the same values at least. You guys are always oriented toward serving others, working hard, and being loyal to the people around you. I don't see why it wouldn't work. As long as you don't diminish her faith and she respects your choice," Christie says wisely.

"That's true. But, eventually, it will be up to Regina," I say.

"Have you ever talked to her about your feelings?"

"Not yet. I have been taking time to think about it. I had a breakup three months ago, and I wanted to be certain that I wasn't using Regina for distraction. Before, I wanted to be certain that my feelings toward her were because of who she was and not because of my particular situation. And I wanted to let her get to know me better. But now I think I am sure."

"That's a very thoughtful consideration. It's good that now you are certain of your feelings."

"Do I have competition, by any chance? Is there any other guy who is pursuing Regina right now?" I realize that I am starting to become competitive again.

"I am not sure. But I have never seen her have a strong connection with anyone else like she has with you."

"Thanks for saying that. It makes me feel relieved."

Five minutes before the concert starts, Ethan finally arrives.

"Hey, guys." He takes the seat beside me. "How are you doing?"

"Good. You?" I say.

"Good, thanks. I am glad that I made it on time."

We change the conversation topic once Ethan joins in. Ethan doesn't know about my feelings toward Regina. I don't know why I haven't told him yet. Maybe because I am afraid he also has feelings for her. He hasn't brought up the issue about wanting to become a priest again. I hope he will not pursue it, though.

Then the orchestra members start entering the stage. I cannot wait to see Regina.

There she is.

She carries her violin and takes a seat in the front row of the second violin section. She wears a long black dress with spaghetti straps and is not wearing her glasses. In my eyes, she looks very pretty.

After all the orchestra members arrive, they start tuning their instruments. The lights in the concert hall are dimmed, and the conductor enters the stage. The audience begins to clap.

Beethoven's Symphony No. 5 starts playing. Although I am enjoying the music, I cannot take my eyes off the second violinist, who is sitting in the front row and playing her violin passionately.

Chapter 33
Regina de Luca
La Maison Symphonique
Saturday, Second Week of July

I feel relieved by the time I finish the concert. The audience gives us a standing applause. But what makes me particularly happy today is that I know, somewhere, Olivier, Christie, and Ethan are among the audience. This is Christie and Ethan's second time watching the orchestra's performance, and this is Olivier's first time. I really hope he enjoyed it.

We bow toward the audience and leave the stage. I put my violin inside its case and chat a bit with other orchestra members to evaluate our performance. Overall, we are all very satisfied, especially with Symphony No. 5. After that, I quickly walk to the lobby as Olivier, Christie, and Ethan are waiting.

I see them right away. It feels very good when your friends are there to support you.

"There she is! Congratulations on a great performance, Regina," Ethan says.

"Yeah, that was really good. Especially Symphony No. 5. I've never seen it played so lively like that," Olivier says.

"Thank you very much on behalf of the orchestra, as I cannot take the credit myself," I say with a smile.

"Let's go somewhere to eat and celebrate! You must feel so relieved!" Christie says.

I nod enthusiastically, and we leave the venue.

As my parents are never here to watch me, sometimes I feel a bit sad because nobody is there to celebrate the after-concert. But today, I feel very thankful for my friends.

***

Regina de Luca
Restaurant at St. Laurent Street

"So, is there any sign that the orchestra will appoint you to become a permanent member?" Christie asks me when we are in the middle of eating our steaks. The four of us decided to eat at this restaurant, only a five-minute walk from *Place des Arts*, and famous for its steak. After the concert, I really need some energy.

"I am not sure. I don't think it's going to be anytime soon. I still have to improve my technique and musicality," I answer.

"It's their loss if they don't select you," Olivier adds. I smile at him. He always thinks highly of my musical ability, even more than I do.

"As long as you play the violin from the heart, you will shine with any orchestra, regardless of whether it's permanent or contract, first or second violin," Ethan adds.

"Yeah, I agree. Right now I am just so grateful for the opportunity, you know? Being able to stay in Montreal, playing with them. Although my future is still uncertain, I am very thankful to God."

"I wish I could be as optimistic and as grateful as you, Regina," Olivier says. "Although, I have been wondering about this question for quite some time, and I sure hope you guys can provide me with an answer. Say, all the good things that happen to us are due to God. What about the people who live in poverty for their entire lives? Like people in Africa or India. What do you think? Why does God let some people achieve their dreams and experience a good life while others don't have any opportunity at all?"

The other thing I like when talking with Olivier is that his questions can actually make me reflect on my faith while finding an answer. Once I find the answer, it strengthens my faith, too. I am someone who is more emotional than logical. But I know Olivier is the other way around.

Ethan jumps in while I am still formulating my answer.

"I don't have the perfect answer for that, but I think you may be judging people's level of happiness from your own standard. I know a lot of rich people who have already achieved their dreams, and they are still not happy. They are worried about their position and status, fight with their family, et cetera. But some of the poor families, though they don't even have food to eat, they suffer together as a family, and they are very grateful once they have something to eat. They may not have the opportunity to pursue a career like we do, but they also don't have to deal with office politics, deadlines, grueling paperwork, and all that."

"So you are saying that everybody has their own cross?" I ask.

"Kind of. Also, remember that many rich people committed suicide during the 2008 economic crisis and the Great Depression. These people were not poor, and they still committed suicide, while there are poor people out there who suffer more but don't commit suicide," Ethan continues.

"I see your point," Olivier says.

"And I don't know if you believe in heaven or hell or not, but we Catholics believe that our lives in this world are only temporary. We may suffer throughout our lives or we may live a happy and fulfilling life. Nevertheless, both happiness and misery are temporary. What counts is how we make the best of our circumstances while we are alive," Ethan explains.

Olivier seems to digest his explanation. "Yeah, that makes sense. I am sorry if I sound like I'm questioning your beliefs."

"No, not at all. We are happy that you ask these questions. We ask the same questions, too, and we don't know all the answers."

I jump in. "For me, I may not know the answers to your questions, but I still choose to believe. God is so much smarter than we are. Since I am only His creation, I will not be able to fully understand Him, my creator, simply because I am limited. It would be silly of me to think I can equal God's intelligence and know everything."

Christie jumps in. "Yeah, me, too. Sometimes, there are Church teachings that don't make sense to me at all. Sometimes I ask the priest, and sometimes I just give up. In the end, I realize that I am too ignorant and immature as a human being to understand."

"Yeah, the smarter and the more mature we are, the more we realize that we don't know a lot, and there are things that we may never understand as a human." Olivier agrees.

Suddenly, Olivier's body tenses up as he looks toward the entrance door. I follow his gaze and find a couple who have just entered the restaurant. A handsome guy and a beautiful woman. I look at Olivier again. He seems to recognize the couple. There is a little bit of pain in his face. I think I can guess who that couple is. Luckily, they don't seem to notice our table.

"I think we should leave now," Ethan says. He notices what's happening, too. He gets up and walks to the counter to pay the bill. I feel sad for Olivier. That couple must be his ex-girlfriend and his best friend. His ex is extremely beautiful, stunning even, and elegant. No wonder Olivier is so heartbroken.

"It's gonna be okay," I try to assure him.

"Thanks." Olivier is just staring at his plate. He has lost his appetite.

Christie whispers, "Can someone tell me what's going on?"

"It's my ex who ended up with my best friend," Olivier says calmly.

"The sooner we leave this place, the better," I say to Christie. We gather our stuff and leave when Ethan comes back.

Outside of the restaurant, Ethan presses Olivier's arm. "Are you okay?"

"Yeah, I think so. I just wasn't expecting them, you know."

"You'll be okay. Think about the beautiful concert and our good meal." Ethan tries to lighten up the mood.

"You are going to be okay, Olivier. You have us," Christie adds.

"Thank you for cheering me up, everyone. Really appreciated," Olivier says.

"I will drop you guys off. Let's go," Ethan says.

We follow Ethan to his car.

***

Regina de Luca
Plateau Mont-Royal

Olivier doesn't say anything in the car. I see sadness in his eyes. It makes me sad, too.

We arrive in front of our place and say goodbye to Ethan and Christie. Then we climb the stairs.

"Regina, I know it's late. But do you want to come over?" Olivier asks me when we are in front of his unit.

"Okay," I say.

We enter his unit and sit in his living room. I don't say a word. I just want to be there for him. Olivier seems to be busy in his thoughts. He offers me a cup of tea. Luckily, tomorrow I don't have any performance schedule, so if I cannot sleep well tonight

173

because of the tea, at least I can wake up later tomorrow and go to Mass in the evening.

"Do you want to play your violin? I know you've just had a performance. You must be tired."

"Don't worry. I think that's a good idea." I take out my violin.

Olivier sits in front of his piano and helps me tune my violin.

We play Schubert's Serenade for piano and violin duet. Two musical instruments and two people create a melody. We unite our hearts through this beautiful piece. I feel like I can see through his mind and his heart when we are playing a duet like this. I feel his emotions. I'm sure that he feels mine.

After that, we continue with Bach's "Ave Maria." This song reminds me of Mother Mary, a motherly figure who brings all my prayer intentions to God. She knows what I need. She knows my feelings toward Olivier, while I myself don't understand very well.

I care a lot about Olivier. When he is happy, I am happy. When he looks sad like this, it breaks my heart, too. I don't want to see him hurt. I know that I love him. But I don't know what to do with my feelings.

"Thank you for being here, Regina," Olivier says when the song finishes.

"Anytime. You can always talk to me."

"I was not sad because of Isabelle. I don't have feelings toward her anymore. I was just sad because they betrayed me. They were the people I used to cherish. It will take time to heal."

"Yes. Give yourself some time. People will always come and go in your life. It's normal to be sad when you lose someone you cherished. But now you have me, Ethan, Christie, and other choir members. You are not alone."

"Thank you, Regina. It means a lot to me." He looks me in the eyes.

Olivier reaches for my hand. He embraces me tightly, and I hug him back. He puts my head on his chest. I can feel his heartbeat.

Then he kisses my forehead softly. I am touched by this emotional gesture. I feel very connected with him. I want to share his sadness, too, and I don't want to leave him alone.

After that, his lips move toward my nose slowly and then to my lips.

I feel like my world stops. We kiss slowly. It is such a beautiful and emotional kiss. I can smell his cologne. I can feel his vulnerability. I hug him tighter. He does the same. We feel each other's body and emotions. We feel connected and loved.

Chapter 34
Olivier Lefebvre
Plateau Mont-Royal
Sunday, Second Week of July

The next day, I am still thinking about Jean-Luc and Isabelle, but it's not as painful as when I saw them yesterday. I know they are together now, but seeing it with my own eyes was different than just knowing it. To console myself, I play piano for a few hours in the morning. I expand my classical repertoire to Bach, Beethoven, and Chopin. In the afternoon, I practice some choir songs for our next performance.

I am glad Regina, Ethan, and Christie were there last night to support me. I also felt strongly connected with Regina. We played music together, and I hugged and kissed her. I wanted to express my love and gratitude, and I was glad that she returned my kiss. I feel like there is hope between us.

Today, I decide that I am going to attend Sunday Mass on my own. I don't necessarily go to church for spiritual reasons. For me, going to church is like attending a seminar. I hope that by listening to the readings and the homily, I can get some inspiration on how to see my life in a more positive way. Plus, I have started to like the soothing music. I find that what they teach in the Church is relevant to me. For example, the lessons about humility, kindness, and not judging others really inspire me. As someone who is very logical, I find that the teachings have great merit. But whenever they talk about Jesus, I have a hard time understanding or believing. When I was a kid, I used to believe that Jesus performed miracles; he was the Son of God who saved humans from their sins by dying on a cross, and he was resurrected from the dead. Now that I am an adult, it's not easy for me to believe these kinds of stories. But then, the conversation with Regina, Ethan, and Christie last night made me doubt my own intelligence as a human. Their explanations also made sense. What if we humans are too ignorant to understand the ways of God? Regardless, I accept what I can accept and I leave what I cannot accept.

At 4 p.m., I start to get ready to go to church.

***

Olivier Lefebvre
Basilica St. Augustine

Today, the readings and the homily talk about forgiveness, which I find quite inspiring. In the first reading from the Book of Leviticus, what resonates with me is this passage: "Do not nurse hatred in your heart for any of your relatives" (Leviticus 19:17). "Love your neighbor as yourself" (Leviticus 19:18). If I am not mistaken, the context was, at that time, the Israelites had just escaped from Egypt, and then, during their forty years of wandering in the desert, they fought among each other. That's why God encouraged them to just love one another.

The Gospel had an even more powerful passage:

"But I say to you, Do not resist one who is evil. But if any one strikes you on the right cheek, turn to him the other also; and if any one would sue you and take your coat, let him have your cloak as well; and if any one forces you to go one mile, go with him two miles. Give to him who begs from you, and do not refuse him who would borrow from you. "You have heard that it was said, 'You shall love your neighbor and hate your enemy.' But I say to you, Love your enemies and pray for those who persecute you, so that you may be sons of your Father who is in heaven; for he makes his sun rise on the evil and on the good, and sends rain on the just and on the unjust. For if you love those who love you, what reward have you? Do not even the tax collectors do the same? And if you salute only your brethren, what more are you doing than others? Do not even the Gentiles do the same?" (Matthew 5:39-47)

I know that this passage is the teaching of Jesus. I have been involved with the choir for some time now. And I know Jesus presented his teaching in a very clever and logical way like in this Gospel. So, should I just let Jean-Luc and Isabelle hurt me? Should I pray for them and wish them happiness? Loving someone like Regina or Ethan is easy. But how could I keep loving Jean-Luc and Isabelle after what they did to me? There is probably no point in hating them because I will only torture myself; they don't even think about me.

Although Jesus' teaching is inspiring, when it's time to recite the creed, I cannot do it yet. As it says:

I believe in God,
the Father Almighty,
Creator of heaven and earth,
and in Jesus Christ, His only Son, our Lord,
who was conceived by the Holy Spirit,
born of the Virgin Mary,
suffered under Pontius Pilate,
was crucified, died and was buried;
He descended into hell;
on the third day He rose again from the dead;
He ascended into heaven,

and is seated at the right hand of God the Father Almighty;
from there He will come to judge the living and the dead.
I believe in the Holy Spirit,
the Holy Catholic Church,
the communion of Saints,
the forgiveness of sins,
the resurrection of the body,
and life everlasting.
Amen.

I still have a hard time believing that Jesus is the son of God and rose from the dead. Therefore, I cannot recite this creed. However, the thing about humans' ignorance is still somewhere at the back of my head.

After church, I go to the third-floor balcony to practice the organ a little bit. Our next choir schedule will be next week. I am pretty much ready with all the songs, but I just need to try them out on the organ. I usually feel much more confident when I get a chance to try out the organ before the performance, as I only play all the songs on the piano at home.

When I arrive on the third-floor balcony, I see two familiar figures in the pews. They seem to be having a serious and intimate discussion. Their heads are very close to each other. The man seems to be sad about something, and the woman is caressing his back. Then he puts his head on the woman's shoulder, and she hugs him.

They are Ethan and Regina.

Chapter 35
Olivier Lefebvre
Squash Court
Wednesday, Third Week of July

I tie my shoelace tightly before entering the squash court. I arrived thirty minutes earlier to smash the little black ball on my own. Ethan will probably arrive shortly. I invited him to play squash after work hours.

What I saw on the choir balcony has really bothered me for the past few days. I am still traumatized by Jean-Luc and Isabelle's betrayal. I cannot stop myself from thinking that maybe Ethan and Regina are betraying me, too. I felt like someone stabbed me in the chest when I saw them together on that balcony. Shocked, I didn't breathe for a few seconds. I have never told Ethan about my feelings toward Regina, but Regina must have known my feelings toward her. We have grown very close these past few months, and we even kissed. Although I haven't asked her to be my girlfriend, I hope she is not someone who acts casually with any guy. Or did I misread her?

I keep hitting the ball to distract myself. It's been a while since the last time I played squash. Now that I have pretty much recovered from my injuries, I want to push myself to my maximum limit. My left leg still hurts when I exercise. It's going to be harder to chase the squash ball, but I don't care at this point. For my remaining kidney, I need to ensure that I don't let the ball hit my right side and I am properly hydrated. I just want my life to get back to normal. Although there will be no more hockey or skiing for me, I still want to do what I can.

I asked Ethan yesterday if he wanted to play squash with me. He agreed. Also, I decided to ask him directly about his relationship with Regina. I am tired of all of this negative thinking. If they indeed like each other, I am going to withdraw and let them be happy. Of course, I will be jealous, but I tell myself that if I really care about Regina and Ethan, I will have to let them go. It is going to be hard for me to accept, but I will try my best. After all, Ethan and Regina embrace the same faith. Maybe Ethan decided not to become a priest for the sake of Regina.

I hear a knock on the glass door. Ethan is there. I open the door.

"Hey, thanks for coming," I say.

"No problem. How are you doing?"

"I am good. You?"

"Good, thanks. What makes you suddenly want to play squash? Is your leg okay now?" He frowns with concern.

"I think it is okay."

We warm up by doing a light rally. I have never played squash with Ethan before, but he seems pretty good.

When we get to the actual game, I realize that he is very good. He moves faster and knows how to position the ball so that it is more challenging for me to hit it back. If I hadn't injured my leg, we would probably be at the same level. My competitive spirit is triggered again.

It's only been ten minutes, and I am already sweaty and out of breath, although I know that Ethan went easy on me. My left leg also starts to hurt because I keep making sudden stops when chasing and hitting the ball.

"Let's take a break." Ethan is frowning at my leg.

"Okay."

We exit the court and drink our water. We don't say anything in the beginning. I don't know how to ask him about Regina.

"Is something bothering you, Olivier? You don't look like yourself these days. Yesterday you looked a bit withdrawn during our choir practice. Now you look frustrated. What's going on?"

I don't answer directly. I need to prepare myself mentally before asking him the question that has been bothering me since last Sunday.

"Is there something going on between you and Regina?" I finally ask.

"Regina and I? We are friends. I thought we all were. Why?" Ethan's eyes narrow.

"I saw you hugging each other on the choir balcony last Sunday. I thought there was something going on between you two."

Ethan doesn't answer right away. He seems to be thinking.

"I asked Regina's opinion about my plan to enter the seminary," Ethan blurts out.

I didn't expect this. "What? What did she say?"

"She fully supported it. She is the first one, aside from my parents, who supports what I am about to do."

I sigh with relief knowing that Ethan and Regina are just friends. "So you have made up your mind?"

"I think so. I will finish my third year by June next year. Then I will enter the seminary. It's getting clearer and clearer which path I should take. I have followed your advice by the way. I have tried to make the most out of my job. And I feel better now. However, the calling is still there. And I am scared, Olivier. Am I really going to serve God completely and not have a wife or children?" Ethan puts his face in his hands. He looks stressed.

"But if this is truly God's calling, you should be excited, right? Because God loves us, and He would not force us to do something that we don't like?" I don't know why I said that again to Ethan. God's calling. I don't even know if God's calling exists. Last time I only used this term to convince him not to quit his residency. If I want to pursue a certain profession, I think that's because of me, not because God is calling me.

Ethan's eyes widen. "Hey, Olivier! That's true. Why didn't I think about it before? Although it's scary, what if, in the end, I will really enjoy taking this path?" He smiles like he is daydreaming. Well, this is not what I was expecting. My point is that because he is scared, maybe being a priest is not God's calling for him.

"Think about it more. Pray, whatever you need to do. Regardless of what your choice is, I will support you." I feel like a bit of a hypocrite, although I will still be his friend if he becomes a priest.

"Thank you so much!" Ethan says. Now his face lights up. "Oh, and back to your question. No, I am not in a relationship with Regina. If you like her and she likes you, she is all yours." Ethan smiles.

I feel relieved.

Chapter 36
Regina de Luca
Basilica St. Augustine
Thursday, Third Week of July

Olivier seems to be happier today at choir practice. Last Tuesday, he looked very sad and disturbed. He gave me a polite smile when he saw me, and on the way back to our place, we biked together but didn't talk much.

But today, he looks normal again. I am relieved, although I am wondering what happened to him these past few days.

Today's choir rehearsal went well overall. Only the tenors and altos had a bit of difficulty in some songs, but that's normal. Just like when I play the second violin in the orchestra, sometimes playing the harmony is more difficult than playing the melody. So it is for the altos, tenors, and bass in a choir. It's hard to get the right pitch for the harmony because it's less intuitive than the melody. Also, it's hard to not get distracted by the sopranos' melody.

However, on the positive side, Olivier seems to get more and more comfortable as an organist. I see a significant improvement in every rehearsal. It is like he is singing through his music, and he looks extremely cool behind the organ, like he is in his own world and enjoying the music.

I think pretty much all the girls in the choir have a crush on either Ethan or Olivier. Ethan, being the conductor, appears very attractive. But so does Olivier when he is playing the organ. I admit that I feel butterflies for Olivier. I sometimes want to believe that he has feelings for me. That kiss the other day! I still remember it very well. It gives me butterflies in my stomach every time I think about it. However, I know that, for some people, kissing doesn't mean that they want to be in a relationship. So, my rule of thumb is that if the person hasn't said anything about love or commitment, that means he only sees me as a friend. And I don't want to start overthinking and expect too much.

We are currently singing "Look at the World" by John Rutter. This is such a beautiful song. I try to reflect on the lyrics.

This song makes me think about all the beautiful things I experience in this world, like nature, the city I live in, my friends, and my music. What I like about singing in the choir is I can be reminded of all good things on a regular basis. These days, what we see in the news—poverty, murder, fights, disease, and natural disasters—can make me feel frustrated. Also, my daily routine can make me feel mundane. So, I really need this regular reminder of all the good things that are still happening.

Once the rehearsal is over, I see Genevieve approaching Olivier. She says something into his ear, and he laughs. I never saw him laugh like that when he was with me. Then he says something informal in French that I cannot understand, and now it's Genevieve's turn to laugh.

I try not to look in their direction. I am wondering if I should just leave first without waiting for Olivier. When I am about to go down the stairs, I hear Olivier calling me.

"Regina, wait."

I turn to him. He is collecting all his stuff really quickly and says to Genevieve, "See you on Sunday." Genevieve looks a bit disappointed and leaves.

"What's up?" I ask him.

"Do you have some time to talk?" Olivier asks.

"Yes."

He pulls me to the corner to have more privacy. I am curious and nervous now. But I am excited at the same time. He, too, looks a bit nervous. This is the first time I've seen him uncertain like this. He usually always appears confident.

"I have been thinking about this, Regina. I really enjoy spending time with you. You have a good influence on me. I feel like I became a better person after I met you."

"Oh, really? I am happy to hear that. I didn't realize." I smile at him.

"Yes. That being said, are you, by any chance, open to a relationship? Like more than friends…with me?" He speaks nervously, but he looks at me with eyes full of hope.

My world stops. I open my mouth in surprise. I didn't expect this at all. I mean, I definitely have a crush on him, but I would never have pictured myself being his girlfriend. I think he is out of my league. He is upper class, sophisticated, cool, and very accomplished. And who am I? I am just a mere Italian immigrant and a violinist who is trying to survive and support myself.

This feels like a dream. So, this is how joyful it is when the person you have crushed on actually likes you back and wants to pursue a relationship with you. I have never felt so happy except when I got accepted into the music school or got an offer from the orchestra. Maybe this is even better.

As much as I want to say yes right away, I have a lot of things to consider. If I pictured dating just for fun and getting to know each other, I would have said yes right away. However, I've always pictured myself dating someone seriously. The goal is clear: it's for marriage. I don't want to date just anyone I like and then break up later on because we are not compatible. It's a waste of time and energy. When I date someone, I have to be able to see the future with the person.

Do I see a future with Olivier?

It makes me sad that on this part, I haven't been able to see my future with him. I mean, I've always pictured myself dating someone who embraces the same faith. Not because I think people with other faiths are wrong. Not at all. It's just so much easier when you date someone with the same belief, right? I know that having faith is always up and down. I imagine that if I dated someone with the same belief, we would be able to support each other spiritually when one is down.

But with Olivier, will that happen? Right now and in the next few months when we will still be in a honeymoon phase, the difference in our faiths will not be a problem. However, once the relationship becomes more serious, I am pretty sure that issues will come up. Also, I prefer not to have sexual relationships before marriage. Where does he stand on this? So, I am not sure what to do.

"I… Would you mind giving me some time to think about it?" I ask him carefully. I don't want to hurt his feelings. But he looks sad right away after hearing my response.

"Oh, yes, for sure. No problem and no pressure." His face looks defeated. It loses color right away, although he is still smiling.

"But don't get me wrong. I really like you. I…I always have butterflies when I am around you. I feel like you are so cool and sophisticated." I feel so embarrassed acknowledging this in front of him. But I don't want to hurt him. "I admit that I have a crush on you." I look at my feet when I say it.

The color in Olivier's face seems to come back. "Thank you for your honesty. Then, may I ask what is it that makes you hesitate? Is it because I am not a believer yet?"

It's a hard question to answer. If I say yes, then I will sound like I am not tolerant of people with a different faith. In fact, I am. It's just that I have to give more consideration if the person who has a different belief will be my boyfriend.

I nod reluctantly. "I think you are a great person, Olivier, really. Even though you are not a Catholic, the way you care for people, it's already reflecting what Catholic teaching is all about. You are always willing to help and to serve others, even when it's inconvenient for you."

"Thank you again. It's okay, Regina. I respect your decision. Don't worry. Please think about it, but no rush at all." He smiles politely, and I throw him my apologetic smile.

"I hope I don't make you uncomfortable by my confession," Olivier continues.

"Not at all. In fact, my crush on you is just getting stronger," I confess shyly.

"Haha. You are funny. Okay, let's go before it's too late. We are still friends, right? Nothing changes?"

"Nope. Not at all. Your confession made me happy."

We walk together to where our bikes are parked. I really wish I could hold his hand, but I don't want to give him a false hope. Olivier seems to read my mind.

"Can I hold your hand although you haven't given me an answer?"

I don't answer. I grab his hand and give him a quick kiss on the cheek.

He looks very happy.

Chapter 37
Olivier Lefebvre
Plateau Mont-Royal
Friday, Third Week of July

I am in the middle of playing Liszt's Liebestraum No. 3 on the piano. *Liebestraum* means "love dream." At this point, I really hope that Regina will accept my feelings, and I can give all my love to her. But I know that she is conservative. Based on her reaction, I know that she takes relationships very seriously. For her, being in an exclusive relationship is not just trial and error. She wants to be certain of it.

I ask myself what I am looking for in a relationship. I also want a serious relationship. However, I wouldn't think as far as marriage yet. As such, I would not mind being in a relationship with Regina, who is a very devoted Catholic.

I haven't really thought about marriage. Although, Regina has a point. If we are already in a relationship but then we discover that we are not a good match, it will be a waste of time, energy, and emotions. I know how a breakup feels.

Suddenly, a new thought comes across my mind. Why don't I just convert? What difference would it make in my life? Nothing really. I know a lot of my friends who are "technically" Catholics. They were baptized; they received their first Communion, and they even made their Confirmation, although they don't go to Sunday Mass anymore. Me, I was baptized already. I just haven't received my first Communion and Confirmation. I am not sure how it will work for me. Am I already a member of the Church? Maybe I should ask Ethan. It's only 8 p.m. now. I call his number.

"Hey, Olivier."

"Hey. Do you have time to talk?"

"Yes. What's up?"

"I have a question for you. If I was baptized in a Catholic church when I was a child, wouldn't I be a Catholic?"

"Hmm...technically, yes, I think. But you did not receive your first Communion or Confirmation, correct?"

"Yes. That's correct. So, what should I do to become a full Catholic?"

"Don't quote me on this as I am not a priest—yet, but I think you can start learning about the faith teachings. Like what is it that we believe in? Who is Jesus? Then you can go to your first Confession, and after that, you can receive your first Communion. Then maybe the priest will recommend you attend the RCIA or Rite of Christian Initiation for Adults class to prepare for your Confirmation. But again, I am not an expert here. There is a canon law for this which I don't remember off the top of my head," Ethan explains.

"Oh, I see." That doesn't sound complicated. I don't mind going to confession.

"Why do you ask this?" Ethan asks.

"Just curious."

"Is it because of Regina?" I really can't hide anything from Ethan.

"Yes."

"I honestly think you shouldn't think about conversion just because you want to date someone. It has to be coming from your own heart. Convert because you truly believe in God, and you are ready to accept Jesus in your life. Just because you were baptized and started attending Mass, it doesn't mean that you are a Catholic if you don't truly believe and accept the teaching."

I try to digest what he said. I have to admit that Ethan is right. I should not be this impulsive.

191

Chapter 38
Regina de Luca
Basilica St. Augustine
Sunday, Third Week of July

I have decided to give Olivier my answer today after our choir sings during the Mass. I try to concentrate on the Mass and singing with the choir. It's hard, especially while Olivier is there, looking gorgeous and immersed behind his organ.

I ask God today to give me clarity on whether Olivier and I are meant to be together or not. As much as I want to be with him, ultimately, I must let God decide because He knows what's best for me, even more than I do. God will also know what's best for Olivier.

At the end of the Mass, Ethan gathers us all.

"Hi, everyone. Thank you for your hard work today. You guys sang beautifully," he says. "I have a quick announcement. A parish in *Mont-Tremblant* has invited our choir to perform in Chapelle Saint-Bernard at the end of September. I just wanted to give you a quick heads-up. Please let me know if you are interested in performing there. I have to know how many people are able to participate before booking the accommodations. Also, if we are going to go, we will spend probably around five days there."

Most of us shout in excitement. This trip sounds very exciting. It will be our first choir performance outside of Montreal, too.

"Are you coming?" Christie asks me.

"Yes! I hope so. I will ask my orchestra leader. I hope I can get some days off."

"Yeah, me, too."

Genevieve, Carla, Luiz, and Sam also seem super excited, although I notice that Genevieve is a bit cold to me these days. Maybe it's because of Olivier.

Genevieve walks toward Olivier right away. She seems to be asking him whether he will join them in *Mont-Tremblant* this September or not.

I wonder if I should talk to Olivier some other time. I see that they both are walking in my direction as they are heading downstairs.

Unfortunately, I have to cut them off. "Olivier, can I talk to you?" I say nervously.

"Yes, of course. See you later, Genevieve," Olivier says. Genevieve doesn't look happy, but she has no choice other than to leave us alone.

"Hey, what's up?" His face lights up when talking to me.

"Do you want to go to a lookout with me?"

"Which lookout? Now?" He looks curious but enthusiastic.

"It's in Outremont. It is about twenty minutes by bike, though, and maybe a bit of walking and hiking, too. And, yes, now if you are free," I say.

It only takes him seconds to decide. "I am free. Let's go." He smiles at me and then puts his arm around my shoulder, and we walk toward our bikes. I am nervous about what I am going to say to him.

***

Regina de Luca
Belvedere Outremont

It's been a while since the last time I came here. I think it was when I just graduated from McGill.

193

The view is very nice. I can see the boarding school and the music school as well as the north side of Montreal. Plus, I am here with someone I really like.

"Wow. I have never been here before, although I grew up close by. Thanks for showing me this view. It's really a hidden gem," Olivier says.

It was quite a long ride from the church. We had to park our bikes at the foot of the mountain because it's hard to bike up unless you are a pro. Then we had to walk and hike for 40 minutes to the lookout itself. But I am glad that Olivier didn't complain.

"That's where I went to school." I point out the boarding school I attended when I was fifteen to seventeen.

"You must have trained really hard back then. Otherwise, you wouldn't be where you are now," Olivier says.

I smile at his comments. I like that he always gives me encouraging and kind words. "Olivier…" I start. He is staring at me. I think he can guess why I brought him here today.

"Yes? So, what is your answer? Do you want to be my girlfriend, Regina?" His eyes are full of hope. My chest feels heavy.

"I am sorry." At first, I looked at him when I said it. But then I cannot bear to see the disappointment in his eyes. My eyes are already full of tears. I realize that I love him, and I really want to be with him. It's hard for me to do this, but this is the right thing to do, at least for now.

Olivier lifts my chin softly with his fingers. He can see that I am tormented.

"It's okay, Regina. I understand." He gives me a hug when he sees me start crying. Again, I am touched by his gentleness, even though I have just rejected him.

We hug for a few minutes. I am glad that he doesn't just walk away. He is still standing here comforting me.

"What would you think if I decided to convert?" he asks.

"No, please don't do that. Only if you really believe and accept it."

"It's hard, Regina. Especially if you grew up here. Also, I don't know if you are aware of what the Catholic Church did in the past—the abusive practices toward the local and indigenous children, all the corruption and everything."

"I know. I am aware of that."

"I know it is not fair to judge and generalize that Catholics are bad based on history. After meeting you and Ethan and some other members of the choir, it really changed my perspective about the Church. But I am just not there yet."

"Yes, I understand. There is nothing wrong with it," I say. "As much as I really care about you, maybe it means that I am not the right girl for you at this point. Maybe, someday, you will find another girl who has the same point of view as yours." Although when I imagine it, it hurts a lot.

"And you will find a devoted Catholic man." He sounds very sad.

"Right now, I can only think of you. I am so sad that we are not together, but, regardless, I still care about you, Olivier. A lot."

"Me, too." He hugs me again.

I know that our relationship may change from now on. We cannot be as close as before. That's why I brought him to this special place. This could be the last time we share an intimate moment together before we move on.

Chapter 39
Olivier Lefebvre
Plateau Mont-Royal
Sunday, Third Week of July

Right after we arrive home, I play Liszt's Consolation No. 3.

This is the first time I have been rejected by a girl. It hurts, but I kind of understand where Regina is coming from.

I cannot imagine myself loving someone other than Regina. It will take some time for me to move on. Wow. We are not even in a relationship yet, but she has already affected me strongly.

What would Jesus do in this situation?

I don't know why I suddenly think about Jesus. Regina is really devoted to her faith. To Jesus. He is someone she looks up to. I am wondering what kind of person Jesus is. I try to remember the readings in the Gospel that we hear every week during Mass.

Jesus was poor. While I have everything I need.

He is full of love. He always shows compassion to those who are poor, sick, or neglected. Aren't I full of love, too? Only to certain people.

From what he taught to his disciples as well as how he answered the Pharisees and the Sadducees, it seems he is full of wisdom. Sounds like Ethan instead of me.

He is always forgiving. Even when the Jews and the Roman soldiers humiliated him, tortured him, and crucified him, he still forgave them. I couldn't do that. I even haven't fully forgiven Jean-Luc and Isabelle.

The conclusion is that I am so far from Jesus and the ideal man who Regina would fall in love with. That's why she rejected me.

How can I be more like Jesus? Could receiving the Holy Eucharist really work? What if I just go to Confession and then receive my first Communion like Ethan said? Nah. There were many people receiving Holy Communion, but they still didn't behave like Jesus. They were far from holy.

I don't know what to think. I keep banging my fingers on the piano keys to let out my frustration. I need to distract myself. I keep remembering the moments when Regina was here, playing her violin while I was accompanying her on the piano. Or when she was singing. I don't know if we can still do that or not.

I decide to go to the office and work. It's only 5 p.m. now. Yeah. Why not?

I gather the stuff I need and ride my bike to the office. I've biked a lot today. This is what I need. My left thigh is hurting again because I overexerted myself, but who cares at this point?

When I arrive in my office, I remember that day when I brought Regina here and to the rooftop restaurant on her birthday. It seems like she has been present in all aspects of my life. Now it's hard to forget her.

What would Jesus do in this situation?

I cannot picture Jesus being bitter if he got rejected by a girl. He probably would just give his unconditional love even though his love was not reciprocated. I don't even know if Jesus ever fell in love in a romantic sense or not.

I look at the stunning Montreal view from my window. The sky has turned dark blue, and the night lights illuminate the city.

I know what to do. I will continue to love and care for Regina in the way that a friend would do. I will still be there for her if she needs me, although I am not going to approach her if it makes her feel uncomfortable. Love is not about possession. Love is about giving.

Just like when Jesus gave Himself to others without expecting it to be reciprocated.

Thanks for the inspiration, Jesus.

Chapter 40
Regina de Luca
Basilica St. Augustine
Thursday, Fourth Week of July

The past few days have been hard for me. I have missed Olivier a lot. We haven't spoken to each other since last Sunday when I decided that I could not be with him.

Sometimes, I hear him playing piano downstairs. The pieces he plays these days are very sad. I find myself doing the same thing on the violin.

When Olivier arrives at the church for our choir practice, I give him a sad smile, and he smiles back with sadness in his eyes, too. My feelings toward him haven't changed at all. They're even stronger. Now I can only admire him from afar, as he doesn't belong to me. Well, he never really belonged to me.

Once Ethan and the remaining choir members arrive, we begin to warm up our voices.

The first song we practice is "Make Me a Channel of Your Peace." I really like this song.

Make me a channel of Your peace
Where there is hatred let me bring Your love
Where there is injury, Your pardon, Lord
And where there is doubt true faith in You

Oh, Master, grant that I may never seek
So much to be consoled as to console
To be understood as to understand
To be loved as to love with all my soul

Maybe I am intolerant. Olivier accepts that I am a Catholic, even though he is not. But he still wants to be with me. What about me? Just because he is not a believer, I don't accept him. Maybe I am too selfish. Maybe I only think about what's good for me, and I don't consider his feelings. I want to be understood, but I am not understanding. Just like in the song. I want to be loved, but I don't love Olivier enough as I cannot accept our differences. I am so lost.

After the rehearsal finishes, I quickly pack my stuff. I am not sure if I am going to ride back home with Olivier or not.

"Regina, Olivier, can you both come here for a second please?" Ethan calls.

"What's up?" Olivier and I are now standing in front of him.

Ethan looks at us back and forth. "Are you guys okay?"

"Yes," we answer in unison.

Ethan tilts his head and squints, unconvinced.

"Anyway, I saw that you both signed up for *Mont-Tremblant*. I am excited! So, in addition to the Mass on Sunday, we will have to recite a Rosary and have adoration on Saturday. That being said, I am thinking that Regina can sing a solo piece before the Rosary, and Olivier can be the accompanist. What do you guys think?"

Olivier looks at me, and I look at him. I don't know what to say. I don't know if this will make him uncomfortable or not.

"Fine by me. Regina?" Olivier says.

"Yes, sure. What song do you have in mind, Ethan?"

"How about 'Ave Maria'?"

"Oh, I like that idea," I say enthusiastically.

Olivier jumps in. "I like it, too. I accompanied you last time for your violin, so it will be just a refresher for me."

"Perfect. I can always count on you guys. Thank you so much." Ethan's face lights up. After that he leaves the two of us alone.

It's awkward between me and Olivier now.

"Let's ride home?" he asks me carefully.

"Sure."

***

Regina de Luca

Plateau Mont-Royal

On the way back home, we didn't talk much as we were on the bikes. Now that we are in front of our unit, I am not sure what to do. Should we just chitchat as usual, like nothing happened? I told myself I was just going to treat Olivier the same way I treat Ethan, Luiz, or Sam from now on.

"Do you want to come over for tea and maybe practice a bit?" Olivier asks politely. As much as I want to say yes, I think about his invitation more carefully. If this were Ethan, Luiz, or Sam, would I say yes? I think so.

"Okay."

Once inside, he makes me a cup of tea. I look around his place. I have been here so many times. I wish we were still like before. It used to be so fun to spend time with him here. Before, every time we agreed to meet here, I was already super excited hours or even days before I actually met him. I also prepared the dishes that he likes, and he was always genuinely excited to try my cooking. Aside from practicing together, I liked accompanying him, working until late while I read, played violin, or just cheered him up. It was just last week that we were still doing stuff together, but it seems ages ago. I am wondering if we can be like that again. I wish he never asked me to be his girlfriend, and I wish I never said no.

He gives me a cup of tea, and we drink in silence.

"I miss you, Regina," Olivier says honestly.

"I miss you, too, Olivier. I mean it."

He only sighs heavily. "Let's practice?"

"Okay."

He opens the piano lid, and I stand beside him. He plays the intro for "Ave Maria," and I start to sing.

> *Ave Maria*
> *Gratia plena*
> *Maria, gratia plena*
> *Maria, gratia plena*
> *Ave, Ave Dominus*
> *Dominus tecum*
> *Benedicta tu in mulieribus*
> *Et benedictus*
> *Et benedictus fructus ventris*
> *Ventris tui, Iesus*
> *Ave Maria*

When I finish singing, I realize that I have tears in my eyes. I feel like I have to be strong like Mother Mary. I feel so lost at this point, especially about my feelings toward Olivier. So, this is how it feels when you love someone, but you cannot be together.

Olivier sees me crying silently. He slowly rises from his seat and gently hugs me. I bury my face on his chest. I can feel his warmth. I don't know how long we hug, but I just don't want this evening to end.

Olivier then starts to kiss me gently. In the beginning, I don't know what to do. I would like to kiss him back, but I don't want to give false hope. At the same time, I also feel a strong urge to follow my emotions.

We kiss each other more passionately than before. I can feel him breathing harder and faster. He caresses my back intimately. I have never been this close with a man before. Am I willing to give myself to this person who is not my husband? He is not even my boyfriend.

Olivier starts to unbutton my shirt. I quickly pull back from him. Olivier must see fear in my eyes. What is he thinking? What am I thinking?

"I…I'm sorry…I…thought you were okay with this." His face is flushed; he's embarrassed. I quickly button the top button of my shirt.

"I cannot do this. I am sorry." I step away from him.

"That's okay. I am sorry if I scared you. I cannot control myself. I apologize." He looks genuinely apologetic.

"It's okay. I will go now. Bye, Olivier."

Chapter 41
Regina de Luca
Montreal—*Mont-Tremblant*
Friday, Fourth Week of September

We are currently on the way to *Mont-Tremblant*. It is a 2.5-hour drive from Montreal. Genevieve, Carla, and I are carpooling in Christie's car. Today is a nice day. The more north we travel, the more we see yellow and red leaves. Fall season has begun.

It has been two months since I spent time alone with Olivier. After that 'almost' intimate moment, we haven't talked properly or texted each other. We only nod politely during choir rehearsal. We don't ride home together anymore. This makes me really sad. The only thing left of him is his music from downstairs, which I often listen to. Other than that, we are just like landlord and tenant. Maybe it's best like this.

What makes me really uncomfortable today is, throughout this ride, Genevieve cannot stop talking about Olivier. They appear to be very close now. The reason Olivier and I don't ride home together anymore is because after choir rehearsal, he and Genevieve always chat for a long time. I figured that I better just leave and ride home on my own.

"He is really sweet. One time he told me that he likes talking to me because it feels like home. We speak the same language, laugh at the same jokes, and everything. I feel like he is truly my soulmate." Genevieve looks enthusiastic and…in love.

It hurts. But I try to be happy for them. Maybe Genevieve would make a better girlfriend for Olivier than I would. With regard to communication, although I have been living in Montreal for nine years now, I still don't understand all Quebec expressions. Sometimes, I noticed that Olivier made an effort to speak more formally to me so that I could understand. But with Genevieve, he can be himself.

"How about you, Regina? Are you seeing someone else?" Carla asks me. I know she is curious if I am still close to Olivier or not.

"No. I don't really have time for dating. I have to practice for the orchestra if I want to keep my job. Also, I am taking on more students."

"Good for you, Regina. Anyway, I think Olivier is the sexiest man alive. His body is soooo good," Genevieve continues.

"What? Have you guys had sex already?"

With her eyes on the road and her hands on the wheel, Christie looks surprised.

"Sorry, I cannot tell you that. It's between me and Olivier." Genevieve smiles secretly.

"Well, congrats to you guys. Just be careful of his scar," Christie says.

"Scar? What scar?" Genevieve asks curiously.

Obviously, Genevieve hasn't seen him without clothes. Otherwise, she would know about the scar on his left side and left thigh. Although I don't care if they have had sex or not, I feel relieved for some reason if they haven't.

"Oh, you don't know?" Christie fishes.

"It's because it's dark," Genevieve says nervously. "How do you know about his scar?"

"I have seen it once. Regina, too. Right, Regina?"

"I forgot." I try not to put oil on fire. After that, Genevieve talks about something else.

Before going to *Mont-Tremblant*, Ethan proposed that we stop by at a cool lookout spot called *Le Sentier des cimes Laurentides*. It's basically a spiral observation tower in the middle of the forest. The tower is about twelve stories high, and we can enjoy the view from the top.

We soon arrive at the parking spot. I cannot wait to get out of the car and get away from Genevieve. I am quite sad how our friendship has turned into a competition. We used to get along so well. I guess we are just human. Whether it's a friendship within a church group or any other group, there will always be friction. I keep reminding myself to love everybody. I don't want to feel jealous or competitive, but sometimes, it's hard. I feel inferior to Genevieve, who is much prettier than I am.

Once Christie finishes parking her car, she walks with me to wait for the others to arrive. At least I still have Christie by my side. It looks like Carla is more loyal to Genevieve than to me. I hope we all can be friends like before.

"I don't know how you could put up with Genevieve's comments about Olivier throughout the ride," Christie whispers. It looks like she is more frustrated than I am.

"Haha. It's okay. We don't need to listen to her."

"But is there something going on between you and Olivier lately? This summer, you were like a honeymoon couple, but I noticed that you guys are a bit cold toward each other now. And he is always talking to Genevieve after choir rehearsals."

I haven't told Christie what happened between me and Olivier.

"We decided not to be together because of our difference in faith," I finally explain.

"Oh, whaat? But…" Christie, with wide eyes, doesn't know what else to say. "But he was very caring and genuine toward you. He adored you so much. And he even goes to church every week. Isn't that enough?"

"He told me that he was not a believer. And stop, he didn't adore me like that," I say.

"He did. Let me tell you something. He fancies you a lot, especially when you play the violin. He told me one time that he went to watch your orchestra performance without you knowing."

"What? When was this?" Wow. This is news for me.

"I think it was a long time ago."

"Yeah, but it doesn't change anything." Although, I am a bit flattered. I thought the only time Olivier watched my orchestra performance was that one time with Christie and Ethan. The day he saw his friend and his ex together in the restaurant. The day we had our first kiss that night in his apartment.

"Well, ultimately, it's up to you. But I feel like you shouldn't let go of this opportunity. He is a really good guy. He is willing to serve as our organist, even though he is not a believer."

"I know he is a good guy."

"Oh, there they are." Christie points out a car that has just entered the parking lot. It's Ethan's car. He is carpooling with Olivier.

Olivier looks very nice today in a blue shirt, jeans, and a long black coat. September can be a bit chilly, especially in the mountains.

Genevieve doesn't waste a single second and approaches Olivier right away. Meanwhile, Ethan waves and walks toward us. We are still waiting for a few more choir members to arrive.

"Hi, Regina. Hi, Christie. How was the ride?" he asks with his usual smile.

"It was good. Although Genevieve was a bit annoying," Christie complains.

"Oh, why?"

"She was talking about Olivier all the time."

Ethan chuckles. "Yeah. I think it's obvious that she is really into Olivier."

Finally, all the members arrive, and we end our conversation as Ethan has to lead the group.

Chapter 42
Olivier Lefebvre
Le Sentier des cimes Laurentides
Friday, Fourth Week of September

On the way up to the top of the observation tower, Genevieve keeps talking to me. I feel a bit suffocated, to be honest. For the past few weeks, we have gotten to know each other better. She always wants to talk to me after choir rehearsals, although I am usually tired and just want to ride home—with Regina. However, I want to respect Genevieve's feelings.

I like talking to her. She is funny and has a lot of interesting stories. Moreover, I can speak like myself again. When I talk to Regina and Christie or some other non-native French speaker, I have to speak more formally and try to control my native Quebec accent. Even Ethan, who speaks perfect French, sometimes doesn't get the expressions I use. Maybe because he hangs out more with Anglophones than Francophones.

But with Genevieve, I can talk more naturally with my heavy Quebec accent without having to hide it. However, I would rather speak more formally with Regina and feel connected. I don't have any feelings for Genevieve, although she is attractive. She is just not the one for me.

It has been two months since that night with Regina when I almost couldn't control my lust. I felt so stupid and embarrassed. What was I thinking? I knew that Regina was a very devoted Catholic. She would not want to do it. Then I figured that I have to keep my distance from her; otherwise, I was just torturing myself. Even these days, listening to her beautiful violin music and her soft voice makes me sad. I miss her so much. My feelings for her are still very strong. I don't even remember if I felt this passionately toward Isabelle before.

Now, every ten minutes, I look for Regina. Because the walkway to the top of the observation deck is like a spiral slope, we can easily see people above or below us. There she is, still one level below me, chatting with Ethan very seriously. I don't want to lose sight of her. I wish I was there with them. But Genevieve has been monopolizing me since I arrived.

During the ride from Montreal to *Mont-Tremblant*, I told Ethan about what happened between me and Regina. He seemed like he'd already guessed what had happened, but he didn't say anything. I didn't tell him about that night when I almost lost control of myself, though. It was too embarrassing.

I am curious about the Catholic teaching regarding sexual relationships. Why is sex before marriage not allowed? What is the reason? Are all Catholic women like this? Or at least the majority?

I wait until Genevieve finishes talking before I ask this question.

"Hey, Genevieve, there is something I am curious about regarding Catholic teaching," I start.

Genevieve looks a bit surprised. We never really talk about faith. "Oh, what is it?"

"Why is sex before marriage not permitted?" I ask bluntly. I can see her suddenly getting excited. I hope she doesn't think I would like to have sex with her or something.

"Oh. Um...I don't know. Because it's a sin? I honestly don't know. But, for me personally, I don't mind." She looks deeply into my eyes.

Okay, it seems that I am asking the wrong person.

***

Regina de Luca
Le Sentier des cimes Laurentides

I walk with Ethan on the way up to the observatory tower.

"So how are you doing these days, Regina?" Ethan asks.

"Not bad. How about yourself?"

"Not bad. I am starting to like my job more."

"Oh really? What makes you like it more?"

"Actually, Olivier was the one who made me become motivated again."

"What did he do?"

"He reminded me that my current job is also God's calling, and I should be at peace with my job before considering changing my path. It's weird that he mentioned God's calling when he'd declared that he himself wasn't a believer," Ethan says.

This is true, I think. I wouldn't expect that Olivier would come up with God's calling.

"That's good advice."

"Yeah. Now that I am a third-year resident, I have more responsibility and I am more confident in my skills, so I enjoy it more now. Before, there were so many things that I didn't know. I still don't understand many things, but at least it's getting better."

"Are you going to change your mind about entering the seminary?" I ask. He told me that he was thinking about becoming a priest and entering a seminary next year, but he was scared. I was surprised but enthusiastic when he told me this.

Wow. God's plan is always working in an unexpected way. I feel like Ethan has the character to be a good priest. He is caring and compassionate. And he has already had experience dealing with patients. He has good social skills, which will make him a good priest, although a lot of women will probably be heartbroken because dating Ethan is no longer an option. I used to have a crush on him, too. But not since Olivier entered my life.

"No. I will still enter the seminary in the fall of next year. So, I am planning to take a year off from my residency. After that, we'll see. Either I finish the remaining two years of my residency or just continue in seminary," Ethan answers.

"That means you still have plenty of time to decide. I will be curious about what it's like to enter the seminary. Tell me more about it next year," I say enthusiastically.

"Okay, I will. And by the way, about Olivier…"

"What about him?" I ask curiously.

"He told me what happened between you guys. I am not trying to meddle in your business, but I think he is a good guy, and he is very genuine toward you."

"I know. But I feel like there will be issues in the future if I date someone with a different belief. Our fundamental values are already different."

"What if it's different only on the outside but similar on the inside? Also, you have to consider it from Olivier's point of view. He had a bad experience with the Catholic Church."

"Oh, what kind of bad experience?"

"He saw a priest sexually assault a boy when he was eight years old," Ethan says.

I am shocked. Olivier never told me this.

"However, because I needed an organist, he stepped out of his comfort zone to help me out. I know that he practices diligently every day, and he always gives his best during our choir performances in the midst of his busy schedule as a partner. He also rides a bike to the church despite the pain in his leg just to attend our rehearsals and performances. I know he declares himself as a nonbeliever, but I think he actually believes more than he shows us."

I didn't realize the depth of Ethan and Olivier's friendship.

"You're probably right, Ethan."

Then we arrive at the top of the observatory. The view is beautiful. I can see the leaves have turned yellow, orange, and red. I can see the Quebec mountain range. I feel the wind in my face.

Olivier is already there and still talking with Genevieve. Christie is also already there talking to Luiz, Sam, and Carla. Even when it's not going very well between me and some people in the choir, I am still happy to be in this beautiful place with them.

"We should take a group picture here," I say.

"That's a great idea. Let me gather everyone." Ethan says.

Chapter 43
Olivier Lefebvre
Mont-Tremblant
Friday, Fourth Week of September

Mont-Tremblant is always full of tourists. But, this time, I don't mind. I enjoy being with the choir. I have so many memories with Isabelle here, but for some reason, I am no longer sad.

We check into the hotel. I share a room with Ethan on the fourth floor overlooking the southeast. I can see the village, the resorts in the middle of the mountain, and the mountain range from afar. It is very peaceful.

After lunch, we go to the St. Bernard Chapel to practice. This is also where we will be doing the Rosary and Adoration on Saturday and singing during Mass on Sunday. I have practiced all the songs and feel pretty confident about it. But most importantly, I will be accompanying Regina on her "Ave Maria" solo on Saturday, as well as Luiz and Christie for "The Prayer Duet" for the Communion song on Sunday. I feel honored to accompany them, as they are extremely talented singers in my opinion.

After choir rehearsal, we eat dinner. I am glad that I get a chance to sit with Regina, Ethan, and Christie, even though it's a bit awkward between me and Regina. I still have a huge crush on her despite the fact that she has rejected me. Every time I am with her, I feel a bit nervous, and I am always self-conscious. Is my hair all in the right place? Is my shirt wrinkled? I just keep hoping to no avail. Regina has made it clear that she doesn't want to be with me, although sometimes I find her glancing at me. Once, I caught her gaze, and she blushed and quickly turned around.

After dinner, some of us want to explore the village at night. I pass because I need to go back to my room to check my work emails.

I am on the way to my room when someone calls me.

"Olivier?"

It's Genevieve. Honestly, as much as I like her as a friend, she is starting to get on my nerves. She keeps following me and wants to talk to me. But I want to respect her feelings and be polite.

"Yes? What's up?"

"Can I come in, too?" Genevieve asks, pointing at my room. I hesitate. What does she want?

"Okay. But I'm gonna work. It's boring," I say. And this is also Ethan's room.

"It's not going to be long," she insists.

"Okay." I give up. I let her enter my room. I hope she is not going to stay too long.

Once inside, she doesn't waste a single second. She throws herself at me and starts kissing me. I am shocked. I don't have this kind of feeling toward her.

"Genevieve, wait." I try to release myself.

"Isn't this what you want? You asked me about having sex as a Catholic before. This is my answer. I don't mind." Then she starts kissing me again.

Honestly, I am not sure what to do. On one hand, my feelings toward Regina are very strong. However, it's been nine months since I have had a sexual relationship with someone. Last time was with Isabelle before my accident. For the past few months, whenever I felt horny, I had to relieve myself. When I almost had sex with Regina, I relieved myself again after she left.

Should I just keep going with Genevieve?

She starts taking off her dress while still kissing me. Then she pushes me to the bed. Now she is standing only with her red lace underwear in front of me. She has perfect curves. In normal times, I would feel very aroused. But today, I feel nothing.

Genevieve kisses me again and then starts unbuttoning my shirt. By the time she unbuttons the last button, I realize that I don't want just anyone to see my scar. Although Ethan and Regina have seen it, and probably Christie, too, I don't care if it was them because I trust them. But, for some reason, I don't want Genevieve to see it.

"Genevieve, stop, please." I extricate myself from her.

Her gaze falls to the ground, hurt. "Why?"

I try to cover my left side with my shirt so that she doesn't see it. But it's too late. She sees it and freezes.

"Is that from your car accident?" she asks carefully.

I don't answer. I hate when people see my scar and probably realize that I don't have a left kidney. That makes me feel very self-conscious and insecure.

What's worse, after that, I hear a swipe key, and someone enters the room.

Ethan and Regina.

They both stand, their eyes and mouths open at seeing Genevieve half-naked and me with my shirt unbuttoned. Regina especially. Her expression is one of betrayal and sadness. She quickly turns around and leaves. Ethan looks disgusted and leaves, too.

I feel so bad. "Genevieve, please leave." I can hardly control my anger.

"Okay," she replies coldly and quickly puts her dress back on and leaves.

Now I don't know what to do. I just want to chase Regina and explain that nothing is happening between Genevieve and me. Well, we kissed, but she was the one who kissed me. I was just playing along. But deep down, I regret it so much. I feel dirty and ashamed of myself.

I sit on the bed, not sure how to clean up this mess.

I hear the swipe key again, and Ethan comes in. His mouth is rigid, and he glares at me. This is the first time I've seen him mad. Really mad.

I quickly button my shirt.

"What was that, Olivier?" Ethan asks coldly.

I finish buttoning my shirt and say, "Nothing happened. It's just a misunderstanding."

"Are you kidding me? We are not in the middle of a romantic vacation. We are coming here to sing as a choir. What were you thinking?!" He sounds very disappointed.

"Oh, yeah? What about you and Regina? Why did you bring her to our room?" I raise my voice, too. I hate seeing them close. Although I know that Ethan said he wants to become a priest, it seems to me that he always pays extra attention to Regina. It makes me jealous, too.

"Don't you dare change the subject. You know better than everybody else that Regina and I are just friends!"

My temper flares. "Stop being so judgmental and acting holy all the time, Ethan. Whom I want to have sex with is none of your business!"

"First of all, this is *our* room. Not your honeymoon suite. Second, I brought the group here, and I am responsible for all of you. I will not tolerate improper behavior. Please be respectful and find an appropriate time and place next time."

Then he storms out of the room and slams the door.

I still cannot believe what I just saw. Olivier being intimate with Genevieve? I feel like someone has stabbed me in the chest. All the perfect images I imagined about Olivier are gone. He is just a typical guy who'd have sex with anybody. He said he was not a believer; now I believe it.

I don't want to cry right now. I feel stupid for crying for someone like him. I rejected Olivier, so whoever he has sex with is none of my business. But why does it still hurt?

I cannot get rid of the image of Genevieve only in her underwear and Olivier with his shirt open. They are such a perfect couple. I feel very jealous.

I try to clear my mind. I sit on one of the benches in the village. It's already dark now. Only the streetlights illuminate the village. I don't want to go back to my room yet. Christie will ask what happened, and I don't want to tell her what I saw.

Suddenly, Ethan appears in front of me.

"Hey. Can I sit?" he asks.

"Of course." I move a bit to give him some space.

We don't say anything in the beginning. Earlier, Ethan was going to show me a music sheet for my possible next solo. That's why he invited me to his room. I expected that I would find Olivier there because he said earlier that he would have to work. But apparently, that was a lie. Olivier would like to have sex with Genevieve; that's why he left right away after supper.

"How do you feel?" Ethan asks.

"Not so good," I confess. "I know I rejected Olivier, and he has the right to have sex with anyone he wants. But I don't know why it hurts so much."

"I think it's because you still love Olivier. Otherwise, you wouldn't feel this devastated."

"Maybe. It's hard to forget him."

Ethan sighs. "I was angry at him earlier. I even yelled at him. But now that my head is clearer, knowing Genevieve and Olivier, I would say it's Genevieve who initiated it."

"You think?"

"Yes. I know that Olivier doesn't have any feelings toward Genevieve. But, for some men, you don't really need to have feelings toward a woman in order to have sex. It would make me disappointed, too, if it turns out that Olivier is one of those guys."

"Yeah. But it's not our place to judge," I say.

"You are right."

"Thanks for clarifying, though, Ethan."

"No problem. Just focus on your own solo tomorrow, okay? Don't think about anything else."

***

Olivier Lefebvre
Mont-Tremblant

I cannot sleep well. First of all, I am not used to sleeping in a T-shirt. I am sweating already, and it feels very hot. I keep changing my sleeping position to make myself more comfortable. But Ethan is there on the other bed, and I don't have privacy. Secondly, I still feel extremely guilty about what happened. I hope I didn't hurt Regina's feelings. But most likely, I did. Thirdly, I am still not talking to Ethan. Since he returned to our room, we have avoided each other's gaze, and we haven't said a single word to each other. I don't like this. We cannot keep ignoring each other, especially when we are roommates.

"Ethan? Are you asleep?" I dare myself to talk to him.

"Not yet." I cannot see his face, as he is facing away from me.

I take a deep breath. "I am sorry for what happened earlier."

He doesn't reply. So I continue. "Please, understand. I haven't had any sexual relationships for the past nine months. Although I don't have feelings toward Genevieve, I thought I would just take the opportunity that she offered. But I felt nothing, really."

I hear him sigh. "Olivier, you don't need to justify yourself. I don't care whom you have sex with. Just do it at a proper time and place. Also, please don't play around with women's feelings. Especially if they are my choir members."

"I don't mean to." How do I make him understand? "Seriously, Ethan, I know you are a devoted Catholic. You believe in no sex before marriage. But do you really follow it? Seriously? You've never had sex throughout your twenty-eight years of life? How do you do it?"

It takes some time for Ethan to answer.

"I had one hookup in undergrad. And I did it with my ex-girlfriend back in med school. I wasn't proud of it," Ethan admits.

"Then after that? How do you restrain yourself?"

"I focus on other stuff. My career, my studies, and I do a lot of sports. I find distractions helpful."

"But what's the reason behind this restriction? It sounds ridiculous to me. Why can't you have sex even with your own girlfriend?"

"I wish I could answer that. Maybe the reason is people might think they love each other just because they have had sex, and they end up being with the wrong person, the person they don't actually love. Restraining our sexual urges teaches us to differentiate between lust and love. Lust is using the other person to satisfy yourself. Love is when you truly give all of yourself to the other person."

"Okay. But if this is with your girlfriend, you know that it must be love, right? Why can't you give all of yourself to your girlfriend?"

"A union between a man and woman is sacred and, in doing so, the spouses renew their marriage vows. It is also a gift from God that needs to be treated with the highest respect. A girlfriend is not a spouse. Performing this act with someone who is not your spouse is a lie and shows that you don't understand how sacred it is," Ethan explains.

I digest his words. There is a point there. It's indeed beautiful to share the ultimate expression of love with just one person, who is your spouse. But it's too late for me. I have had sex with seven women in my life.

"Okay. Thanks for your explanation. I'll stop bothering you, and I'm gonna go to sleep now. Good night."

Chapter 45
Regina de Luca
Mont-Tremblant
Saturday, Fourth week of September

Tonight I will sing my solo for the Rosary and Adoration. I haven't practiced with Olivier for quite a while now. After all the things that happened, I don't think we are comfortable enough to practice together. However, for the sake of tonight, we really have to practice at least once.

Today, all of us will take the gondola up the mountain to enjoy the view. But after that, Ethan has advised that we practice for a couple of hours before the Rosary and Adoration itself. So, I can worry about my practice session with Olivier later.

Christie and I gather at the base of the gondola. We arrive before everybody else. I haven't told Christie what happened between Olivier and Genevieve yesterday. I don't want to spread gossip. It's not my business.

At around 11 a.m., everybody has gathered at the base. Olivier and Genevieve seem to avoid each other. Olivier talks more with Luiz and Sam now.

Ethan distributes our tickets, and we line up for the gondola ride. I try to enjoy my surroundings as much as possible. This is my second time in *Mont-Tremblant*. Last time I came here was with my secondary school friends six years ago. The view will be good from up there, and I am excited to see it again.

As the gondola can fit six people, Ethan, Christie, and I end up in the same gondola as Olivier, Luiz, and Sam. Olivier and I are avoiding each other's gaze. I just focus on enjoying the view. The higher we go up, the more beautiful the view is. First, we see the colorful village getting smaller and smaller. After that, we see the mountain ranges and Lake Tremblant. When I went here last time, it was during winter. *Mont-Tremblant* turns all white in winter. This is a popular ski resort. But in September, it offers a different kind of view, with beautiful autumn colours. Both views are very pretty in their own way.

"Hey, do you guys want to come back here for skiing this winter?" Luiz asks.

Sam jumps in. "Yeah, that would be a good idea. Although I cannot ski, I always wanted to learn."

"How about you, Olivier? Are you good at skiing?" Luiz asks.

Olivier doesn't answer at first. He looks a bit sad instead. I know why.

"I don't ski anymore, unfortunately." With only one kidney and the injury to his left leg, skiing is probably not a good idea for him. I forget that even though Olivier seems to have recovered from his injury really well, it must still be hard for him to adjust to his new life, with all the dietary restrictions and sports limitations. This makes me feel bad, especially when we are being cold toward each other like this.

Once the gondola reaches its peak, we enjoy the view and take a few group photos together. After that, we sit in the chalet and drink hot chocolate.

The practice with Olivier that evening is not as bad as I thought it would be. He is still being polite to me. Maybe a little bit too polite, but I can feel the distance between us. I also try to be as normal as possible.

We rehearsed "Ave Maria" before the Rosary, and I think it went really well despite only practicing twice. Olivier played his music well and with so much emotion.

At 7 p.m., everybody gathers at the chapel. All of our choir members are there, even though they will not be singing this time. Only Olivier and I will perform tonight. Some locals and tourists will also join our Rosary and Adoration.

When it is time for my solo, I take a deep breath to calm myself. Olivier starts the intro beautifully. Then I start singing.

When I sing "*Ave Maria,*" I try to imagine Mother Mary. I want to be like her. She was a very strong woman and very loyal to God. She said yes to God's calling to be the mother of Jesus, even though she was fifteen and a virgin at that time. I cannot imagine how she felt when Jesus was tortured and died on the cross. Mary must have relied on God a lot during difficult times. That's why she is full of grace and blessed by God. Having a figure like Mother Mary reminds me to be courageous and pure like her. Although, at this point, my problem is very trivial compared to Mother Mary's. I just have to have the courage to accept my feelings for Olivier while, at the same time, try to control them.

I feel lucky to have a motherly figure who is very close to God herself. As a Catholic, I don't worship Mary, but I honor her and try to follow her good example. It's like how sometimes I ask my friends to pray for me for support. Why don't I ask the Mother of God herself to pray for me, too?

After my solo ends, we continue with the Rosary prayer. I like this prayer. Because of its repetitive nature, it feels like meditating. It makes me so much calmer. I have a feeling that everything will be fine.

Then during the Adoration, Olivier plays some Taizé songs that are very calming. They are also repetitive, but it helps me stay focused during Adoration. There is a consecrated host on the altar, which I believe is truly the body, blood, soul, and divinity of Christ. This Adoration reminds me to give all of myself to Jesus. I want to serve Him. I want Him to use me. Why? Because without Him, I would be so lost. He has opened the way for me to become a better person. Through my relationship with Him, I realize my shortcomings. Maybe I am too egoistic. Maybe I am too ambitious. Maybe I am full of jealousy. By praying to Him and asking for His guidance, I feel supported. I believe that Jesus was also human and faced the same temptations as I do in this world. This gives me hope that I can be like Him, too. I ask myself—have I behaved according to the spirit of Jesus? Maybe not. There are two priests available for confession. I decide to take this opportunity.

I enter the small room with a priest there. In the church, usually there is a confessional with a lattice so that you don't see the priest's face. However, because it is such a small chapel, there is no confessional box.

I make the sign of the cross and start my Confession.

"Father, I have recently fallen in love with a guy. He is a nonbeliever although he is a good person. At one point, he confessed his feelings for me, and I rejected him. But now, whenever I see him getting close to someone, I feel jealous. I really need help to control my feelings. Am I being selfish? What should I do?"

The priest looks at me with sympathy. "Thank you for your honest confession. Loving and caring for someone is such a good thing. Jesus loves everybody regardless of what they believe. However, when love seems to turn into possession, that's where we need to draw the line. Love is selfless while lust is selfish. Selfishness is when you use the other person to make yourself feel good. If you truly love him, you should respect his belief and let him choose what's best for himself. That's selfless love."

"That's true. If I really love him, I should be happy for him regardless of whom he chooses, right? Even if someone else makes him happy." I imagine Genevieve's face.

"Exactly."

Then the priest gives me a penance, and I go back to the Adoration. All my negative feelings feel trivial when I am in a praying and meditating mode. I really want to be selfless and wish the best for everybody. For this choir, for Olivier, and even for Genevieve. If they have the same values and are truly meant for each other, why would I be concerned? As long as they both are happy. As the priest reminds me, love is not about possession. Love is thinking about the other person's happiness before your own. I truly believe it. I feel at peace.

***

Olivier Lefebvre
St. Bernard Chapelle, *Mont-Tremblant*

At the beginning of the Rosary, I almost fall asleep. I don't see why they keep repeating the Hail Mary prayer ten times every decade. And since there are five decades, at the end, they recited the Hail Mary prayer fifty times. I just don't get it. However, I try to be respectful.

Then for the Adoration, I have to repeat a song at least five times. That's what Ethan suggested. At least the Adoration songs are typically very short.

I also don't see the point of Adoration. Based on what I observe, it seems that Catholics truly believe that the host on the altar has Jesus' presence. This is beyond my capacity to understand. But, strangely, I feel calmer than usual.

Chapter 46
Olivier Lefebvre
Mont-Tremblant
Sunday, Fourth Week of September

A few hours before the morning Mass, I take a walk. I feel relieved that Genevieve is not following me around anymore, although I feel bad for her after what happened last Friday.

I walk toward the small deck by Lake Tremblant to enjoy the view. When I arrive, I freeze for a second. Someone is already there.

Regina.

It's too late to go back because she has heard my steps and turned around. We stare at each other, not sure what to do. If this was during a rehearsal, it would be easy. We would simply need to make music. But when it is just us, surrounded by this beautiful lake view, I am at a loss.

I decide to just approach her. "Hi, Regina."

"Hi, Olivier." She smiles politely.

We don't talk for the first few minutes as we enjoy the lake view. It's very peaceful. A mountain range surrounds the lake.

I try to start a conversation. "You sang beautifully yesterday."

"Thank you. Your playing is getting better and better. It's so full of emotions now. Like you created the perfect atmosphere for the song."

Her compliment sounds genuine. I didn't realize how much I miss Regina. She is always encouraging and supportive. "Thanks for your kind words, Regina. Maybe it's because I started recording myself to improve." Then, it's silent again.

"And by the way, nothing happened between me and Genevieve. I hope you don't misunderstand," I say carefully.

"Oh, don't worry. You don't need to explain to me. It's none of my business."

"But I don't want you to misunderstand. Although you have made up your mind, I still want to make a good impression on you." She gives me an unreadable look.

Suddenly, her phone beeps. She looks at her phone screen and freezes, her face is full of shock and horror.

"Are you okay? What happened?" I ask her worriedly.

She doesn't answer. She starts trembling. I step forward and look at her phone. There is a text message written in Italian. Although I don't speak Italian, I still understand what the text means because Italian is very close to French.

Regina, can you come home right away? Dad had a heart attack.

I hold Regina's hand all the way from the lake to my room. She still looks extremely shocked and lost. I quickly formulate a plan in my head.

When we enter my room, Ethan is there. He notices the tension between us.

"What's going on?" he asks.

"Regina's dad had a heart attack. I will book a ticket for her now. And she probably needs to return to Montreal soon," I say quickly. Ethan looks surprised and stressed, too.

"Oh, no. I am so sorry, Regina." Ethan gives her a hug.

"That's okay," Regina says. She looks like she is about to cry now.

I open my laptop and start searching for flight options. Unfortunately, there is no direct flight from Montreal to Naples. The earliest flight will be at six tonight, and it costs so damn much because of the last-minute booking. But I book it anyway.

"Regina, are you okay with flying tonight at 6 p.m.? That's the earliest flight I could find. You will have a layover in Munich and arrive at Naples tomorrow morning."

"That's okay. Thank you so much, Olivier." Regina is sobbing now. I can feel her pain and sadness. It breaks my heart.

"Ethan, can we borrow your car so Regina can return to Montreal as soon as possible?" I ask.

"Yes, go ahead and take my car. But who is going to drive?"

I don't reply at first. I haven't been driving since my car accident, and I don't think it's a good idea for me to drive. But this is an emergency for Regina. I will do everything for her.

I take a deep breath and say, "I will."

Ethan doesn't answer at first. He seems to be thinking. "Do you still have flashbacks or bad dreams about your car accident?"

"Flashbacks sometimes, bad dreams not so much."

"Have you been near the accident site lately?"

"No." I never want to go near the part of Sherbrooke Street where I had the accident.

"Have you driven a car since your accident?"

"No."

"Do you have difficulties sleeping?"

"Not really, no." Especially whenever Regina plays her violin and sings, I find myself sleeping very well.

"How do you feel about your accident or anything related to it? Do you feel agitated, tense, or angry?"

"No. It doesn't affect me anymore. I even dropped the lawsuit."

"Is there any memory loss related to the incident?"

"Not that I am aware of."

"Do you have negative thoughts about yourself?"

I lose my patience. "Are you for real, Ethan? Stop trying to diagnose me. Just let me drive Regina to Montreal."

"Olivier, I don't care if you wreck my car. I care if you hurt yourself...or Regina."

"Okay, I see your point. But I can drive."

Ethan sees the conviction in my eyes. Then he gets up, grabs his car keys, and gives them to me.

"Regina, why don't you start packing now? I will come and get you in about thirty minutes, okay?" I say.

"Okay. Thanks." She wipes the tears from her face and leaves.

Once Regina leaves, I transfer the recorded files of all the music I was supposed to play for today's Mass to Ethan. Although I am leaving, I don't want the choir to sing without accompaniment. Ethan looks relieved and grateful.

After that, I start packing my things. Some of the choir members will leave tonight. Some will leave tomorrow. I was supposed to leave tonight, but Regina is more important.

Chapter 47
Regina de Luca
Mont-Tremblant—Montreal
Sunday, Fourth Week of September

I am finally on the way back to Montreal from *Mont- Tremblant*. For the past few hours, it hasn't felt real to me. When I received the text from my mom, I felt like my whole world was falling apart. Dad has never had a heart problem. At least not that I am aware of. Why suddenly? He is only fifty-eight.

The last time I saw Dad was last year when I went back to Sorrento. He and Mom were supposed to come and visit me this December. I am so scared for him. What if he doesn't make it? I talked with him on a video call last week. I wish I had called him more often.

I cannot stop crying in the car. Olivier hasn't said anything so far. I appreciate his bravery for driving me to Montreal. I can tell that he is uncomfortable, and he is driving slower than normal. But I can also feel his conviction. He has been very helpful by booking the flight and everything. I can feel his sincerity.

At 12 p.m., we finally arrive in Montreal. I still have six hours before my flight.

"I will help you pack," Olivier says.

I just nod. We enter my unit, and I start packing my things for Sorrento. I don't know how long I will stay there, but I pack clothes for a month.

Olivier starts writing down the necessary stuff for me to pack, which I can cross-check against. He also brings me a glass of water.

"You cried a lot, Regina. You can get dehydrated. Please drink this." Olivier also gives me a pack of Kleenex.

"Thank you, Olivier."

"I am going to order some food in the meantime."

I nod and continue packing. Honestly, I am very grateful that Olivier is here. I cannot imagine having to go through this on my own. I cannot think straight at this point.

After packing, we eat at the dining table. Olivier ordered some sushi and pork bowls. I told him once that besides Italian food, Japanese food is my comfort food. Although I don't have an appetite right now, I force myself to eat.

At 3 p.m., everything is ready, and we leave for the airport in Ethan's car. Once we arrive at the airport, Olivier parks the car and helps me with my luggage. We go up to the international terminal to check in at Lufthansa's counter.

When it's time for me to pass through the gate, we stare at each other. I wish that Olivier could come with me to Sorrento. His presence made this terrible experience 100 times better. When I was sick with COVID, he took care of me so well. Now he has done it again. I feel like I can rely on him.

Although I have rejected him, he still cares about me. He is still willing to help me, including driving me to Montreal even though he is not comfortable driving.

Olivier steps toward me and hugs me tight. "Take care, Regina. Everything will be fine. Text me when you arrive, okay?"

I want to cry again. He is so kind and protective. It's touching.

"Thank you for everything, Olivier. I don't know what I'd do without you, really," I whisper to his chest. I hug him tight, too. He is a huge comfort.

"I will pray for you, Regina."

***

Olivier Lefebvre
Plateau Mont-Royal

I feel exhausted when I arrive home. It's been a roller coaster since this morning. When I drove Regina from *Mont-Tremblant* to Montreal, I was extremely nervous; my heart was pounding and my hands were sweaty. Whenever I saw vehicles coming from the opposite direction, I just wanted to slam my brakes or wrench the steering wheel to the right.

However, for Regina's safety and Ethan's car, as well as my own safety, I forced myself to overcome my fear rationally. I ended up driving as close to the right as possible.

I also kept thinking about those tough months of recovery. I did not want to go through that again. And I would never let Regina get into the same situation. I calmed myself by taking deep breaths several times. I hope it was not too obvious to Regina, as I don't want to add stress to an already stressful situation.

Luckily we arrived in Montreal safely, and I was even able to drive Regina to the airport. Now, I am really worried about her. I hope that she stays calm and arrives in Sorrento safely.

Chapter 48
Olivier Lefebvre
The Royal Montreal Golf Club
Monday, First Week of October

Today is golf day with my dad. It's been a while since I played golf with him. I usually play with my clients. I also like the green scenery at the golf course. It's a way to escape from the bustling city.

My parents are retired. My dad used to work as an investment banker, and my mom was an engineer. I am their only son. I moved out from their place in Outremont when I was in university.

While Regina's dad is hospitalized, I realize that I should be grateful to have a healthy dad. Yesterday, when I arrived home after dropping Regina off, I texted my dad to see if he wanted to play golf with me. He said yes right away. This morning, he picked me up at my place, and we drove approximately forty minutes to the golf course in *Île Bizard*.

I haven't visited my parents that often, especially since I am busy with work and the choir. Before, I used to see my parents once a month or once every two months. The last time I saw my parents was in July. I know that I should show them some gratitude and pay attention to and take care of them for what they did for me after my accident. They let me stay at their house for a month and supported me during my recovery.

Today, we will be playing on the blue course with eighteen holes. I am quite good at golf. This is a sport that requires concentration and consistency and trains mental toughness. When I see my shot was good, I want to maintain it. But when

I see my shots are consistently worse, it may ruin my confidence.

My dad is a better golfer than I am. But today, I feel a bit competitive again.

"How's work, Olivier?" my dad says when we arrive at hole one, and he takes out his driver.

"It's good. Everything is under control."

"You visit us less often these days. I thought work was keeping you busy."

"I have to attend a lot of client networking events. So, yeah, that's keeping me busy. Also, I have other commitments, too." For some reason, I am not ready to tell my dad about volunteering at the church. He will not be happy with that.

"Are you seeing someone right now?" My dad hits his first ball straight and high, even while he is talking to me. I am impressed.

"No. Not really. Why?"

"Oh, just wondering. So, what are these other commitments?"

"I started playing piano again," I say. Now it's my turn to hit the ball. I take a deep breath and try to perfect my posture before hitting the ball.

Nice first shot—far and straight like my dad's.

"Piano? What made you start playing piano again? I thought you played hockey with your group of friends."

"Not anymore. They can be rough sometimes. I only have one kidney, Dad. Remember?"

"Oh, true. But I thought you were no longer interested in piano."

My dad doesn't really like me playing the piano. For him, it's not manly. It was my mom who wanted me to take piano lessons when I was young.

"I am still." We drive the golf cart to where our balls fell.

"What else are you busy with?" my dad asks.

"I am busy hanging out with some friends."

"Which friends?"

"Do you remember Ethan O'Sullivan?"

"Yes. That Irish boy who beat you during the exams?"

"Yes. Apparently, he is a pretty nice guy. He was one of the surgeons who operated on my leg." For some reason, I don't like it when my dad makes a reference to Ethan as being Irish. Now that I am hanging out with more people from diverse backgrounds, whether they are Quebeckers, Irish, Italian, Asian, Francophone, or Anglophone, I am more tolerant. Everybody deserves respect, regardless of their race or the language they speak.

"Who else do you hang out with?"

I don't know why he asks so many questions.

"There is Regina, my tenant. She is a violinist with *Orchestre Symphonique de Mont-Royal*."

"Hmm… Is something happening between the two of you? Is that why you are playing piano again?"

Damn. My dad is smart.

"Nothing is happening between us. But, yeah, you are partially right. I was inspired by her whenever she played her violin. She also sings very well. Sometimes I accompany her singing with my piano." I feel so proud whenever I talk about Regina. I feel happy whenever I share with someone about our collaboration.

"Where does she sing?"

I don't answer at first. I don't want to give too many details, but my dad seems to be extra curious about my personal life today.

"In a choir."

"So, you are part of a choir now?"

"Yes. I am the organist."

"Where do you guys perform?"

I cannot avoid his questions any longer. My dad probably knows that I am hiding something from him. That's why he keeps probing.

"In a church."

My dad was in the middle of hitting the ball when I said it. Now I see that his ball is going in the wrong direction. Instead of straight, it goes to the far left.

"What did you just say? Church?"

"You heard me."

"So, you are part of a church choir? A Catholic church?" my dad asks in disbelief.

"Yes. But I am not practicing the religion or anything. I am just helping the choir."

"What's wrong with you, Olivier? You've started hanging out with these people, going to the church, even playing the organ."

"What's wrong with that, Dad?" I am about to hit the ball, but I am so irritated, I face him instead of the ball.

"Don't you remember what happened to you when you were eight years old?"

"Yes. But that has nothing to do with this."

"You are behaving strangely these days—this is not your usual self, Olivier. Are you still doing your regular checkups after the accident?"

"Dad, I lost my kidney and broke my ribs and my left femur during the accident, but I didn't hit my head. Stop talking to me like this."

"I am just worried about you, son."

"I am not a child, Dad. I can decide what activities I want to pursue. And honestly, the Church is not as bad as I thought."

"I just don't want them to brainwash you. They used to be very oppressive and abusive, do you know that?"

"Yes, I am aware. As you said, they used to be."

"The only reason they are not anymore is because of the *Revolution Tranquille*. They lost their power. If not, I guarantee you, they would still be as oppressive and abusive as they used to be."

"But that has nothing to do with the faith, Dad. Those who were oppressive and abusive were just some bad clergy. Not every member of the Church is like that. Some of the priests are actually really cool and wise."

My dad is looking at me with pity. He must think there is something wrong with my head. When he does not say anything else, I switch my focus back to the ball.

The second shot is not as good as the first one.

"I still think that you need a checkup."

"I think it's you who should start being open-minded. Everybody makes mistakes. The priests, the nuns, the apostles, even politicians, businessmen, and teachers. We, ourselves, are not perfect, Dad. Who are we to judge others? I don't care about the past scandals of the Catholic Church. I only want to grow as a good person. I want to follow good teaching."

"You can be a good person without going to church."

Yeah, say it to yourself. I don't want to say this in front of him. Before, I didn't realize how judgmental my dad sounded, because I used to be the same. All we cared about were money, power, and social status. Going to church actually makes me realize that I am not perfect, and I should humble myself.

For the rest of the game, my dad beats me in every single hole. It is the worst golf game I have ever played.

I don't feel good after my dad drops me at home. Obviously, our relationship is strained now. He doesn't like my involvement with the Church. I feel like I need to talk to someone.

Regina.

I really miss her. I wish she were upstairs, and I could talk to her. But I don't want to bother her. Obviously, she is dealing with something more distressing than a mere fight with a dad. This morning, she texted me the moment she arrived in Naples. By now, she probably has reunited with her family. I sent her a quick text message asking how her dad is doing.

Ethan and the choir also arrived in Montreal last night. However, Ethan has to go to work early this morning. So, he hasn't had a chance to pick up his car, which is still parked in front of my place now. He said he probably can pick up the car later today.

I check my work emails on my phone. There are no urgent emails from my staff or my clients, so I can take it easy for the rest of the day. As a partner, a golf day with my dad could be categorized as "business development." But we didn't really talk about any potential clients today. Instead, we debated the value of the Catholic Church.

Suddenly, my doorbell rings. Who would visit me at this hour? Maybe a delivery guy.

When I open the door, I am surprised to see a familiar man standing in my doorway.

Jean-Luc.

I've imagined what I would do if Jean-Luc appeared. The most common scenario is to hit him in the face. However, even though now is the perfect opportunity, I just stand there looking at him, without doing anything.

"Hey, Olivier. Long time no see," Jean-Luc says. His face doesn't show confidence or arrogance as usual. Instead, today, he looks defeated.

"What do you want, Jean-Luc?"

"I'm no longer with Isabelle."

"I don't care. It's not my business anymore."

"Please, can I come in?"

I sigh and let him in. We sit in the living room. As much as I don't like Jean-Luc being here, I cannot just forget that he visited me the moment he heard that I was in an accident. He took turns with my parents, who usually visited during the day, and Isabelle during the evening. He also helped me rearrange my plex, including the room we are currently sitting in.

"Olivier, I am so sorry for what happened between Isabelle and me. I really wanted to tell you, but you were beaten up after the accident. We didn't want to hurt you even more. But whenever I consoled Isabelle and drove her home, we couldn't ignore the attraction. I know I was such a jerk." Jean-Luc sounds full of regret.

I don't know what to say. He reopens the old wound that I have worked so hard to close. I want to scream at him, but suddenly I remember something.

Jesus. What would he do in my situation?

"Jean-Luc, I accept your apology."

"What?"

"Do I have to repeat myself?"

"I...I didn't expect that you would forgive me this easily."

"Go and don't repeat your mistake."

"Are you joking, Olivier? You're not mad at all?"

"I was mad. But not anymore."

"Wow. I am really speechless. I have known you since we were kids. You were not someone who forgave easily."

"Consider yourself lucky then."

Weirdly, we end up catching up like old friends. He has been nominated as a partner this year and is waiting for the announcement at the end of the year. I know that he is a good personal injury and criminal defense lawyer. He is a smooth talker. Maybe that's why Isabelle preferred him over me.

Apparently, Isabelle ended up with another principal dancer at her company. But Jean-Luc had already fallen out of love with her.

A few months ago, I would probably be happy that their relationship did not work out. But it's not my business anymore, and I don't feel affected at all.

Although the trust between us has been broken, I don't hold a grudge toward Jean-Luc anymore. When he leaves my place, I feel at peace with an old wound. And I feel lighter.

Chapter 50
Regina de Luca
Sorrento
October

I sit on one of the benches in Villa Comunale Park in the heart of Sorrento, where I can see the Bay of Naples, Mount Vesuvio on the other side, as well as some smaller islands. The bay is very beautiful and blue. This is where I've gone whenever I've felt down since I was a kid. Finally, I am home. I hear people around me speak Italian again. But for some reason, I don't feel like I'm home.

The past few days have been a roller coaster. As soon as I arrived in my hometown, I went straight to the hospital to visit my dad. I kept asking my mom to give me an update on Dad's condition throughout my journey from Montreal to Sorrento. At least I knew that he was still alive.

Once I saw my dad lying in the hospital bed, I couldn't hold back my tears, and I hugged him right away. It had been a year since I'd seen him, but he looked like he had aged several years. Luckily, his condition has stabilized. My mom and I are comforting each other.

Finally, after five days, the doctor said my dad could go home. He was given some medications and was advised to go to cardiac rehab regularly. Although my dad's condition is stable now, the heart attack badly damaged his heart. The doctor said that his quality of life may not be the same as before. I feel guilty for not being by his side when the heart attack happened. I cannot imagine how my mom handled this by herself.

Olivier, Ethan, Christie, and other choir members keep asking about my dad. I am grateful that they care about me and have sent them an update about his condition. Especially Olivier—he sounded very worried from his texts. He texted me two to three times per day, asking where I was and how my dad was doing.

I miss Olivier already.

I wish he were here by my side during this difficult time. I didn't realize how much I needed him until now. I have sent him the money for my ticket and my rent for the month of October, although I will probably stay here in Sorrento until the end of October. Olivier sent the money back right away. He said he didn't want me to pay for the ticket that he booked. He probably guessed that, as a contract musician, I don't get paid for the days I don't perform or attend rehearsals. Thanks to him, I have fewer things to stress about.

I've never encountered someone as genuine as Olivier. Although I have rejected him, he still treats me very kindly, which shows that he truly cares and is not being kind to me just so that I'll be in a relationship with him.

As much as I miss my life on the other side of the Atlantic Ocean, what happened with my dad made me realize something. What is it that I value in my life? Yes, I have a great career as a violinist in Montreal. I have my choir friends there. If I only think about myself, there is no doubt that I will choose to stay in Montreal.

But what about my parents? Who will take care of them here? Would it make sense to get them to move to Montreal? I know the answer is no. My parents would never be happier anywhere else.

I get up and walk toward Piazza Tasso, the center of Sorrento. I try to enjoy my surroundings—the colorful old buildings, bars, restaurants, shops, and narrow alleys. I also try to find food that I can buy for my dad tonight.

When I immigrated to Canada at fifteen years old, of course, I didn't think about these things. Now that I am older, I realize that I should not be living for myself anymore. I have to consider my parents, too. Even if it means that I should let go of my dream life in Montreal, as well as Olivier.

***

Olivier Lefebvre
Montreal
October

I don't know which is worse—having Regina living on top of my unit but not talking to each other, or talking to each other when she is on the other side of the Atlantic Ocean.

I think I prefer the first.

I would rather be close to her than apart, although we are not in a relationship. Honestly, I wish she had someone who could take care of her, especially during this time. I don't feel at ease knowing that she is in Italy taking care of her parents by herself. Although we text each other every day now, I called her once because I really wanted to hear her voice. We ended up talking for one hour. But I have to restrain from calling her again as I know that she is busy with her parents.

For the past few weeks, I have tried to continue my normal routine. I have to force myself. I work longer hours than usual in the office because I know that my unit will sound empty at night without Regina's violin music. I really miss her and her music.

Recently, I managed to acquire two client engagements. One is a valuation for a large manufacturing company, and the other is a valuation for a clothing retail chain store. As such, the next few months will be busy for me. I hope this will be a good distraction from thinking about Regina.

I also play piano more regularly these days. I finally mastered Liszt's Romance "*O Pourquoi Donc*" after two full months of practice. I really like this piece. It represents my feelings toward Regina.

Choir rehearsal is also not as fun as when Regina was there. At least I get to see my other friends like Ethan, Christie, Luiz, and Sam. Genevieve and I did not speak to each other after what happened at Mont Tremblant, but I couldn't care less. I am more sad that I have to ride back home by myself instead of with Regina.

Ethan knows that I am feeling a bit down without Regina, so sometimes we hang out at my place or at his place. Sometimes, we invite Christie, too. At least these two people are going through the same thing as I am. We all care about Regina, and her absence affects all of us deeply. Ethan and I also play squash more regularly now. Unfortunately, Christie doesn't like playing squash.

Even more pathetic—every Sunday after church, I ride my bike to the Belvedere *Outremont*, where Regina rejected me. I stand there just to enjoy the view for ten or fifteen minutes. This is Regina's favorite place in Montreal. She told me that she'd come here often, especially when she'd still been in school, so I wanted to do the same. I don't know how else I can feel close to her. I wish I was in Italy supporting her.

One day, on the way back from the Belvedere, I noticed a retirement home not far away, called *Maison St. Luc*.

I suddenly had an idea.

Chapter 51
Olivier Lefebvre
Maison St. Luc
Sunday, Third Week of October

For the past couple of weeks, I have been volunteering at *Maison St. Luc*, a nursing home for palliative care patients, twice per week. The nursing home is a very peaceful resting place for people in their final days. It has rooms with en suite bathrooms, a common area, a cafeteria, a library, a quiet area, and even an exercise room. The garden at the back of the home is very nice, too, even in fall.

Initially, I was only playing piano in the living room. The residents really liked it and invited me to their rooms to chat sometimes. Some of them are in pain, and sometimes, they scream. I can only console them by holding their hands.

Aside from volunteering with the choir, I have never volunteered before. All my life, I have only lived for myself. Now, I see that serving others can also make my life more fulfilled.

I chose a nursing home because I know that Regina is taking care of her dad right now. I wanted to know what she has been going through so that I can relate to her experience and support her. In addition, my relationship with my dad is still cold since we golfed.

It is not always easy to volunteer here. Other than playing the piano, sometimes, I help the residents eat and clean up their vomit. I help the nurse clean them after they have bowel movements. As a professional in the financial industry, I had never imagined myself doing this. However, I quickly dismiss this thought. I remind myself that when I become old, I will also be like them.

There is an old man I've become friends with. Michel used to be the CFO of a multinational company. Now, he is dying of stage four stomach cancer. In the beginning, we got along well because we could talk about business and finance. But after that, our conversations became more spiritual. Surprisingly, I liked it.

In the middle of a discussion, Michel says to me, "You know, throughout my life, I have been so cocky. I never believed in God. I looked at the Catholic Church in disdain because of what they did in the past. But now that my life is coming to an end, I kind of wonder how I could've lived, you know? What's the point? Just work, have fun, have a family, raise your kids, and you think you are successful. Until this cancer hit me, I never realized that maybe I haven't been the person I was supposed to be, you know?" Michel confesses this to me as I am feeding him an easily digestible porridge.

"I think you are too hard on yourself, Michel. You did a lot. You became a CFO. You raised your kids well. You have contributed enough to society," I say.

"Honestly, you haven't met my kids. Looking at them now, I realize that they are just like me when I was young. I'm not proud."

"What makes you say that?"

"The more my kids grow up, the worse they become. They don't behave well. They are rude and aggressive to others. Also, they make fun of the Church. They prioritize the wrong things in life. It's all about appearance. Prestigious job, expensive house, great kids. It's all about themselves and how they appear in front of others. If society went south, they would go down with it. People are so lost these days." Michel sighs.

"But what else matters besides having a good job, buying properties to live in or to invest in, and raising a family? Isn't it better to do that than nothing?"

"Yes, you should fulfill your basic needs. But after that, it's about living for the greater good, not just for yourself. Take pride in your work; don't just work in a particular field because it's prestigious. People nowadays complain about how much they hate their jobs. Well, why did they choose their career in the first place? People think that by having a family, they will be happy. No. They don't realize that a calling to have a family is a calling to sacrifice yourself. And if you are not ready, your kids will suffer. People nowadays think that jobs and family make their lives fulfilling. But actually, it's the other way around. It's through working hard in your prestigious job and working day and night to raise your family that you make your lives fulfilling through sacrifice and love," Michel says.

I digest Michel's words. There is wisdom in them. I ask myself: Why did I choose my current profession? Is it for the prestige or because I want to make a positive impact on society? I cannot say anything about having a family because I don't have my own family yet. But I can draw a parallel situation with my friends and Regina. Do I want them in my life to make myself happy and entertained or so that my presence can make their lives better?

"But, Michel, shouldn't it be going in both directions? Like we do something to make our lives fulfilled and to make other people's lives better, too. It should be give and take, no? We are just human. We cannot always give without receiving anything back. Otherwise, we will get burned out."

"You are right, Olivier. However, people nowadays don't realize that they need to give, too, not only take. We shouldn't be entitled all the time. Let's take an example: you see how so many people are divorced or separated. That's because they feel they are being treated unfairly; they don't get what they expect in a relationship. But the point of entering into a relationship is you have to be ready to get hurt. We often get hurt by those we love. Running away is no protection. To truly love means to accept and forgive those who hurt you, as you want to be accepted and forgiven. That's what builds a real relationship."

I cannot agree more. I love Regina so much to the point that it hurt physically when she rejected me and when she left for Italy.

Michel told me that he divorced twice. So, he may have learned the hard way.

"I see your point, Michel. But honestly, hearing you talking like this, I would think you have lived your life meaningfully. Maybe it's not perfect. But you acknowledge it, and it's never too late."

"Yes. Before I was diagnosed with cancer, I was living like a shit, even though I was successful. After I was diagnosed, I turned to God again. And I think about the criminals who were crucified with Jesus. One of the criminals repented only at the last minute and said, 'Jesus, remember me when you come into your kingdom.' And Jesus said, 'Today, you will be with me in heaven.' It gives me hope that no matter how badly I was living my life, I will still be forgiven."

"Are you practicing your Catholic faith now, Michel?"

"Yes, I started praying and reading the Bible again. But I miss going to church. I remember the beautiful choral songs. Back then, I didn't understand anything. But now, I have started to believe again," he says. "Are you a believer yourself, Olivier?"

I don't answer right away. Am I a believer? I remember my life before I joined the choir versus now. Do I want to go back to my previous life? No. I was exactly what Michel described—only living for myself and my pride. But can I really say with conviction that I believe in God and Jesus now?

"I am still finding the truth, Michel," I answer honestly.

"Take your time. But don't wait until you are dying like me."

Right after he says that, he chokes on his food and starts coughing and vomiting the porridge and blood. I call the nurse and quickly grab the stainless steel bowl beside the bed.

This is not the first time I've seen Michel like this. The first time he vomited, it got on my shirt, and I had to clean myself and change my clothes. Now every time I come here, I change into scrubs right away.

A nurse named Natalie comes, and we clean Michel together. His breathing is ragged. We know he doesn't have much time left. Compared to the first time I saw him, he has lost more weight and sleeps longer than usual. Although I have only known him for a couple weeks, I feel deeply affected by his suffering.

"Olivier?" Michel calls weakly after he is stabilized.

"Yes?"

"Would you mind calling a priest to come here this Sunday? I will offer my last Confession, and I would like to receive my last sacrament," Michel whispers, and then he falls asleep.

I approach Ethan right after our choir practice. "Hey, can we talk?"

"Of course. What's up?" He puts the music sheets into his bag and then focuses on me.

"What would you think if the choir performed at a palliative care home this weekend?"

Ethan thinks for a moment. "Hey, I think it's a really good idea, Olivier. Which palliative care home are you referring to?"

"*Maison St. Luc*, the one in Outremont."

"I personally don't mind. I can ask the group if you want."

"Yes, please."

"What makes you suddenly come up with this?" Ethan smiles in curiosity.

"Oh, I have been volunteering there for the past couple of weeks. And one of the patients there is dying and said he missed the choir at the church."

Ethan doesn't say anything at first, looking at me with an unreadable expression.

"I am really proud of you, Olivier. I never expected you to volunteer at palliative care. Is this because of Regina?"

"Yes and no. I know Regina's father is getting better. At least he was the last time we talked. But, yes, I want to feel closer to her by taking care of older people." I shrug.

"That's great. Maybe that's God's calling for you on top of being an organist at the church. I wish I could do the same." Ethan smiles. We walk downstairs together.

"You have already done a lot in the hospital, Ethan," I remind him.

"I hope so. By the way, how's Regina?"

"She is holding up well, I think. Her father is stable now. But I really hope that she will return soon. It's not the same without her."

"Yeah, we all miss her."

***

Olivier Lefebvre
Maison St. Luc
Sunday, First Week of November

When I arrive at *Maison St. Luc*, Michel is sleeping. His skin is extremely pale, and his breathing is slower.

Last Wednesday, I visited Michel again. I knew his time was approaching. We had a good conversation. I started telling him about my life, including my car accident early this year, which paved the way for me to return to church. I also told him about my feelings toward Regina as I needed fatherly advice that my own father wouldn't give me.

"Wow, I don't think I have ever loved someone as strong as you do," Michel said.

"Maybe I am just stupid. Waiting for someone who will never accept me."

"I would rather be stupid than never learn to love unconditionally."

"You think?"

"Yes. Being in love with someone is a calling from God, too. Whether it's a calling to be hurt or to be loved, let the other person decide. Just like God never forces us to love Him back. It's a genuine love, when there is no force."

"You are right. She's in Italy, taking care of her sick father. I wish she were here, and you could meet her, too."

"Is that why you started volunteering here?"

"Yes. I want to understand what she is going through."

"Regardless of whether you end up with her or not, look how she has influenced your life."

"I know. Not only this. But also in terms of my growing faith. I used to be very prideful, thinking that faith was silly. But her devotion and humility really opened my eyes. The way she lives her life opened my mind and heart toward Catholic teaching."

"There you go. Trust God. Let Him decide whether you and this girl are meant to be together."

"Thanks for listening, Michel."

"I think today could be his last day. Have you contacted the priest?" Natalie's voice brings me back from my lamentation. Natalie and I got along right away because we both like to play piano. She, too, plays a lot of classical music. Her favorite composers are Bach and Beethoven.

"Yes. He will come shortly, in about twenty minutes. Also, my choir group will be arriving soon."

"Choir group? You are part of a choir group?" Natalie's eyes widen with surprise.

"Yes. I am not singing, though. I am just the organist."

"Wow, that's so cool."

We talk about my choir group for the next ten minutes. Natalie seems to be super interested. She was baptized, received her first Communion, and was confirmed; however, it's been a while since she went to church because of her work schedule.

"Olivier, I just want to let you know that you have made such a difference in Michel's final days," Natalie says suddenly.

"How so?"

"First of all, his family never visits him—not his children or his ex-wives. So, when you started showing up, his face lit up. He finally found someone he could talk to. His mood has improved so much since he met you."

"Thank you for saying that."

"Also, I know that he is a very smart man. He must have had a very successful life before he ended up here."

"Yeah, maybe. One day, each of us ends up in a place like this, too."

"I just hope that I will be surrounded by my family," Natalie adds somberly.

Twenty minutes later, the priest arrives. Father Joseph is probably in his forties. I found his name in the St. Augustine Parish. He brings a big bag, which I guess consists of the Holy Communion, the chalice, oil, holy water, and the Bible.

"Thanks for coming, Father. Please follow us," I say.

"Sure," Father Joseph replies. Natalie and I lead him to Michel's room.

"Should we wake him up now?" I ask Natalie.

"Let's wait until the choir arrives. We'll listen to the choir first before the last sacraments."

"Okay, perfect."

Shortly after, Ethan, Christie, and the other choir members arrive.

However, someone I didn't expect also shows up.

Regina.

I cannot believe my eyes when I see Regina standing there. Isn't she supposed to be in Italy right now? She looks the same as a month ago, the last time I saw her. Today, she is wearing a very beautiful blue knee-length dress. And she is smiling at me.

I don't waste a single second. I walk toward her, and she walks toward me, and we embrace each other tightly like we haven't seen each other for years. We don't care if other people in the room are watching us now. We are like a reunited couple.

I see in her eyes that she has missed me as much as I've missed her.

"Regina! How come you are here? When did you arrive?" I cannot hide my excitement.

"This morning! I wanted to surprise you!" Regina smiles at me. I have never felt this happy before.

"How's your dad? Is he okay now?"

"Yes, he is fine. He is stable for now. Thanks for asking." We still hold each other in our arms.

"I am glad to hear." I tighten the hug. I don't want to be separated from her even for a second.

"Okay, enough, you two. We have to get ready," Ethan says with a teasing voice.

I turn toward Ethan. "Did you know that Regina was arriving today?"

"Yes, I did. She asked me to keep it quiet because she wanted to surprise you."

"You guys are *soo* romantic," Christie adds.

"You knew about this too, Christie?"

"Yes, I did. Sorry, Olivier. It was meant to be a surprise."

I am not mad at them for hiding this good news from me. In fact, I am very touched. This amplifies my excitement of seeing Regina.

Then we all enter Michel's room. Natalie has woken him up. He is a bit disoriented at first, but he still can recognize people. I introduce Michel to our choir while holding his hand. I hope he still can understand what's going on.

Our choir gets ready. We will perform one song for Michel, "Still," by Reuben Morgan. After the keyboard has been set up, I start the intro. Then, our choir starts singing.

From behind the keyboard, I can see tears in Michel's eyes. I didn't realize that this moment would be so emotional for everyone. Regina and Christie, the lead sopranos, also start tearing up. Today, we don't sing with our best technique, but we sing with the most profound emotion.

The atmosphere in the room is intense but peaceful at the same time. We know that Michel doesn't have much time left. He is very close to death. I was wondering, where is he going? Will he meet Jesus? Does heaven exist? For some reason, I feel the divine spirit in this room more than I have ever experienced. A very profound love is present.

After the choir finishes, we gather outside Michel's room and let him be alone with Father Joseph for his last Confession.

Nobody says much. We are busy with our own thoughts. Some of us have never seen a person dying like this. It reminds us of our own mortality. Where are we going after death? How did I live my life on earth? Have I done enough?

Regina approaches me and takes my hand. "Olivier, it's so good what you have done today." She lays her head on my shoulder.

"Thanks. I just hope that Michel did not suffer. We have known each other for less than a month, but we have talked a lot, and he inspired me."

"You inspired all of us, too. I am glad you got a chance to meet him."

Then Michel's door opens, and Father Joseph calls me. I take a deep breath, gather my courage, and walk into the room.

I am surprised when I see Michel. His face has changed. He is awake and seems very peaceful. He smiles at me when I enter the room.

"Olivier." He offers his hand, and I sit on the chair beside the bed and hold his hand.

"How are you feeling, Michel?"

"Never better. The girl who was singing in the front in a blue dress—is she the girl you fell in love with?"

I am surprised he is still this alert to recognize it. "Yes. Good guess, Michel." I nod.

"She looks like a very pure girl. I hope you will end up together."

"She is. Thanks, Michel."

"Olivier, I just want to let you know that although I am sad that my son and daughter cannot be here, I am happy you are here." Michel closes his eyes.

"Yes, me, too. Please rest in peace, Michel." I suddenly feel a lump in my throat. Within a short period of time, I have developed a strong affection toward this man who has acted like a father figure to me for the past few weeks.

Then we know it is time.

Father Joseph approaches Michel and makes the sign of the cross on Michel's forehead with his thumb, which has been anointed with oil.

"Through this holy anointing, may the Lord in His love and mercy help you with the grace of the Holy Spirit. May the Lord who frees you from sin save you and raise you up."

"Amen," Michel says.

We then recite the Lord's Prayer together.

Father Joseph continues, "Behold the Lamb of God, behold Him who takes away the sins of the world. Blessed are those who are called to the supper of the Lamb."

Michel finally receives his last Eucharist.

Warmth spreads all over my body. I feel the power of profound love. I see Michel's face, I can see that he has been loved profoundly. His face looks like he is sleeping peacefully instead of dying. He radiates beauty.

Five minutes after the last rites, Michel passes away.

Chapter 54
Regina de Luca
Maison St. Luc
Sunday, First Week of November

My flight arrived in Montreal this morning at nine. I only notified Ethan and Christie because I wanted to surprise Olivier. We spoke on the phone yesterday before I boarded my plane, but I didn't tell him anything.

When I arrived at my unit this morning, I was relieved that Olivier was not there. Ethan told me that Olivier was probably in the church. He usually attends the morning Mass. Ethan also told me that the choir would be singing in *Maison St. Luc* today, and it would be cool if I suddenly showed up.

And it worked.

The moment I saw Olivier standing there, I realized how much I had missed him, even though I'd been gone for less than a month. He looked great as usual. His hair was a bit shorter than the last time I saw him. He was wearing a white shirt and black dress pants. When we hugged, I remembered how good he smells. He seemed very excited to see me. He didn't expect to find me there.

I could see that Olivier has been gradually changing. In the beginning, when we first met, he was a bit cold and distant. Probably he was still depressed because of his injury. The more I knew him, the more he hung out with our choir group, and the more I found him relaxed, friendly, and, I would say, even more humble, too. Before, I felt like he was keeping his distance from people who were not like him (rich, powerful, smart, and gorgeous), but now, he is friendly with everybody, even with a dying man.

I would never have imagined Olivier volunteering in a palliative care home. It must have required a lot of self-sacrifice. He must have gotten his hands dirty. I was very impressed.

I can see that Jesus is working through him. Jesus actually lives in him and is transforming him into a different person.

This makes me realize that there are people who think they are not believers, but deep down, they live the way Jesus lived. There are also people who declare that they are believers, but they don't live the way Jesus lived. I realize that what's important is action and not just words. Olivier has proven himself through his concrete actions. He inspires me.

When Olivier walks out of Michel's room, we know what's happening. Olivier's face looks sad but at peace. We look at him, waiting for his confirmation.

"He is gone."

Olivier and I are sitting in the garden at the back of *Maison St. Luc*. Ethan is talking with Father Joseph, and Christie and the rest of our choir members have left. Natalie, the nurse who was taking care of Michel, is calling the funeral director and Michel's son and daughter. I am not sure if Michel's ex-wives are going to come or not.

"How are you feeling, Olivier?" I ask him. For the past few minutes, he has been staring at the beautiful plants and flowers in the garden. He seems lost in his own thoughts.

"I am okay. I didn't realize how much Michel has impacted my life for the past few weeks."

"In what way did he impact your life?" I ask.

"He made me rethink my priorities and consider my life more deeply. Have I lived my life accordingly so that I will have no regrets when it's my time to go? I don't know how he was living his life before, but I am glad that he died peacefully. He didn't suffer or anything."

"That's good."

"How about yourself, Regina? Sorry to drag you into all of this. I know you must still be tired from your flight, and you must still worry about your dad."

"Oh no, I am happy that you did all these things, and I feel fulfilled too. This is my first time singing in a palliative care home. Thanks for inviting us here. And yeah, I was a bit tired, but it's okay. My dad is fine now. But I don't know if he can have the same quality of life as before. The damage to his heart muscle is pretty bad; we monitor him closely for heart failure. He also has problems with his heart rhythm now."

Olivier looks worried. "I'm so sorry. It must've been hard, right, leaving him there?"

"Yes, it was."

"Can they immigrate to Canada? Can you sponsor them?"

I don't answer him at first. I haven't told him the reason I returned to Montreal. And I don't know if this is a good time to tell him.

"They would prefer to live in Italy. It's been their home throughout their lives."

"I see. So what's your next plan? Maybe visit your parents more often? Like two or three times per year? I think it's doable."

This may be the right time to tell him. Sooner or later, I have to tell him.

"Olivier, there is something I haven't told you."

His eyes narrow. "What is it?"

"I came back to Montreal but not to stay."

He tilts his head, confused. "What do you mean?"

I take a deep breath. "I came back to pack my remaining stuff and resign from my job. I am going back to Italy. For good."

Chapter 55
Olivier Lefebvre
Maison St. Luc
Sunday, First Week of November

What? I cannot believe what I have just heard. Regina is going back to Italy for good?

I am shocked and sad at the same time. I was hopeful about us when she showed up this morning, standing there in front of me. I thought this could be a new beginning for us. Even if we are not in a relationship, I really want Regina's presence in my life. I cannot imagine my life without her.

But I cannot be selfish, right? She needs her parents, and her parents need her. But I need her, too.

"It's very sudden. When are you going back to Italy?"

"In two weeks," Regina says sadly.

Two weeks? After that, she will be gone forever? I feel like my world has just shattered.

"Can you stay here longer? Maybe one or two more years? Please?" I beg her.

"I wish I could. Unfortunately, I cannot take a chance. The doctor said that next time my dad has a heart attack, there is the possibility that he may also have a stroke, or it can even be fatal."

I don't know what else to say. I feel sad for Regina and her family. I suddenly feel hopeless. What am I going to do without her? No more violin melody and no more singing from the unit above me for the rest of my life. No more bicycle rides with her. No more choir rehearsals and church Masses with her. How can I fill this emptiness?

I don't realize I am breathing harder because I am panicking. My chest starts to hurt, but I try to control myself. I slowly reach for her hands.

"That's okay. Let's enjoy the next two weeks together, shall we?" I say slowly and try hard to hide my grief.

She nods and lets tears fall from her eyes. She holds my hand really tight.

"I wish we could spend more time together. I really like you, Olivier. I love you."

I am speechless. This is the first time she has said that she loves me.

I kiss her hand gently. She has opened up about her feelings toward me. I am going to do the same. There will be no holding back between us, especially for the next two weeks.

"I love you, too, Regina." I wipe the tears from her cheeks. Then I hug her tight and let her cry on my chest.

Two weeks. Although it's short, I will make the best out of it. We can even go to the countryside or to Quebec City. We can go out for dinner like a regular couple. We can do a lot of fun activities together.

"Let's go home and make a list of what we want to do for the next two weeks." I try to remain positive. I can feel Regina nod against my chest. I caress her head gently.

I don't know how long we hug each other before we hear a commotion from inside. Regina and I quickly release each other and walk back to the home.

Michel's son and daughter have arrived. They are in Michel's bedroom. The son is a big guy, probably weighs about 200 pounds. He looks to be in his 30s. The daughter looks forty-ish. Her face is full of anger.

It appears that they have attracted quite a lot of attention. All the staff and even some patients are watching curiously from outside of the bedroom.

"Who the hell told you to give my father the last sacraments? He is not a believer!" Michel's daughter shouts to Father Joseph.

Before Father Joseph can answer, I step in. "Your father asked me to call a priest to give the last sacraments." I try to remain calm.

"Who the hell are you? You son of a bitch! How dare you interfere with our family matters."

Ethan tries to jump in. "Madame, please calm down. It's your father himself who requested it."

Natalie jumps in as well. "I was your father's nurse. I can testify that it was, indeed, your father who requested it."

Michel's daughter doesn't seem to hear. She starts to throw things at us—books, plates, utensils, et cetera.

I quickly step in front of Father Joseph, Ethan, and Natalie to cover them. They had nothing to do with this.

"Call security, quick," I say to Natalie. She nods and leaves right away. I also motion to Father Joseph and Ethan to leave the room.

When I turn back to face Michel's daughter, she has just thrown a heavy tray at me. I don't anticipate this. Before I can move, Regina quickly jumps between me and the flying tray.

The tray slams her back really hard.

"No!" I scream. What has she done? I grab Regina's arms and look into her face. "Are you okay? Are you hurt?"

She shakes her head. But I can see that she is in pain. I quickly take her to Ethan. "You guys should leave now. Ethan, please take care of her while I solve this." He nods and pulls Regina toward him.

Things are getting out of control now. Michel's daughter starts throwing bigger things at me like chairs and tables. Michel's son looks like he is enjoying a show.

I dodge the flying furniture and manage to grab the crazy woman and push her against the wall. "Stop it! You'll go to jail for assault," I say firmly.

She tries to break free, but I am stronger than she is. Unfortunately, her brother sees my holding her as an attack. He runs over, grabs my collar, and throws me against the bed, where Michel is lying dead.

I lose balance and fall to the floor. I am not a match for Michel's son. He is too big and strong. I have to get out of here. Before I can move, he strangles me and punches me hard until I hear my ribs crack.

I freeze when I hear the crack. I know what it is. Bone fractures. It all happened very fast. A few seconds ago, Olivier was still holding Michel's daughter. Then, he was punched to the floor and Michel's son broke his bones.

Although I am not a match for Michel's son, I run toward the bedroom. I need to save Olivier.

Luckily, some of the male staff also come forward to stop this. And finally, the two security officers arrive. They quickly handcuff Michel's son and daughter and drag them out of the room.

I see Olivier lying on the floor, coughing and gasping for air while clutching his midriff and wincing in pain. I flashback to what happened earlier this year—him in the ER, injured after his car accident—has happened again. My heart skips a bit, and I quickly kneel beside him.

"Hey, Olivier. You are going to be okay. Look at me." I grab his wrist, trying to find his pulse.

"Damn, is my kidney...still there? If not, it's my turn to...receive the last sacraments." He seems to have trouble breathing. Every breath is painful for him. At least he still has a sense of humor.

"Can you point out to me where exactly he hit you?" I ask.

"Here." He points at his upper right abdomen.

"Do you mind if I take a look?"

"No, go ahead."

I sigh with relief when his ribs still look normal from the outside, other than the redness. I don't see any deformity. It's most likely a hairline or non-displaced fracture. But I need to examine him for internal bleeding. Especially his kidney.

I help him stand slowly. He yelps in pain.

"Do you need a wheelchair?" I ask.

"No way. I can walk."

I help him walk slowly. Once we are outside the bedroom, Regina runs forward. Natalie follows close behind.

"Is he okay?" Regina looks panicked.

"He will be okay. Don't worry," I assure her. I turn to Natalie.

"Is there an empty bedroom we can use? Not too far, please."

"Follow me," Natalie says.

Once we are inside the room, I help Olivier lie down on the bed with minimal movement of his ribs. "Also, would you mind getting me a vital signs kit?" I ask Natalie.

"Okay. I will be back."

"Is his kidney safe?" Regina asks worriedly.

"I don't know yet. I need to examine him." I am as worried as she is, but I try not to show it.

"Regina, you also need...to get checked. That woman threw...a heavy tray at you," Olivier says.

"It's nothing really. I am more worried about you," she says.

Natalie comes back with the kit.

"Natalie, can you please examine Regina's back as well? She got hit by a tray earlier."

Natalie nods again. "Come, Regina, follow me."

After they both leave, I turn toward Olivier and quickly unbutton his shirt to examine him. The area around his fractured ribs is still red. It looks like it's going to be bruised and swollen soon. But the rest of his abdominal color is good.

"You are tough, Olivier. Especially after getting your ribs broken twice this year." I try to sound encouraging, although I hate to see another injury on his body. I listen to his abdomen and chest, too. Nothing sounds alarming. But I cannot know for sure.

"Do you feel nauseated?" I ask. He shakes his head. "This is going to hurt, okay?" He nods. I carefully palpate his ribs and his abdomen. He groans in pain. There is abdominal tenderness, but no rebound tenderness, rigidity, or distension.

Lastly, I check his vital signs. His blood pressure is slightly high. At least there is no sign of internal bleeding. Temperature and blood oxygen level are good. Heart rate is a bit fast, which is expected. Respiratory rate is still high.

"Here is what we are going to do," I say after I finish buttoning up his shirt. "Let's go to the hospital to get an X-ray and some other tests. Even though there is nothing alarming other than your ribs, I just want to be certain. I'll drive you to the hospital now."

"Okay. Thanks, Ethan. I hope…I don't need to stay…overnight."

"I would recommend staying overnight for monitoring. You will also need a painkiller."

Olivier's shoulders slump. Unfortunately, I still have more orders. "And no exercise or strenuous activities for the next two months."

"What?" He frowns.

"What can you expect? Even breathing causes you pain now."

"But, I want to do more things…with Regina. Do you know that…she is leaving in two weeks?" Olivier sounds panicky now.

I don't answer at first. I know about this. Regina has told me. "Yes, I know. Can you guys just relax at home then? Cook, watch movies, talk, and so on?" Although Olivier and Regina are not in a relationship, I know how much they love each other. It's undeniable. Overcoming his terrible anxiety, Olivier drove Regina to the airport the other day, and today Regina threw herself in front of flying objects to protect Olivier. I was very happy when I saw them reunited this morning, even though I knew it would only be a short reunion.

Olivier looks defeated now. It breaks my heart.

Chapter 57
Regina de Luca
Plateau Mont-Royal
Third Week of November

For the past two weeks, it was both up and down for me and Olivier. Fortunately, he didn't suffer anything worse than a hairline fracture from the assault.

Still, his movement became extremely limited. He couldn't really turn his body or bend over, even though he was on painkillers all the time.

I helped him do stuff that he couldn't do with broken ribs, like cleaning his place and helping him dress. He was not embarrassed in front of me, but I knew that he didn't like to rely on other people. Sometimes, I caught him looking frustrated and depressed because of his limitations, but I knew that he tried to hide it from me because we have such a short time together.

The upside was that with me being his caregiver 24/7, I ended up living in his place. This brought us closer than ever. We opened up more. At night, I accompany him to his bedroom, although we didn't do anything other than chatting until late at night, holding hands, and kissing. Had he not injured his ribs, I wondered if we still could restrain ourselves from making love while we were together in bed like this. But at the end of the day, I always return to his couch.

Sometimes, I played my violin for him. Sometimes, he accompanied me on the piano, although he was extremely careful not to move his body too much. Olivier was only working when I was away for my farewell with the orchestra or to sort out other matters. He worked from home for the past two weeks because we wanted to maximize our time together. I never imagined that leaving him would be this sad.

Last week, I arranged for my bicycle to be shipped to Italy. This bike is precious to me as it was a gift from Olivier. Whenever I ride this bike in the future, I will always remember Olivier and the fun times we spent biking around Montreal together.

I doubt there will be a man in my life who loves me as much as he does. When I was in Italy, I realized that even if he would not convert, I would still choose to be with him. It doesn't matter what he said he believed in. His action clearly shows what he believes in. He believes in love. And God is love. Jesus is the most loving person. Olivier's actions reflect Jesus Himself at times. For example, before leaving *Maison St. Luc* to go to the hospital the other day, he decided not to sue Michel's son. He held no grudge at all.

Natalie told us that the reason Michel's son and daughter were so hostile and violent was because they didn't get any inheritance from Michel. All his estate went to charity. They thought we were from the charity. So it has nothing to do with the last sacraments that Michel received. It was nothing personal against us.

"Regina, can I ask you something?" Olivier asked one night. He could only face up while sleeping to minimize any unnecessary movement on his ribs, so we were just holding hands while talking.

"Yes?"

"Never risk yourself trying to protect me again like last time. You don't know how scared I was when that tray hit you," he said.

"Don't think about it. It's all good. I didn't want you to get hurt." I lay on my side and leaned on my elbow so that I could look straight at him.

"But I also don't want you to get hurt. One person getting hurt is enough." He looked me in the eyes while lying on his back.

"But you risked yourself, too, trying to protect me. Remember when you took care of me when I got COVID and when you fought those drunken guys at the bar? Or when you drove me from *Mont-Tremblant* back to Montreal even though you were scared of driving?"

He didn't answer at first. "It's different. Let me protect you. But don't try to protect me."

"It's not fair." I caressed his black hair and his forehead. Even with the light turned off, I could still see how handsome and genuine-looking Olivier is.

"Promise me you will find a good woman," I said.

"I think I should find God or faith first before falling in love with someone else."

Again, I was surprised that he said these things. "I like that idea. As much as I want to be with you, we have to trust God's plan instead of our plans. If we are meant to be together, God will make it happen. But if not, I still think it's a blessing that we crossed paths. You have made a difference in my life."

"So have you. I wish I could live with you in Italy. But if not, I sincerely hope that you will find a good Catholic man who can take care of you." His voice was trembling, and tears were slipping down the side of his face.

I suddenly felt his pain. My chest hurt, too.

That was the first time I saw him crying. He pinched his nose as a cover to clear the tears from his eyes. A lump rose in my throat and tears stung my eyes.

"Instead of trying to find a Catholic man, I hope I will find someone as sincere and as kind as you. I'm sorry that I didn't realize this earlier." I wiped the tears on his temple.

"It's okay. Our care for each other is more important than our relationship status. I treasure every moment we have together." He also wiped the tears on my cheek. I put my arms around his shoulder, put my cheek on his forehead and hugged him tight.

For the remaining two weeks, I will love him and fully take care of him until I can no longer do it.

***

Olivier Lefebvre
Belvedere Outremont

For the past two weeks, we have come to the lookout often despite my little struggle to climb up due to my broken rib. This is our favorite place. Today is the last day we can be here together. Tomorrow, Regina will leave for Italy. Ethan will pick us up and drive us to the airport. Christie will join us, too.

We are currently enjoying the north view of Montreal together as usual. The sunset is very pretty. I don't know if I will come back here once Regina leaves Montreal for good. Coming here will remind me of her. But it may also make me feel close to her.

We sit on the boulder, and she leans her head on my shoulder. I put my arm around her.

"Don't hesitate to contact me while you are there, okay? If you have any problem, I can fly over," I say to her.

"Okay. You, too, promise?" She gazes at me.

"Sure."

I feel emotional again. I try so hard to hold back my tears. I know Regina will tear up, too, if she sees me crying.

"I am going to miss you a lot, Regina."

"Me, too." She starts tearing up again. I can feel her body shaking against mine.

I hug her tight. I don't care about the pain in my rib. The pain of losing her is much greater.

***

Olivier Lefebvre
Pierre Elliot Trudeau International Airport

Finally, it's time to say goodbye to Regina. Ethan and Christie picked us up this morning. Nobody really said anything on the way to the airport. No one wanted to get emotional.

Ethan parks the car, and we all go up to the departure terminal. Ethan and I each carry Regina's two big suitcases. After that, we check them in. Christie insists on carrying Regina's violin while Regina wears her heavy backpack. I am impressed that these are pretty much all her belongings.

When it's time to get into the security check, I realize that I have no idea when I'll see Regina again in person. My chest hurts, and I am breathing faster.

Christie starts to sob and hugs Regina.

"I wish you the best, Regina. Thank you for being my best friend for these past few years. I couldn't have wished for a better friend."

Regina starts to cry, too. She hugs Christie. "Me, too. Thank you so much, Christie. Please continue to live well and touch other people's hearts with your beautiful voice."

After that, Ethan hugs Regina. He has tears in his eyes, too, and his jaw clenches. "Please continue to play violin and sing well. Thank you for your service and dedication to the choir. And for being my best friend, too."

"Thanks, Ethan. Thank you for the opportunities, and please continue to lead the choir well."

Then it's my turn to say goodbye.

I hug her tightly. She hugs me tighter. I feel pain in my ribs, but I don't care. I kiss her on the lips. I know that this is going to be our last kiss. I can feel her tears on my lips, too. I try hard to hold back my tears. My heart is beating very fast, and I can feel Regina's fast heartbeat as well.

Finally, we release each other. We look each other in the eyes one last time. Her eyes are full of tears, which I slowly wipe from her face.

"Thank you for everything, Regina. And thank you for loving me."

With only a mute nod, she waves at us and turns to the security line. Even after she passes security on the other side, she turns to us again. We wave for the last time. I try to memorize the picture of her.

After that, she is gone.

I feel extreme emptiness in my chest. When I broke up with Isabelle, I thought that was the worst. This is a hundred times worse than that. How can I continue my life without Regina?

I cannot do this. This is killing me. I am overwhelmed with sadness until my legs cannot support my body anymore. I drop to the ground on my knees.

"Olivier, are you okay?" Ethan looks at me with wide eyes. He and Christie are both supporting my arms and helping me get back on my feet. I am still trying to catch my breath.

"I am sorry. I am okay." I try to stand steady. I feel suffocated. I cannot breathe. My chest hurts. My vision starts to blur because of tears, and my body is shaking.

"Don't hold it in, Olivier. Let yourself cry. It's okay to be sad." Christie cries and she hugs me, as does Ethan.

I finally let myself cry in their embrace.

One year later
Chapter 58
Olivier Lefebvre
Paris
Mid-November

I am in the middle of reviewing a performance report from our office in Paris, but my mind is somewhere else. I am waiting for a text. A text from Regina.

It has been a year since we last saw each other. Although I have been continuing my life as normal, it has been extremely tough. There are no more violin melodies or beautiful voices singing from upstairs. Right after Regina left, I rented out my third-floor unit.

I continued playing organ for the choir, too. Ethan and Christie noticed how devastated I was after Regina left. They were as sad as I was. The good thing was, we had a new member join. Guess who? Natalie.

When she saw us singing in the nursing home, Natalie was really touched. Then she decided to join in. She could play the organ as well as sing, although she preferred playing the organ. So, when I was busy at work and did not have a lot of time to practice, we split the songs. When she was not playing the organ, she was singing with the sopranos. Christie seemed very happy that Natalie joined us. She was lonely, too, without Regina.

After Regina left, Ethan created a chat group, which included him, me, Regina, and Christie. At least we were still connected. However, sometimes Regina replied late, or we replied late, too, because of the time difference. Nevertheless, we continue to support each other.

I restrained myself from calling Regina. I wanted her to adjust well to her new life. I didn't want her to keep thinking about her life in Montreal because of me. But she told me that after eight years of living abroad, moving back to her country gave her what's called reverse culture shock. She had to adapt again to her new life in Italy.

Because there was no career opportunity in Sorrento, Regina ended up living in Rome and working with the St. Lucia Orchestra, which is one of the best orchestras in Rome, even in Italy. I was not surprised. I knew that she was very talented. Also, this time, she is part of the first violins and a permanent member. I could not be happier for her.

I myself continued working hard for the firm. I took more clients, attended more networking events, and had more one-on-one conversations with the managers and senior managers, even with the associates and senior associates as well. Before, I used to be extremely strict and distant with my employees. Now I have become approachable, although I made it clear that I still expected a high performance standard. After a few months, I could feel that their attitudes had changed. They became more motivated, and they spoke up more and dared to share their ideas. Some of the ideas were actually good.

The managing partner noticed how the figures for our valuation department had increased significantly. I earned a higher bonus and enjoyed more benefits. Although I should be proud of myself, somehow, I had a feeling that there was someone helping me. I felt like this wasn't all because of me. Maybe God was helping me.

Two months ago, the managing partner called me into his office and gave me surprising news. Our office in Paris wanted me to join them there. Apparently, they had noticed my excellent performance, especially for the past year, and they wanted me to identify how I could improve the valuation team in Paris as well. I wasn't sure what to say. So I told the managing partner that I would think about it.

Obviously, there would be pros and cons of living in Paris. The first pro would be living closer to Regina. However, it will still take a two-hour flight to get from Paris to Rome. But at least Rome and Paris weren't separated by the Atlantic Ocean. This would also be a boost to my career, especially to have an international experience. This would be an opportunity for me to step out of my comfort zone. I have never lived outside of Montreal before. Compared to Regina and Christie, who moved here when they were young and did not even speak French at the time, the prospect of moving to Paris did not seem too scary. At least people in Paris speak French.

However, there were also some cons. I have visited Paris several times before, but I was never interested in living there. It's very crowded and not as clean as Montreal. The housing is also much more expensive there. Not to mention the cultural difference between us Quebeckers versus Parisians.

Also, what about my family and friends here? My father and I finally are getting along again after what happened at the golf course. As long as I don't mention faith or church, we have been on good terms. He is happy that my career has been progressing well. My mom and I have always had a good relationship. She was always more laid-back and accepted everything that I did. She doesn't mind that I go to church every Sunday because I am curious about the teachings of Jesus.

I also get along very well with my fellow choir members—not only Ethan and Christie but also Natalie, Luiz, Sam, and even Genevieve. She is now dating someone outside of our choir group, and we laughed about what happened in *Mont-Tremblant*. It would be hard to leave these people.

Uncertain about what to do, I lit a candle and prayed after Mass. I needed more clarity from God. Before, I didn't believe that He could actually get involved in my life. Now, I just wanted to believe in God because I had no one else I could rely on. Besides, I had nothing to lose by believing in God.

As usual, Ethan helped me make the decision, just like I did when he decided to take a year off from his residency. He entered a religious order seminary this August and has started the novitiate stage. I saluted his decision, although I still couldn't believe that he decided to give up a wife and family. He can't even date now.

"I hate losing an organist, but I can see that you are actually interested in taking this offer," Ethan said when we were hanging out in my place.

"Logically, it doesn't make sense for me to move there. Yes, it may look good on my resume, but at this point in my career, I don't think I really need this boost on my resume anymore. Is it worth it to move across the Atlantic, or can I just continue enjoying my life here?"

"Maybe it's worth it. You are going to be closer to Regina. Are you still in touch with her?"

"Yes, I am. But she is living in Rome. If I were to live in Paris, would it make a difference between us?"

"Yes, it will. You guys have something very strong. I can feel it."

"Anyway, how do you enjoy the seminary?" I asked him, and his face lit up.

"It's very interesting. I really like it so far. It's so quiet and peaceful. We are learning about the order's spirituality as well as deepening our prayer life. This is something I have been curious about but never had time to explore. I was scared of taking a year off from my residency in the beginning, but now I am starting to see that maybe this is God's plan for me. It required a leap of faith, but I believe in Him. He would never call me to do something that my heart does not desire." Ethan appeared to be daydreaming.

Wow. I did not expect an answer this enthusiastic. I thought becoming a priest meant that you were going to have a miserable life. Ethan is currently living with some priests and other candidates in the seminary. He rented out his condo to a tenant. They limit the use of technology there. I can't imagine living like that, but Ethan seems happier these past few months. And more relaxed, too. Maybe this is really his calling.

"Do you miss your job? Like being in the OR?" I asked him.

"Sometimes. However, this new learning provides different types of challenges. I cannot wait until I learn philosophy and theology in the next few years."

"So you will give up your medical career?"

"I don't know yet. Maybe not. I may go back and finish my residency next year and get my medical license before continuing priestly formation if the order allows it. Honestly, taking this year off to be in the seminary really opened my eyes. I will never see the world the same again, including how I practice medicine."

"I hope they will allow you to finish your residency. Who knows? Maybe one day your surgery skills will still be valuable even when you become a priest."

"Absolutely. But if God wants me to be something other than a surgeon, then I will accept that. Now that I'm following God's will, I feel more at peace than ever. So, you see, don't be afraid to take the opportunity that God has given you."

"You think moving to France is part of God's plan for me?"

"I don't know. You have to discern about it. Only you know. Pay attention to how you feel. Maybe you feel scared about taking this opportunity. But what if you don't take it? Will you regret it?"

So here I am, living in Paris. I moved here exactly one month ago. My firm provided me with a furnished apartment in the 1st *arrondissement*, although my office is in *La Défense* area. I prefer this way because I like the old Paris, not the modern Paris like in *La Défense*. Every day, I commute to work using the metro. It takes me thirty minutes, but I don't mind. Even though during rush hour, the metro can be very crowded, and I can't find a seat, I can't complain. I complain less these days, and I try to be grateful for what I have.

Life in Paris is very different than back home in Montreal. Although everybody speaks French here, I have to refine my French a bit so that my Quebec accent is not so obvious. In the office, it's even more challenging. As a foreigner, the local people will not easily trust your judgment and expertise. I have already established my reputation back in Canada. However, here, I need to prove myself. Some people talk behind my back, too. Only the managing partner in the office knows my accomplishments, and he holds me in high regard. He gave me a nice-looking office on the fiftieth floor of our building in *La Défense*. From my office, I can see old Paris, including the *Arc de Triomphe*, the Eiffel Tower, the Seine River, and even the *Sacre Coeur* at Montmartre.

After work, I usually stroll along the Seine River, then go sit in the park. Sometimes, I sit on the *terrasse* of a *café* and enjoy coffee; other times, I stroll through the museums and enjoy the artwork. The Louvre is still my favorite museum here.

In the beginning, I was a bit lonely because I didn't know anyone yet. I also haven't met other Canadians or Quebeckers. However, I did find a church community during my first week here. I surprised myself. I guess I started to have a sense of belonging in the Church, as going to church has become part of my lifestyle.

I usually go to Saint Paul Saint Louis Parish, which is located in the 4th *arrondissement.* On Sunday, if I feel like taking a walk, I walk along *Rue Ravioli* to the church. Sometimes, I enjoy lunch in *Le Marais* after church. I have slowly become accustomed to my new lifestyle in Paris and have established a routine.

To keep myself in shape, I jog along the Seine River every morning before work. Since I broke my ribs, however, it has never felt the same, so I no longer do any sort of muscular exercise in the gym. However, I still bike around the city sometimes, which also reminds me of good old times in Montreal with Regina.

Finally, my phone beeps, and I receive the text that I have been waiting for.

Hi, Olivier! I have just arrived in Paris. See you in about an hour.

I quickly gather my stuff, leave my office, and walk toward the *Esplanade La Défense* metro. Paris weather in November is a bit cold. I tighten my coat. It's almost sunset now. Today, I will meet Regina at the top of the *Arc de Triomphe.* I want to be there first so that I can welcome her.

I walk out at the *Charles de Gaulle–Etoile* metro, which is the stop for the *Arc de Triomphe*. I line up at the bottom of the *Arc de Triomphe*, pass the security, show my ticket, and then go up the stairs. It's quite an exercise to go up, but I am too excited to care.

Once I am there, I am surrounded by the beautiful view of Paris. I can see the *Champs-Élysées* in the east, the Eiffel Tower and Montparnasse in the southeast, my office in *La Défense* in the west, and *Sacre Coeur* in the northeast. I can't wait until I can share this view with Regina.

Suddenly, I hear someone calling me from behind.

"Olivier?"

I am surprised by the beauty of her voice, and I turn around.

Regina is standing there. It feels like a dream. I didn't realize how much I have missed her. She is wearing her winter coat, and her hair is longer than the last time I saw her. The wind blows her hair. She looks very different. Very mature. My world stops, and then suddenly, we rush into each other's arms.

We hug each other tightly. I cannot believe this is happening. Our chemistry is as strong as before, like the past year of separation never happened. I know right away that she is still mine. And I am hers.

When we release each other, we gaze into each other's eyes.

"Regina, I am so happy to see you."

"Me, too, Olivier." She smiles with tears of happiness. My heart melts with gladness.

"I thought you had just arrived. How come you are already here?" I ask.

"I wanted to surprise you and arrive before you."

It's no surprise that we thought the same thing.

"I am happy that you look great and healthy," Regina continues.

"So do you. You are very beautiful. You really look like an Italian lady," I say. She laughs.

"You look like an important Parisian businessman."

Now it's my turn to laugh.

I grab her hand and give her a quick tour. I point out the *arrondissement*, where I live, and *La Défense*, where I work. She is going to spend two weeks in Paris. I cannot wait to share my city with her.

"Are you happy living here, Olivier? It must have been hard leaving your hometown," she says once we have completed our tour.

"It's a bit lonely. But I focus on my work, so it isn't too bad. I want to experience what you experience, Regina. By living alone, I rely on God more as I cannot rely on anyone else."

"I am glad to hear it. I will always be there for you, too." She looks me in the eyes.

Then I kiss her on top of the *Arc de Triomphe*.

Chapter 59
Regina de Luca
St. Peter Square, Vatican City
Second Week of December

I'm in the middle of a break before playing Handel's "Hallelujah" with the St. Lucia Orchestra and St. Lucia Choir at St. Peter Square. Today we are performing for the public for free. I like performing in an open space like this. It's a different experience than performing in the concert hall. I have been part of this group for a year, and I could not have hoped for a better orchestra group.

Today's performance is particularly special for me because three people in the audience have come all the way from abroad: Olivier from Paris, as well as Ethan and Christie from Montreal. Yes, they are all here today. I am very excited.

The past two weeks were like heaven. Two weeks ago, I met Olivier in Paris on top of the *Arc de Triomphe*. It has been a year since we last saw each other. He looked more handsome than I remembered in his business suit and long coat. It felt like a dream. I still remember his scent and his hug. It felt like home.

After we enjoyed Paris from the top of the *Arc de Triomphe*, we had dinner in his favorite restaurant in Paris in the 1st *arrondissement*, near where he lives. After that, we walked along the Seine River and enjoyed Paris at night. We also saw the Eiffel Tower's glorious light.

We caught up that night at his apartment. When he invited me to Paris, he clearly told me not to book a hotel because he wanted me to stay in his apartment. His place is a two-bedroom apartment in a prime area in Paris, but he told me that it's his company's, not his own. He hasn't decided yet how long he is going to stay in Paris.

Then, for the next two weeks, we explored Paris together. He showed me the places he visited regularly: the church he went to every Sunday, his favorite café, and the garden he always sits in. I could imagine that he must feel a bit lonely, just like when I moved to Rome last year. At least my parents are only a short bus trip from Rome.

I still feel our connection is very strong. Even stronger. It seems that our separation for the past year only made us realize how significant we are to each other.

"So, are your parents okay with you living in Rome?" Olivier asked one day when we were at Pont Alexandre III, just enjoying the view of the Seine River.

"Yes. They are even okay with me returning to Montreal, but I cannot leave them alone in Italy. At least Rome and Sorrento are not too far by bus."

"I see. So your long-term plan is to live in Rome, right?"

"Yes. For now. How about you?"

"I don't know yet. I moved to Paris to be closer to you. And I am happy that we can easily meet up like this. But I don't think moving to Rome is feasible at this time. I cannot speak Italian."

"Haha. Yeah, I know. I wouldn't expect you to move to Rome either. I don't mind having a long-distance relationship. Although we may not be close physically, I still feel close to you emotionally and spiritually." I looked him in the eyes.

"Me too, Regina. Give me a few months to a year to figure this out. Maybe I will live in Paris for the next few years. And looking at how much I'm making right now, maybe I can retire when I am thirty-five, which is six years from now. By that time, maybe I could live in Rome."

"Wow. That would be a big sacrifice for you. But, yeah, I am willing to wait, and I am optimistic about our future. But what about your life in Montreal? Don't you miss your life there?"

"Yeah, I miss speaking Quebec French. And I miss our choir. Maybe we can come back to Montreal when we are old?" He smiled.

I noticed that now the way he is speaking is more Metropolitan French than Quebec French, although he has only been here for a month.

"I miss our choir, too, especially Ethan and Christie. Also, is Natalie doing okay with being the organist?" Thanks to the chat group that Ethan created, I am pretty up to date with what is going on with the choir. Natalie, the nurse we met at *Maison St. Luc,* joined the choir as a soprano and organist. Now that Olivier has left, she is the only organist.

"Yes, she is very good. She is happier being an organist than a soprano."

"I feel that God is really watching over the choir. Like when you came at the perfect time when Linda was about to retire. And then you met Natalie, who now is replacing you."

"Yup. Also, Ethan is still able to lead the choir even though he is in seminary," Olivier added.

I am happy that Ethan finally had the courage to take a year off from his residency and enter the seminary. Not many people have the courage to do that.

The glorious music starts up again and brings me back to the present moment.

I refocus on the music score in front of me, although I have memorized it all by heart.

Ethan and Christie told us in the group chat that they had just arrived in Rome at midnight last night. So I will meet them right after I finish this concert. Unfortunately, Christie's boyfriend, Luiz, cannot join us because he cannot leave his restaurant during the busy season.

Right now, Olivier, Ethan, and Christie must be seated together somewhere in St. Peter Square. I cannot wait to join them.

Once our orchestra finishes, I quickly pack my stuff and look for Olivier, Ethan, and Christie. I don't have to look hard. They hurry to my orchestra seat.

My eyes are full of tears when I see them standing there. Just like before when they attended my orchestra performance back in Montreal. They look the same.

I quickly run to them and hug them.

"Regina! I missed you a lot," Christie cries. Her cheerful spirit is still the same. I missed that so much.

"I missed you, too."

Ethan steps forward and hugs me, too. "I am sad that you left us, but I am happy that you have found a place where you can still shine, Regina." He is radiating an aura of wisdom and calmness. I cannot wait to ask him about his new life in the seminary.

"Be careful, guys, don't suffocate her." Olivier smiles. He arrived in Rome two days ago, a few days after I returned from Paris. Now it's his turn to visit my city. He is staying at my place while in Rome, even though he has to sleep on the couch.

I cannot believe we are all here. The four of us reunited in front of St. Peter's Basilica, the seat of our Church that began over 2000 years ago. We have decided to do a quick tour inside the Basilica, as this is Christie's first time in Rome. We enter the Basilica and admire the Renaissance architecture: the tall and impressive dome designed by Michelangelo; the relics of St. Veronica, St. Helena, St. Longinus, and St. Andrew that support the dome; as well as the Altar of the Confession, which was built over St. Peter's tomb. We also visit the Sistine Chapel, where the conclave, or the election of the pope, is held.

Once we finish our tour, I hold Olivier's hand, and we walk with Ethan and Christie to explore Rome together. I am excited to show my city to them. First, we cross the Tiber River via *Ponte Vittorio Emanuele II* to go to downtown Rome. Then, we sightsee: to Piazza Navona, the Pantheon, Trevi Fountain, the Roman Forum, and the Colosseum. When it's time for dinner, I bring my friends to my favorite pizza and pasta restaurant that I visit regularly. We catch up about life while eating. Ethan shares about his new life in the seminary; Christie shares about her new relationship with Luiz; Olivier shares about his new job in Paris; and I share about my new life and my new orchestra here in Rome. Knowing that each of us encounters our own ups and downs in our new roles makes me feel less alone.

Although we live in different parts of the world, I thank God that no matter where we live, we still can support each other, and no matter where I live, I can still experience friendship love as well as romantic love.

After dropping Ethan and Christie at their hotel that evening, Olivier and I walk up the Spanish Steps and enjoy the beautiful night view of Rome.

Once we are at the top, I put my head on his shoulder and sigh. "When Ethan and Christie go back to Montreal and you go back to Paris, I will be very sad. In the future, every time I pass the places that we visited today, it will remind me of today." Once Olivier returns to Paris, I can already imagine myself coming back to this beautiful spot by myself to remember this beautiful moment.

Olivier puts his arm around my shoulder. "I know how it feels. When you went back to Sorrento last year, I felt the emptiness. Then when you left Montreal for good, it was worse. Everywhere I went, my place, the church, my office, *Mont-Royal,* and Belvedere Outremont, they reminded me of you. It was extremely hard in the beginning. Even after a few months, the pain of missing you was still there, but I had learned to accept it. Now that we are only two hours away, I believe I will be able to survive."

"I'm sorry that you had to endure that pain. I felt miserable as well after I left Montreal for good. I missed you so much. I kept thinking about you and about the moments we shared together. Also, I was worried about you. What if you got sick again or what if something happened to your kidney?"

He plants a kiss on my forehead. "I was worried about you too. What if you got sick and nobody could take care of you? What if someone hurt you? You know what, I honestly don't mind visiting you here every month. Even if it's only during the weekend."

"Or I can visit Paris more often, or we can meet in the middle. In the end, the connection that we have, the love and care that we have for each other, it's worth fighting for. Although it will be lonely and tough for the next few months or years for both of us, I will never lose hope in our relationship. I am sure that we will find a way to be together again eventually. Or God will show us a way."

"Yes. Speaking about God, I realize how He has been guiding my life, especially for the past couple of years. Now, whenever I feel lonely or lost, I know that His guidance will always lead me in the right direction toward where I should be to grow as a person, toward love, and toward you."

"Really?" My face lights up. I look at him. "How so?"

"In my case, He guided me through the people around me. Through Ethan's words of wisdom, Christie's words of encouragement, and you, Regina. Yes. Through your voice, your music, and your love. For me, you are the voice of angels."

Nydia was born in Jakarta, Indonesia, and moved to Canada when she was 18 years old. In 2017, she graduated from the University of Alberta in Edmonton, then moved to Calgary, Toronto, and finally to Montreal in 2021. Living in various cities in Canada has broadened her perspective as a Canadian author.

Although she was born and raised Catholic, it wasn't until 2018 that she experienced God's love firsthand and decided to serve God through writing. When she is not writing, she spends her spare time reading and playing piano.

The inspiration for her writing includes Montreal and Canada's beauty, her Asian roots, classical music, her travel experience, and her faith and spirituality.

Other publications:

Speaking French in Quebec Changed My Life (CBC, 2022)
Dear God (Bookleaf Publishing, 2022)
Romance Concerto (AOS Publishing, 2024)

Published by
Full Quiver Publishing
PO Box 244
Pakenham ON K0A2X0
Canada
www.fullquiverpublishing.com

www.ingramcontent.com/pod-product-compliance
Lightning Source LLC
Chambersburg PA
CBHW061343310726
48974CB00001B/170